Taken by the Wind

Taken by the Wind

ELLEN HART

MINOTAUR BOOKS ⚇ NEW YORK

TAKEN BY THE WIND. Copyright © 2013 by Ellen Hart. All rights reserved. Printed in the United States of America. For information, address St. Martin's Press, 175 Fifth Avenue, New York, N.Y. 10010.

www.minotaurbooks.com

Library of Congress Cataloging-in-Publication Data

Hart, Ellen.
    Taken by the Wind / Ellen Hart.
        p. cm.
    ISBN 978-1-250-00187-0 (hardcover)
    ISBN 978-1-250-03643-8 (e-book)
    1. Lawless, Jane (Fictitious character)—Fiction.   2. Private investigators—Fiction.   3. Children of gay parents—Fiction.   4. Missing children—Fiction.   I. Title.
    PS3558.A6775T35 2013
    813'.54—dc23

                                                                        2013024381

Minotaur books may be purchased for educational, business, or promotional use. For information on bulk purchases, please contact Macmillan Corporate and Premium Sales Department at 1-800-221-7945, extension 5442, or write specialmarkets@macmillan.com.

First Edition: October 2013

10   9   8   7   6   5   4   3   2   1

For Avery, Dylan, Teddy, Mirabel, and Isaac,
with all my love

And in memory of my brother,
Robert Louis Boehnhardt
1943–2012

Cast of Characters

Jane Lawless: Owner of the Lyme House Restaurant in Minneapolis. Partner with A. J. Nolan at Nolan & Lawless Investigations.

Cordelia Thorn: Theater director. Hattie's aunt. Octavia's sister. Jane's best friend.

Jack Lindstrom: Twelve-year-old son of Eric and Andrew. Gabriel's cousin.

Gabriel Born: Twelve-year-old son of Suzanne. Branch's stepson. Jack's cousin.

Truman Lindstom: Eric's uncle.

Eric Lindstrom: Owner of the Lindstrom Bar & Café. Jack's father. Suzanne's brother. Andrew's husband.

Suzanne Born: Pastor at Winfield Grace Fellowship. Gabriel's mother. Branch's wife. Eric's sister.

Matt Steinhauser: Police officer in Winfield.

Hattie Thorn-Lester: Cordelia's seven-year-old niece. Octavia's daughter.

Andrew Waltz: Project manager for a construction company in the Twin Cities. Jack's father. Eric's husband.

Branch Born: Unemployed landscaper. Suzanne's husband. Gabriel's stepfather.

Aaron Eld: Seventh-grade science teacher in Winfield. Holly's husband.

Avi Greenberg: Writer. Bartender. Jane's girlfriend.

Julia Martinsen: Medical doctor. Humanitarian. Jane's ex-girlfriend.

Octavia Thorn-Lester: Actor. Cordelia's sister. Hattie's mother.

Holly Eld: Aaron's wife.

And if it shall come, when you look abroad over the ruin and desolation, remember the long years in which the storm was rising and do not blame the thunderbolt.

—Clarence Darrow

Taken by the Wind

1

Like bloodthirsty mosquitoes to bare arms, Jack and Gabriel were drawn to the old RV parked in the grass behind the farmhouse. It didn't matter that the guy who lived in it, Jack's great-uncle, Truman Lindstrom, was scary as hell. That was the point.

Standing at the edge of the front porch, Jack gave Gabriel an unexpected shove.

"Hey, quit it," whispered Gabriel, whirling around, his baseball cap nearly flying off his head.

Above them, the sky exploded with thunder. Raindrops began to pelt the dry spring dirt.

"It's your turn," Jack whispered back. "I ran up and touched the door last time."

"Touching his door is totally lame," muttered Gabriel. "We need a better plan."

It was just after dark. Gabriel was staying over at Jack's place, as he often did on Saturday nights. Jack and Gabriel were cousins, and had been best friends since third grade, when Gabriel and his mom had moved back to Winfield. The boys were both twelve now, recently graduated from seventh grade. Gabriel seemed older than Jack because he was bigger—taller and a good twenty pounds heavier—but also because he was more of a jock, one who liked math and science, was generally serious about school, and spent a lot of time reading. Jack's likes and dislikes were less set in stone, with a few exceptions: he was drawn to trouble, didn't like grown-ups, hated the word "no," and detested hearing his two dads fight, as they were doing more and more these days. Jack stayed out of the house as much as he could, especially at night, when the arguments seemed to heat up.

Squatting down next to the arborvitae, Jack whispered, "Let's climb the ladder on the back of the RV."

"Why would we do that?"

They were so close, Jack could smell the Fritos on Gabriel's breath. "Maybe there's some way we can see inside. Don't you want to know what he's doing in there?"

"You mean like torturing animals?"

They'd both seen the animal carcasses in the woods. Since the farmhouse sat on twenty acres, with a wooded area bordering the rear of the property, it wasn't unusual to find dead critters around, though not gathered like that. "Truman's evil."

"Not good evil either. *Bad* evil," agreed Gabriel. "The guy's got rattlesnake eyes."

"I've never been on an RV roof before," said Jack, rising from his squat. "It would be cool."

"What if he catches us?"

"Don't be a wimp. He won't." Jack charged across the grass, feeling his thin cotton jacket billow like a sail in the wind. He liked running about as much as he liked anything. When he'd hear his dads start to fight and he got that sick feeling inside his stomach, he'd sometimes take off out the back door and run until he was bent over double, panting, exhausted. One pain replaced another.

"I am *not* a wimp," called Gabriel, adjusting his hat and racing after him.

They huddled together behind the RV as a bolt of lightning lit up the night sky.

"I'm going up," whispered Jack. "You can stay here or you can come with. But if you come, wait until I get up top before you follow me. Got it?" He figured that the two of them together might weigh the back of the RV down and alert Truman that he was under attack.

Gabriel gave an uncertain nod. His gaze traveled up the ladder.

Jack grabbed the side rail and hefted himself up onto the first rung. When he reached the top, he saw that the roof was made of some sort of rubberized material. He stood up, feeling like he was on top of a mountain, then motioned for Gabriel to follow.

When they were both up top, they crawled slowly past a vent to a skylight toward the front.

"There he is," whispered Jack. He could hear loud music blasting from inside.

Truman was sitting next to a weird, angled table, looking through a microscope.

"What's he looking at?" whispered Gabriel, ducking reflexively at another crack of thunder.

It came to Jack out of the blue. "Germs."

"Germs?"

"He's into chemical warfare. Or maybe he's making a bomb. You ever heard of the Unabomber?"

"You're nuts."

Maybe, thought Jack, but there was something wrong with Truman. Ever since he'd arrived in his RV months ago, Jack had sensed it. The guy wasn't normal.

"I don't like it up here," said Gabriel. "The storm's getting bad. We could be blown off."

"Then go back down." Jack wanted to stay and watch a while longer.

Gabriel was halfway to the ladder when Jack called, "I think he's smoking weed."

"Really? How can you tell?"

Weed was a subject of great interest to both of them.

On his way back to the skylight, Gabriel caught his shoe on one of the vents and landed flat on his stomach.

"Crap," said Jack. Truman was up and out of his chair, staring up at the skylight. "We are so busted."

Jack scrambled down the ladder with Gabriel in hot pursuit. As they ran toward the woods to find a place to hide, the rain grew heavier. Cracks of lightning helped them see their way to a thick section of brush. Hunkering down, Jack felt his heart beat like the bass on his dad's Black Sabbath CDs.

"I lost my hat," whispered Gabriel.

Jack put a finger to his lips. A minute went by. Then two. When he figured they were safe, he said, "Do you think he saw us?"

"He did," came a deep, menacing voice.

Jack shook so hard his teeth rattled. Looking up, he saw Truman part the leaves with a baseball bat. A flicker of lightning lit up his face, all slick with water, his curly dark hair plastered to a monstrous head.

4

"We didn't mean anything," said Gabriel, grabbing Jack's arm. "I hate kids."

Jack tried to speak, but nothing came out. He couldn't believe Gabriel was handling this. *He* was the brave one, not Gabriel.

"You got no right to spy on me."

"No, sir," said Gabriel.

Jack felt Gabriel's wet hat hit his chest.

"If I see you anywhere near my RV again—"

"You won't," said Gabriel. "We're sorry. We've learned our lesson."

Truman looked fifty feet tall. Raising the bat, he held it aloft, a soaked marijuana cigarette dangling from his lips.

Jack squeezed his eyes shut. And waited. When he finally worked up the courage to open them, Truman was gone.

2

Rolling over onto his back and pulling a thin cotton blanket up over his head, all Eric wanted from this bright mid-June morning was a place to hide. Now that Andrew had moved out, something Eric had never wanted, he felt as if he were slogging through each day with such a heavy weight on his shoulders that at night, all he could do was drop into bed and seek a small piece of oblivion in sleep.

Eric and Andrew had been together for sixteen years. They'd tied the knot up in Thunder Bay four summers ago. Growing up in Winfield, a small town about seventy miles southeast of the Twin Cities, they'd gone to the same high school. Andrew had been two years older, so they hadn't run with the same crowd, though Eric had certainly noticed him. It would have been hard not to. Andrew's claim to fame at school had been his musical ability. He played guitar and piano, had an amazing voice, and even wrote songs for the band he and three of his buddies had formed his junior year. Lots of people thought he'd be famous one day. Not that Eric was all that interested in fame. He was, however, very much interested in male beauty.

Andrew dressed like he cared about his looks, all clothes selected to show off his lean, muscular body. At five foot six, he was shorter than most of the other guys, and yet he carried himself with such casual assurance that Eric doubted anybody noticed. It was his eyes that were the most arresting—not just the color, a warm gold, but the way he would fix them on the person he was talking to. He was never in a rush. Always willing to listen. If he was *with* you, you felt his presence. He was very much in the moment.

From an early age, Eric had known he was different, calling himself gay, albeit only inside his mind, since he was thirteen. He would have bet money that Andrew was gay, too, although nobody ever said things like that out loud back then.

Lying in bed on this hot summer morning, Eric was mentally playing with a stupid game show scenario. In front of a crowd of clapping onlookers, he'd been shown two doors and asked to pick one. The first door allowed him to live with Andrew and be unhappy. The second door meant he'd live without Andrew—and be unhappy. There was no door number three. The crowd seemed eager for him to choose, egging him on with calls like "Number one is better" and "Two, man. Pick two!"

Outside the bedroom window, a crow made its usual morning racket. "All right, all right," Eric grumbled, struggling out from under the blanket. "I'm up."

After pulling on a pair of jeans and a T-shirt with the logo of his restaurant—LINDSTROM BAR & CAFÉ—on the front, and pushing into a pair of flip-flops, he made his way past a large hole in the hallway wall downstairs into the kitchen, where he found his sister, Suzanne, sitting at the table with a cup of coffee, staring through half-glasses at a copy of the Koran. Suzanne had been the associate pastor, family outreach coordinator, and choir director at Winfield Grace Fellowship, a nondenominational Christian church, for the last four years. She had a key to his house, not that it was strictly necessary. The doors were rarely locked.

"You thinking of switching religions?" he asked, getting down a mug.

"Just checking out the competition," she said, turning a page.

"Weren't you reading some Buddhist something or other on meditation last week?"

"Inquiring minds."

"Are the boys up yet?"

"Haven't seen them."

Suzanne was Gabriel's mother. She lived in Winfield with her second husband, Branch Born, currently an unemployed landscaper. She'd no doubt come by to pick up Gabriel. Separating the boys, especially when Gabriel was at the farmhouse, was always a hassle.

Jack and Gabriel had spent the night in a tent in the backyard. They explained they were zombie hunters, intending to sleep outside to toughen themselves up until they went back to school in the fall. Eric was amused and decided not to interfere with their plan. Knowing how headstrong Jack was, there wasn't much point. Also, ever since Jack had run away several weeks ago, right after Andrew had moved out, Eric tended to treat him more gently. He was going through a rough patch, as were Eric and Andrew. "Would you like some breakfast?"

"I could be coaxed."

"Where's Branch?"

"Driving up to Prior Lake for a job interview. This one looks promising."

Branch was a sweet, towering tree trunk of a man in his early forties. Suzanne's first husband, Sam McKibben, had died of ALS when Gabriel was just seven—almost six years ago. Because Suzanne had taken the death so hard, and because of her painful loneliness, Eric had been thrilled when she'd been hired by the church, which allowed her to move back home to Winfield. Six months later she'd fallen head over heels for Branch and had married him the following year. Suzanne was a warm, outgoing woman, a natural caregiver, and Branch, far more reserved, was a guy who seemed to need a little extra TLC.

Glancing out the window over the sink, Eric thought about taking Jack with him when he went in to work today. As a boy, Eric had spent many summers working at the restaurant. His grandfather Lars Lindstrom had opened the place in 1948. His dad, Henry, had taken it over in 1974. Eric hoped that Jack, who had once loved going to work with him, happy to help with anything and everything, would one day spend his summers at the café. And yet, in the last year or so, Jack had begun to grouse when Eric took him along. He maintained that he was old enough to stay home alone, and that if his fathers didn't allow it, that meant they didn't trust him, which wasn't fair. Jack was upset by injustice of any kind, especially when it came to the way people treated him. Under ordinary circumstances, leaving him alone wouldn't have been a problem, and yet after his runaway attempt, Eric was worried that he might get it into his head to try it again.

"I'm going out to wake up the kids," said Eric. "They'll be hungry. Maybe I'll make pancakes."

"I'll scramble some eggs," said Suzanne, closing the book and smiling up at him. "I wish Andrew was here."

"Don't start."

"I also wish you'd talk to me about what's going on with you two. I thought you were doing great. Did I miss something?"

"Probably. You've been so preoccupied with what's happening at your church for the last year that sometimes I wonder if you even know what day it is."

"That bad?"

"Pretty much."

"Then fill me in. Tell me why Andrew left."

"It's complicated."

"Isn't everything?"

Eric and Suzanne, fraternal twins, were blond haired and blue eyed, but that's where the similarities ended. While Suzanne was philosophically inclined, an extrovert but also a thinker, Eric was the pragmatist, the realist, a guy who'd rather act than analyze. It took the hard knocks of adult life for them to understand the weaknesses in each position, and yet neither had changed much.

"I'm here for you," said Suzanne.

"In your capacity as pastor, or as my sister?"

"Does it matter? I love you—both of you. Maybe I can help."

Ignoring her, as he often did when he didn't know what to say, he went outside, taking a moment to reel in the garden hose. He didn't like being asked to talk when he didn't feel like it. In that, he was probably more like his son than he cared to know.

Standing outside the tent, Eric called, "Anybody in there

hungry?" When he didn't receive an immediate response, he opened the front flap and looked in.

Empty.

Wondering where they'd gone, he walked around the side of the farmhouse, calling, "Jack? Gabriel? Breakfast. I've got some raw bear meat for you, just what fearless zombie hunters crave." He continued on to the garage. "Jack? *Answer* me." Raising the heavy door, he saw that the bikes were next to the wall. "Where the hell?" he whispered. He called their names one more time, standing in the center of the yard, hoping they'd come racing out of the woods or up from the meadow. When they didn't, he gave up and returned to the kitchen.

His sister looked up from setting the table. "Tell them to wash up, okay?"

"Can't find them. What time did you get here?"

"Half an hour ago, maybe."

"You didn't see them?"

"I assumed they were asleep in the tent."

"Well, they're not."

Suzanne and Eric exchanged semianxious glances.

"I talked to Gabriel last night," said Suzanne. "He knows I've got meetings all day, that he had to be ready to leave here by nine. Like I said, Branch's got that job interview. He was planning to take Gabriel on a picnic when he gets home, maybe do some fishing off the pontoon."

The deal was, Jack was supposed to tell Eric if he went anywhere. It was nonnegotiable after he'd taken off on his bike, intending to ride to a friend's house a good twenty-five miles away, where he planned to hide in the garage. It wasn't much of a plan. When his front tire went flat about six miles out of Win-field, he gave up and hitchhiked back to the farmhouse, admitting under pressure what his intentions had been. They'd driven out to pick up the bike, Jack refusing to talk about why he'd left. Not that it was necessary. It was all about Andrew leaving and they both knew it. "I better go find them," said Eric.

"I'll come with."

"Let's split up. We can cover more territory that way. You check the woods. I'll take the car and head into town."

"I don't get it," said Suzanne, nervously pulling a lock of hair behind her ear. "Gabriel wouldn't just leave."

"He would if Jack made running away sound like an adventure."

" 'Running away'?" she repeated, her eyes widening.

Eric hated being the kind of parent who always jumped to the most extreme conclusion right off the bat, and yet he couldn't stop himself.

"Wait. Let me try his cell," said Suzanne.

"Gabriel has a cell phone?"

"Branch bought it for him. Apparently Gabriel had been after him to buy him one for months. It's cheap, looks like a toy, but it works." She stepped over to the counter and picked up the cordless, waiting through several rings. "He's not answering," she said, her frown deepening.

"Look," said Eric, grabbing his keys and billfold off the kitchen counter. "If you find them, call my cell. I'll do the same." He was worried, for sure, but he was also pissed. Both he and Andrew had talked to Jack about why Andrew had moved out. They'd made it as clear as humanly possible that their problems had nothing to do with him—that they loved him and always would. They stressed

12

that running away was never a solution. Since the split, Andrew had spent every weekend with Jack. In many ways, he was spending more time with him now that he'd moved out than when he was living at home. They were both bending over backward to make their separation as easy as possible for Jack, though they knew it was still taking a toll. It was at moments like this that Eric hated Andrew.

Hurrying down the back steps to his BMW, Eric glanced toward the long RV parked at the back of the yard. He wondered if Truman had seen the boys this morning. It seemed unlikely since Jack and Gabriel gave him such a wide berth. They'd both made it clear that they thought Truman was freaky. Eric agreed that Truman was an unusual man, although because he didn't know him well, and because he was family—his dad's brother—he tried to give him the benefit of the doubt.

Heading down the long graveled drive out to the county road, Eric glanced up at the rearview mirror, his eyes lingering on the farmhouse. Andrew had bought it five years ago hoping that the market would improve and that they could flip it quickly and move on to something a little nicer. He'd painted the exterior a brick red with white trim, replaced the roof, repaired or replaced all the windows, and rebuilt the porch, adding all new screens and some nice outdoor furniture. Branch had landscaped the property, putting in sod, bushes, and flower beds, and erecting an arbor trellis on the south side, complete with a deep purple climbing clematis. It had taken nearly every dime they had. With no money left in the bank to work on the interior, Andrew had taken a project manager position at a construction company up in the Cities.

Eric wasn't exactly the kind of guy who had premonitions,

but he'd had more than one about this place, none of them good. He'd never said anything to Andrew. It just seemed too "out there." Jack must have felt it, too, because from the very beginning, for no apparent reason, he'd loathed his bedroom. It overlooked the meadow and it was larger than any of his other bedrooms, so on the face of it, he should have been happy. But for the first few months, he refused to sleep anywhere but the couch in the living room. He eventually mellowed after they agreed to repaint. Jack wanted black. They agreed on navy blue. The bats in the walls didn't come alive until the following spring. Jack seemed to take those in stride, and usually helped Andrew and Eric catch them when they appeared, most often in the middle of the night.

As he sped along the highway, Eric wondered briefly if he should call Andrew and tell him what had happened. Thinking that there was more than an even possibility it wasn't another runaway attempt, but simply one of Jack's small acts of rebellion, he decided to wait. If he could find his son, they would need to have another father-son talk about why Papa, as Jack called Andrew, had moved out. Eric wished he could tell him that the move was only temporary, but the truth was, he wasn't sure Andrew wanted to come home.

For the next half hour, Eric drove around town looking for the boys at all their favorite hangouts—the bakery, the Hamburger Shack, the 7-Eleven, and finally Marla's Sweet Shop down on Main. Striking out at each place, he decided to head over to Bay Point Park, where he came upon a few teenage girls tossing a volleyball around. For a June morning, it was unusually hot. The beach at the lake would fill up soon enough. He stopped to ask the girls if they'd seen Jack Lindstrom or Gabriel Born. They nodded as if they knew the names, but said that they hadn't seen anyone since they arrived.

"Except for Mr. Eld," said the girl in the red shorts.

"Mr. Eld—the science teacher at the middle school?"

"Yeah."

Jack had been in Aaron Eld's class this past year. If Eric ran into him, he could ask Eld to keep an eye out for the boys. He thanked the girls and drove on, feeling the worry inside him expand like an inflating balloon. After sailing past the playground behind the middle school and finding nobody around, he pulled the car over to the curb to regroup. Summer classes wouldn't start for another week or two. Thinking that he should probably check out the homes of some of Jack's friends, Eric drove up the hill, past the old Carnegie library, and turned left onto Grand Avenue, a narrow, tree-lined street that ran east and west through the town. As he drove along, he noticed a few new FOR SALE and FORECLOSED signs.

Pulling up to the curb in front of a one-story ranch, Eric turned off the engine and jumped out. Next to Gabriel, Corey Willis was Jack's best buddy. Corey was sitting cross-legged in the grass watching his father dig up dandelions. "Hey, you two," called Eric, waving. "Either of you seen my kid? Or Gabriel Born?"

"Nope," said Corey, shading his eyes from the sun. "Not for a couple of days."

"Can't find them?" asked Corey's dad. Eric hadn't told anyone about Jack running away, though word always seemed to spread in a small town.

"Afraid not. Jack's supposed to tell me when he leaves. He didn't this morning." Tucking his T-shirt into his jeans, Eric glanced back at Corey. "You have any idea where they might have gone?"

The kid shrugged. "The 7-Eleven?"

"Already looked there."

He shrugged again. "Sorry."

"If we see them, Eric, we'll tell them to get on home," said Mr. Willis. "Unless you want us to help you look."

"No thanks," called Eric on his way back to the car. It wasn't time to hit the panic button just yet. After stopping by two more of Jack's friends' homes and learning nothing, he headed back to the farmhouse feeling frustrated and rattled, wondering if Suzanne had fared any better than he had.

Eric had moved to Minneapolis after high school to attend the U. He'd ended up with an MBA and was making a good living as a speechwriter for several sustainable agriculture organizations when his father was diagnosed with cancer. He'd come back to Winfield to help run the café for a few months, commuting between his life up in Minneapolis with Andrew and Jack, and Winfield. He ended up talking Andrew into moving back down after his father had passed. That was eleven years ago. They both had fond memories of the town, and thought raising their son here might be a good idea. They worried how folks would react to a gay couple moving in, but eventually came to the conclusion that they couldn't let narrow minds chase them away from their hometown. Lately, Eric was beginning to wonder if the move had been a mistake.

Jack received exactly five bucks a week as an allowance. He wasn't very good at saving money, or at planning ahead. Same with Gabriel. Eric had to believe that if the boys had run off, they would come back when they got hungry or ran out of funds. What preoccupied Eric most on the drive back was the conversation he would need to have with Jack, as well as the punishment he would be forced to dish out. Neither would be a simple matter.

3

By six that night, Eric was charging through the house, picking up magazines and newspapers, busing dirty dishes back to the kitchen, dusting, sweeping, and generally cleaning up. Shifting into Whirling Dervish—mode was something he often did when he was nervous, though tonight his agitation had a more specific purpose.

He'd given himself a mental deadline. If the kids weren't home by eight, he would call the police. When eight came, with no Jack and Gabriel, he placed the call. Suzanne and Branch had arrived around seven thirty. Nobody was doing much talking.

Branch was seated on the wing chair in the living room, focusing all his attention on the TV, while Suzanne stood trance-like next to the window in the dining room, gazing through the screen at the purple twilight. Eric figured she was praying. They'd all been out searching for the boys at one point or another during the afternoon and early evening.

"I still think they'll show up," said Branch. He'd been lobbying to wait a while longer before calling the cops. "I ran off once when I was a kid. I was angry at my dad. I was gone less than a day before I got tired of it and came home. If the cops had been in the living room when I got home, I would have been so pissed."

"There's no harm in talking to the police," said Suzanne, playing absently with her gold necklace. Squinting through the screen, she said, "The squad car's here. Looks like Matt Steinhauser."

"Crap," muttered Branch. "That guy's a first-class jerk."

"You think all cops are jerks," said Eric.

"Yeah, well."

Winfield, Bridger, and Short Creek, three towns within twenty miles of each other, shared a police department. Since Winfield was the largest, nearly three thousand people, the station house was located there. Steinhauser was a licensed police officer, as well as the resource officer assigned to Winfield Middle School. Each of the three schools in the area had a resource officer assigned to it during the school year. Now that school was out, Steinhauser had no doubt returned to the general officer pool.

Rushing to the front door, Eric skidded to a stop, then walked more slowly out onto the front porch. Steinhauser came to the café occasionally, so Eric knew him, though not well. He was in his late fifties. Gray haired. Slope shouldered. A heavy gut spilling over his belt. He was required to wear his uniform while at school, which created a natural distance between him and the students, but because he coached Little League baseball—Gabriel's Little League team—the kids seemed to both like and trust him. Wearing street clothes tonight, his badge clipped to his belt, he nodded as he approached the front steps. "Eric."

"Thanks for coming. Suzanne and Branch are inside. Andrew's on his way back from the Twin Cities." He held the door open.

As always, he was embarrassed by the run-down state of the house's interior. The TV had been switched off and Branch was standing next to Suzanne, his arm held protectively around her shoulders.

Eric was more than a little surprised by the way Steinhauser looked. He hadn't seen him in a couple of months. In that time his ruddy face had become bloated, his eyes sunken, ringed with dark circles. Eric's first thought was that he was ill.

Steinhauser nodded to Suzanne. After eyeing Branch for a few seconds, he said, "Why don't we sit?" He claimed the piano bench, while Eric sat on the arm of the couch and Branch and Suzanne sat on the love seat. "We'll figure this out, don't you worry. About what time do you think the kids took off?"

"I'm not sure," said Eric. He explained about them sleeping in the tent. "Their bikes are still in the garage."

"That's a good sign. They can't get as far on foot. I should probably take a look at the tent."

Eric had already examined it multiple times and found nothing that would suggest anything unusual. The sleeping bags were laid out, rumpled as if they'd been slept in. Gabriel's bag of Fritos was empty, as was a two-liter bottle of root beer.

"Were the boys upset about anything?" asked Steinhauser. "Something that might make them want to run off?"

"Gabriel was fine," said Suzanne. "Right?" she asked, looking at Branch for his agreement. "He likes it out here in the country better than he does in town. And then, of course, Jack's not only his cousin, but his best friend."

"Any fishing poles missing?" asked Steinhauser.

Eric shook his head.

"I already looked around down by the lake," said Branch, an uncharacteristic gruffness in his voice. "No sign of them."

"What about Jack?" continued Steinhauser. "Any issues there?"

"Well," said Eric, clearing his throat. "Andrew moved out a few weeks ago. Jack was understandably upset." He gave a brief explanation of his runaway attempt. "Andrew and I both talked to him about it. I thought we'd ironed out the problems."

"Tell me again how that works? Whose kid is Jack?"

"Biologically, he's Andrew's. Legally, he belongs to both of us."

"Where's the mother?"

"She's a flight nurse at the U.S. air base in Ramstein, Germany." Eric was determined to leave it there. Steinhauser didn't seem to be homophobic, though it was always possible. Minnesotans were known for hiding their lethal opinions behind a smile.

"Does Andrew still see Jack?"

"Every weekend."

"So no cause to think that Andrew took him."

The comment threw Eric. "Absolutely not."

"Has Jack contacted Andrew since last night?"

"No. If he had, Andrew would have told me."

Steinhauser considered the issue. "So, if I'm reading this right, you think Jack was the instigator. He provided the reason for running off. Gabriel just went along for the ride."

Eric stared down at his wedding ring. "I guess."

"Let me ask you something," said Suzanne. "You see Gabriel every week at baseball practice. Have you noticed anything unusual? Anything Branch and I may have missed?"

Steinhauser shifted back in his seat. "Kids his age can blow hot one minute, cold the next. Hard to say what's going on in the mind of a twelve-year-old boy. I like Gabriel and Jack. They're good kids. Good students. My guess is, they'll be back before dark." Rising from his chair, he added, "All the same, before I go, I'd like to take a look at the tent."

"That's it?" said Suzanne, clearly unhappy that he wasn't asking more questions or offering them more information.

"Give it a few hours," said Steinhauser.

"But what if they don't come back?" asked Suzanne.

Hearing the back screen door slam, Eric pitched off the couch and rushed into the kitchen, sure that the kids were home. Instead, he found Truman bent over, talking to himself as he dug through the refrigerator. "What are you looking for?" he demanded, annoyed that his uncle was once again treating his kitchen like a grocery store.

"Something for dinner," Truman said, continuing to mumble.

"We already had this conversation. If you're hungry, go into town and buy yourself some groceries."

"I'm hungry *now*."

Steinhauser stepped up behind Eric. "Who would this be?"

Hearing an unfamiliar voice, Truman turned around. He eyed Steinhauser warily, but said nothing.

"What's your name?" asked Steinhauser.

"This is my uncle," said Eric. "Truman Lindstrom. He lives in the RV behind the house."

"I noticed it when I drove up," said Steinhauser, hooking a thumb over his belt. "You got a Minnesota license for that thing?"

Truman's mouth set angrily. "Just passing through."

"Did you see the kids leave this morning?" asked the officer.

"No. Now if you'll excuse me, I'd like to forage in peace."

Steinhauser stared at him a moment, then motioned for Eric

to follow him back into the dining room. "Not very friendly," he whispered, bending his head close to Eric's. "He lived here long?"

"Since February." Eric and Andrew hadn't been exactly thrilled when Truman had driven in, assuming that he'd be welcome to park on their property.

"You ever been inside that RV?"

"My uncle doesn't appreciate visitors."

"What did your son think of the guy?"

"That he was strange."

"He ever say or do anything that seemed threatening?"

"He's not like that."

"How well do you know him?"

Eric had to admit that he'd only been around Truman a few times when he was a kid. He might be his father's brother, but they didn't seem to have much in common. "Not well."

Steinhauser's cell phone rang. Slipping it out of his pocket, he switched it on and read what appeared to be a text message. "Shit." His face blanched. Running a hand over his mouth, he said, "I've gotta go."

"Problems?"

"Afraid so," he said, already on his way back through the living room. "Now listen—all of you. If the boys don't come home tonight, we'll talk first thing in the morning. I may need to interview your uncle, Eric."

"Aren't you going to examine the tent?" asked Suzanne.

"Leave it up. I'll look at it tomorrow."

4

"Are we all ready for the big reveal?"

Cordelia's voice blasted through Jane's cell phone with more enthusiasm than was strictly necessary for nine in the morning. For multiple reasons, Jane didn't feel quite as confident about the potential outcome of this morning's "reveal" as Cordelia did. "I'm as ready as I'll ever be."

"I've just pulled into my parking space behind the theater. I still can't believe it's mine. Good-bye to my years as the creative director at the Allen Grimby Repertory Theater and hello to my future, the Thorn Lester Playhouse. You like the new name, right?"

"I think it's perfect."

"Yup. Me, too. Sometimes theaters remind me of churches. There's too much reverence in them. I want to shake up the theater world around here."

Jane didn't like to be negative. She hoped her best friend's dream would be everything Cordelia dreamed it would be—and more—

and yet, as much as she resisted the notion, she could foresee problems that could easily sink the enterprise. "You can't leave your sister out of that equation."

"Yes, yes. Octavia Thorn-Lester—the great zircon in the diadem of American theater."

"She is, after all, the one with the money."

"Octavia will get tired of living in the middle of corn country and move back to Europe. Either that or I could always spray a little Roundup in her evening martini."

"How middle western of you."

"I've lived here too long."

"But your sister wants to star in the maiden production next fall, right?"

Cordelia hooted. "I suggested we do *Lost in Yonkers.* She'd be perfect as the grandmother."

"Look, I'm at the Lyme House. A quick conversation with my executive chef and I'll be on my way."

"ETA still ten A.M.ish?"

"That's the plan."

"Mah-velous." As the most feted and admired creative director in the entire Midwest, Cordelia never really moved out of theatrical mode.

"Hey, I'm getting another call," said Jane. "Gotta run."

"Stay classy, Janey. I'm out." She cut the line.

Jane sat down at a table in the empty pub. Her staff was already prepping for the day, restocking the bar, cleaning tables, sweeping the floor. "Jane Lawless."

"Jane, hi, it's Andrew Waltz."

"Hey. Wow, it's been a while. How are you?" Andrew and his partner, Eric, were old friends.

"Not great. I'm hoping you can help me with something. It's . . . personal."

As a much younger man, Andrew had worked on the construction of the Lyme House, Jane's first restaurant, as one of the worker bees. Every evening, she would see this gorgeous blond guy pick Andrew up. One thing led to another and Andrew and Jane eventually came out to each other. They'd become friends and stayed that way for many years, though they drifted apart after Jane's partner, Christine Kane, had died. Andrew did invite Jane and Cordelia to his marriage ceremony when he and Eric—the gorgeous blond guy—finally tied the knot.

"Eric and I split about a month ago," he said quietly. "I ran into Cordelia last week. She may have told you."

"Was it supposed to be a secret?"

"I never tell Cordelia anything I don't want broadcast on national TV."

"I'm sorry, Andrew. Any hope you two can work things out?"

"Hard to say. Maybe. Anyway, the problem I called about is our son, Jack. He and his cousin, Gabriel, took off sometime between Tuesday night and Wednesday morning. They haven't come back. Jack ran away once before—a few weeks after I moved out. Didn't get very far. Eric and I had a stern talk with him about it and he promised he'd never try anything like that again. They slept in a tent in our backyard on Tuesday night. Eric and his sister—do you remember her from the wedding?"

"The minister? She looked a lot like Eric."

"Yeah, that's Suzanne. Gabriel's her kid. Eric and Suzanne talked to a local cop about it last night. The guy thought the boys would be back by bedtime."

"But they weren't."

"No. All of us are nearly out of our minds with worry."

Jane's niece, Mia, had disappeared one afternoon a couple of years back. She'd been playing hopscotch in front of Jane's house at the time, so this was a situation Jane viscerally understood. Just remembering it made her stomach tighten. "What can I do?"

"I want to hire you and your friend, Nolan, to find them. I'll pay you whatever the going rate is."

"How did you know I was doing part-time investigative work?"

"Cordelia."

"Of course."

"I mean, maybe the cop is right and they will come back on their own. Problem is, I can't wait for that. They're just kids. Sure it's a rural area, but that doesn't mean bad things can't happen."

Jane didn't want to ask the next question, and yet to do the job he was asking her to do, she had to. "There's no chance that they were—"

"Abducted?" he said, finishing the sentence with a groan. "Jesus, no. No sign of anything like that." He inhaled audibly, paused for a couple of seconds. "My best guess is that Jack's still angry at us for the breakup and is trying to make us pay. Only this time, he's got his cousin involved."

"Does Eric agree with that assessment?"

"As much as we agree on anything these days."

Jane removed a small notepad from the back pocket of her jeans, and a pen from the pocket of her leather vest. She mainly remembered Jack and Gabriel as skinny, somewhat gawky kids, blurs as they ran past with the other kids at the wedding. Flipping to an empty page, she asked, "How old are the boys?"

"Both twelve. They attend Winfield Middle School, just graduated from the seventh grade."

"Anything else going on? With Jack or his cousin?"

"Suzanne said everything was fine with Gabriel. She's remarried. Gabriel gets along fine with his stepdad. We all like him—his name is Branch Born. Branch and I used to work together, so I know him pretty well. Jack, well, I mean, he's always been a difficult kid. Even as a toddler, you'd put him in a room with a bunch of toys and he'd always find the one dangerous thing to do. He's strong willed. A little on the arrogant side. With the exception of the problems between Eric and me, nothing else was going on with him—at least that we know about. I'm working construction in the Cities right now, but I drove back home last night. The family spent the morning nailing up flyers around Winfield. Friends are helping with the search. Suzanne even has some of the people from her church out looking."

Andrew and Eric's wedding had been a private affair up in Canada, but the wedding reception had been held at a room in the community center in Winfield, so Jane had been there once before.

"We moved into an old farmhouse a couple miles outside of town. I've been rehabbing it in my spare time, which, to be honest, I don't have much of these days. We were hoping to sell it at a profit."

"Flipping houses still works for you?"

"Not like it used to. It was how I kept our family afloat for years. Eric doesn't make much at that family bar and café of his. And until I got this position as project manager, my jobs tended to be seasonal. I lost a couple of properties in the subprime housing mess. Couldn't sell them and couldn't afford to pay the mortgages."

"Ouch."

"Yeah, well. As they say, Wall Street got bailed out. Main Street got fleeced."

"I hear the housing market is rebounding."

"I'm seeing some positive signs. Maybe we'll actually be able to sell the farmhouse one of these days. Anyway, Suzanne has more church members lined up to search later today. What else should we be doing?"

Jane doodled in her notebook. "First off, you and Eric need to talk to all the boys' friends."

"Eric did some of that yesterday," said Andrew. "We'll put our heads together and make sure we've got it covered."

"The police need to take a hard look at your phone records. You want to know if Jack talked to anyone unusual recently."

"Good. I'll make that happen."

"Is there a local TV or radio station in Winfield?"

"Radio."

"Call them. Get them to feature the boys' disappearance. And contact the local newspaper."

"I'm so glad I called you. Anything else?"

"Work up a list of volunteer searchers. You can't lean on the same people for . . . however long it takes to find them. Hopefully, that police officer who came out to your house was right and they'll come home on their own."

"If only," said Andrew, his voice cracking with emotion.

"Text me the address of your place. And your cell phone number and Eric's. I'll make time to come down later in the day. That work for you?"

"I'm grateful."

"Stay positive, Andrew."

"Sure. You're right. It's just—"

"I know. I've been there. We'll figure this out."

Jane would never get used to seeing her business partner and longtime friend, A. J. Nolan, in a wheelchair. An African-American man in his midsixties, a retired homicide cop turned PI, until a few months ago, he'd been vigorous, burly, and tough-minded. Jane had worked well over a year to earn her PI, license from the state of Minnesota so that she could join him, part-time, in their new company, Nolan & Lawless Investigations. She'd owned the Lyme House restaurant in Minneapolis for sixteen years, the Xanadu Club in Uptown for one third of that time. She was a restaurateur by desire and by training, and yet in her late thirties, she found that she had begun to grow restless.

Now in her midforties, she'd fine-tuned her life and was finally on the right track professionally—a dual track that, so far, she'd been able to manage with one significant, forthcoming alteration. In less than a month, the Xanadu Club, her second restaurant, would be sold. She was about to take a bath on the sale, losing money she couldn't afford to, though she saw no way around it. When it came to her work life, Pollyanna, like Elvis, had definitely left the building.

Everything had been going reasonably well until Nolan had taken a bullet to his stomach while saving her life. He'd recently been forced to undergo a second surgery, which had left him with constant back pain and a useless leg. The doctors held out hope for a limited recovery, continued to tell him that the numbness in his left leg would diminish with time and therapy, but looking into his eyes, Jane could tell he didn't believe any of it.

Nolan had every reason to be depressed. His active, consequential life had been stolen from him, reducing him to sitting in a chair, mostly watching TV. He was capable of so much more, though his depressed mental state had prevented him from making the effort. That's why Jane and Cordelia had been working on something they hoped would get him back on track, back to work. There was no reason he couldn't continue to have a full life. It would simply be a different one, with limitations and obstacles he would need to figure out how to negotiate. Easy for Jane to say, as he often pointed out. She wasn't the one in the chair. Comments like that weren't meant to cause guilt. Nolan didn't live his life that way. Still, even without the reminder, Jane could hardly ignore the fact that he wouldn't be in the chair if it hadn't been for her bad decisions. Cordelia liked to point out that Jane hadn't done the shooting, but sometimes that detail seemed a bit too fine.

Ever since Nolan had been sent home from rehab, exactly one month ago, Jane had been spending several nights a week with him, bringing over pastries from the Lyme House, cooking him soups and stews, things he could easily reheat in the microwave when she wasn't around. They'd played a lot of poker, watched a ton of movies—mostly foreign films, his favorites. He'd almost died in the hospital because of an infection, so time with him felt like a gift.

Opening Nolan's back door, Jane slipped quietly into the kitchen, relieved to smell coffee and know that he was up. Cordelia and Jane had kept "the big reveal," as Cordelia liked to put it, a secret, hoping that it might just be the hook that would pull him back to life.

"Nolan?" Jane called. She crossed the hall and found him with his back to her, looking out the window in the living room, gazing mutely at the summer morning from the confines of his chair. "Hi," she said softly, feeling tears burn her eyes. She pushed the feeling away. "Are you ready?"

He didn't speak for several moments. Then, "I don't even know what this is about. Think I'll stay home."

"You can't."

He backed the chair up and turned it around. "Why can't I?"

"Because I have a surprise. It's important."

"I don't like surprises."

"You'll like this one."

He grumbled, his hand crawling up his tie. He'd dressed up for the occasion, even though he didn't know what it was. Jane was touched by the effort. His arms were strong enough so that he could lift himself into and out of the chair without assistance. They'd talked about finding someone to come in to do some of the chores Jane had taken on—washing clothes, changing bed linens, grocery shopping, general cleaning and maintenance. So far, although the idea was on the table, neither one of them had acted on it. Jane wondered if he was afraid that she'd disappear if someone else came on board. He must know that she'd never abandon him, and yet fear made people believe odd things. They'd grown even closer over the last few months. Jane had a wonderful father who lived in St. Paul, a semiretired criminal defense lawyer. In an important way, Nolan also felt like her father. To Jane's mind, it was an embarrassment of riches.

"Have you had breakfast?" she asked, stepping behind him and pushing him into the kitchen.

"Toast and coffee. More than enough. I'm getting fat."

"No you're not."

They stopped so he could press the off switch on the coffee-maker. "Okay, I'll go. But this better be good."

He wheeled himself out the back door and down the short ramp she'd asked a carpenter to build so that he could get in and out of the house by himself. She locked the door behind them and then walked behind him out to her Mini. "I finally found a place that will adapt your car so you can drive again."

He didn't respond. After he'd pulled himself into the front seat, Jane folded up the chair and lifted it in behind him. On the way around the back of the car to the driver's side, she crossed her fingers behind her back, hoping that his mood would improve when they got to the theater.

Cordelia was waiting for them at the top of the ramp that had been built years ago to make the building handicapped accessible. In an uncharacteristic moment of eagerness, Nolan wheeled himself up the ramp, clearly happy to see her.

She leaned down and kissed his stubbled cheek. "Are you ready to be amazed?"

"No," he said, allowing her to wheel him in through the stage doors. "But I would like a tour of the place. You're sure you can make a go of it?"

"What's life without a little risk?"

"That's what I used to think."

"Oh, stop kvetching."

Cordelia was the only one who could get away with talking to him like that. Not only did he allow it, he seemed to enjoy it.

Perhaps as a way to look festive for the grand occasion, Cordelia

33

had wound her head with an India-print scarf, two large peacock feathers sticking out from the back. At Jane's questioning glance, she said, "What? Too too?"

"Is Octavia around?" asked Jane.

"I hooked her up with my real estate agent. Let us fervently pray that she's out looking at properties. I have to admit that I now understand what it was like living in the Balkans before World War One. Assassination plots are in the air, dearhearts. *Everywhere* in the air."

As they were waiting for the elevator, Cordelia's seven-year-old niece, Hattie Thorn-Lester—Octavia's daughter with Roland Lester, the famous Golden Age Hollywood film director—skipped up, a backpack over her shoulders. Hattie had lived with Cordelia for most of her life, mainly because Octavia, with her constant travel, her multiple husbands, and her periodic movie and theater roles, simply didn't have time to devote to a child. So strong was Cordelia's feeling that Octavia was an utter dirtbag when it came to motherhood that she'd figured out a way to force Octavia to give her full legal custody. It hadn't been pretty, but it was a done deal.

"What's up, Hatts?" said Cordelia, giving her a hug, her eyes glowing with fondness. Hattie was done with school for the summer. On certain weekdays she was at Smart Kids' Camp, as Cordelia called it.

"One of the workmen said there were bugs in the basement," said Hattie, hopping up and down, unable to contain her enthusiasm.

Cordelia pressed the back of her hand dramatically to her forehead. "What did we say about this bug fixation of yours?"

"It's not a fixation," said Hattie, tossing her blond curls behind her back. "It's a hobby."

Jane couldn't help but laugh. Two of the best known names in the dramatic arts had produced a child who wanted nothing more than to spend her days studying pigmy hippos or watching the occasional spider crawl across the travertine tile in the kitchen.

"Hi, Jane," said Hattie, spinning around. "Hi, Mr. Nolan."

"Why don't you go watch that DVD I bought you," asked Cordelia. "*Moguls and Movie Stars: A History of Hollywood.*"

"B-O-R-I-N-G, Deeya."

Hattie had called Cordelia Deeya ever since she was a toddler. When she wanted to act more grown up, she used "Auntie Cordelia," though most of the time Deeya sufficed.

Pressing a finger to her niece's lips, Cordelia said sternly, "Never utter that word with reference to the world's great film stars in my presence."

"Can I go down to the basement to look for bugs?"

Cordelia expelled a deep, agonized sigh. "If you must."

"Thank you!"

"Be careful," Cordelia called after her as the little girl skipped away. "There's lots of junk down there." She added to Jane and Nolan, "It's where most of the old stage props were dumped. We haven't even begun to look through them all."

"Such a beautiful little girl," said Nolan, watching her disappear around the corner.

"Yes, she *is* a Thorn," said Cordelia, patting the back of her new hairdo, a dyed pink emo with purple highlights. With the accompanying extra-wide turquoise eye shadow and the long diamond barrette, she looked very "sparkly," as she liked to phrase it.

They took the freight elevator up to the second floor.

"I'm told that the theater is on the third," said Nolan, wheeling himself off after Jane drew back the doors.

"Offices are on the second," said Cordelia. "Retail space on the first. That is, when we get it all redesigned. I'd show you my office, but it's nowhere near ready for visitors."

Jane nose itched at the smell of the drywall dust, wet cement, and new paint.

"So what are we about to see?" asked Nolan, gripping the arms of his chair as Cordelia all but hurtled him down the corridor.

Over her shoulder, Cordelia shot Jane a conspiratorial look. "Just cool your jets for another few seconds and you'll find out." She stopped at the end of the hall and turned him toward an antique door with an opaque chicken-wire-glass panel top. A piece of paper covered the center section of the glass.

"So?" said Nolan with a shrug. "A door. So far, no amazement."

With a flourish, Cordelia tore off the paper. Underneath, in bold gold and black American Typewriter lettering, were the words:

Nolan & Lawless Investigations

Nolan didn't speak for several seconds. Then, "What the hell have you two been up to?"

"Voilà," said Cordelia. "Your new offices."

Jane opened the door as Cordelia propelled him inside.

They were both proud of the effort they'd made. The area was spacious—divided into three separate rooms. The larger office was for Nolan. The smaller one was for Jane. A center section was reserved for clients. The walls had been painted a golden ochre, the oak wood trim restored to its original luster.

"You can leave your house," said Jane, standing next to Nolan, "get in your car—completely reequipped for your use—pull into your dedicated parking space behind the theater, take the ramp inside, and then the elevator up here."

"Easy peasy," said Cordelia. She backed up, flinging her arms wide, doing her best Vanna White imitation as she stood in front of several framed oversized movie posters. "Humphrey Bogart in *The Maltese Falcon*. Alan Ladd and Veronica Lake in *This Gun for Hire*. They were my idea, of course, so you can thank me for creating the proper ambience. I thought they'd help get you in the sleuthing mood."

Nolan gave her a half-lidded look.

"The front office, *yours*, overlooks Harvard Place," she continued. "And the smaller office faces a side street and the park beyond. That's Jane's. The waiting room is for your oodles and oodles of mysterious clients." She dropped down on an extra-long leather couch and crossed her legs dramatically to emphasize her point.

"I've never wanted *oodles* of clients," grumbled Nolan. "I only want the occasional interesting one."

"What*ever*," said Cordelia, waving the comment away.

It was a wonderful setup, in Jane's opinion. She and Cordelia had dithered over an antique desk they'd seen in a local shop, one Jane wanted to buy Nolan. She finally decided it was perfect—a solid, quarter-sawn oak monster. Jane had found an antique Stickley desk for her office. It was being shipped from North Carolina and wouldn't arrive for another couple of weeks.

Nolan glanced at the monster desk as he wheeled himself past it to the window. "I will admit, this is a surprise all right."

"A good surprise?" asked Cordelia, jumping up from the couch and joining him.

Jane held her breath.

"I recognize the effort this took," he said, not exactly answering the question.

"Your computer and all your files will be delivered tomorrow," said Jane. "My office will take a little longer to get set up. The telephone line will be installed by the end of the week. Until then, I figure we can use our cell phones."

"For what?" asked Nolan, wheeling around.

Jane opened one of the bottom drawers of his desk and removed a file folder. Dropping it on the desktop, she said, "This is a list of all the people we've heard from in the last two months looking to hire an investigator."

"How am I supposed to help them?" he demanded, his mouth drawing together angrily. "Without my legs."

"The same way you always did," said Jane. "With your brain. Your eyes. Your experience. Your computer. And your wheels—both your car and your chair. Nolan, listen to me. I know this is hard. I know you're depressed by what's happened to you. But you can still work—still have a life. You simply have to want it." Seeing that he was still resisting the idea, she added, "I can't want it for you. I wish I could, but I can't. It's your decision. We can tell Cordelia to use this space for something else—remove our names from the door. Or—" She hesitated. "We can get back to work."

Scraping the back of his hand across his mouth, Nolan regarded the desk. After a few more seconds, he flipped open the folder. "I *suppose* . . . it seems kind of ungrateful to turn all this down."

" 'Ungrateful'?" repeated Cordelia. "Just think of everything you'll miss if you . . . you look this gift horse in the mouth." As an aside, she said, "Not that I'm sure what 'gift horse' really means."

38

"I can explain it to you," offered Jane. "If you want."

"I'm not big on equine metaphors." Swirling around the room, her hands cupped together, she nearly exploded with excitement. "Just think of the fun we'll have together," she said, flinging her arms wide. "Since I'm right across the hall, I'll be able to offer you my crime-solving expertise whenever you need it."

Nolan cleared his throat.

"And think of the coffee breaks we'll be able to take together."

Jane couldn't tell if Cordelia's hard sell was working or not.

Scanning the room for a couple of seconds, Nolan finally rolled himself squarely behind the desk. "I guess this fits okay. Right height and all."

Cordelia gave Jane one of her infamous semipulverizing bear hugs. "Just wait until you see the coffee machine I'm installing," she said. "The break room down the hall will be *state of the art*."

"Where's Octavia's office?" asked Jane. Octavia had been taking her time selecting one. She'd wanted Cordelia's, of course, but Cordelia had grabbed it first.

"I suggested the broom closet. Seemed like a perfect fit. Now, give me two seconds and I'll be back with the champagne—to cement our new business relationship. Every theater should have a shamus on the premises," she said, charging out door. "Actors," she shouted over her shoulder, "are so full of nasty little secrets."

Jane stepped into the hallway to remind her to bring the flutes, only to find Hattie racing toward Cordelia from the other end of the hall.

"Deeya! Look what I found." She was waving a quart jar over her head.

"I don't want to see any bugs," said Cordelia, hands pressed to her eyes.

"But—"

"Put it in your backpack." She checked her watch. "Time for you to get downstairs. Bolger is picking you up at ten thirty."

Bolger Aspenwall III was Hattie's nanny. He was also working on his MFA in directing at the University of Minnesota.

"He's taking you to the zoo," said Cordelia, disappearing into an open doorway.

"He is?" said Hattie, her face brightening.

"Chuck the bugs before you head back to the mother ship, okay, Hatts? I don't want to wake up with any more emerald ash borers in my bed."

"But—"

"Run along now," came Cordelia's voice through the open doorway. "Enjoy the lions and tigers."

"And the binturongs. They're my favorites."

"Oh, mine, too," came Cordelia's voice, oozing sarcasm. "Be sure to give them my love."

5

"We're wasting our time," said Branch, pulling his truck over to the side of a dusty county road and cutting the engine. "We keep going over the same real estate again and again. It's pointless. If the kids want to hide, it's like trying to find a needle in a haystack. They could be anywhere."

"We have to keep looking," said Suzanne, scanning the fields, all the while trying, with little success, to push away the sick feeling inside her stomach. Her husband didn't seem to understand that driving around was as much about the need for movement as it was about the actual search.

Matt Steinhauser, the police officer the family had spoken to last evening, might not see the boys' disappearance as anything more than a youthful prank, but Suzanne didn't buy it. She didn't believe for a second that Gabriel would put her through something this terrifying just because Jack wanted to make the point that he was pissed at his dads. Her son still had the softness and sweetness of a boy. He wasn't reckless like Jack. Suzanne had seen a quiet strength grow inside Gabriel since his father's death, a quality that Jack, with all his hotheaded bluster, entirely lacked. Her son wouldn't run away unless he was convinced it was the right thing to do. The problem was, Jack was a great spinner of tales. He had a youthful charisma that made him a natural leader—but a boy who was governed by impulses, rarely his better judgment.

Branch pushed the truck's door open, his boots landing with a thud on the dry dirt. Stepping around the front of the truck, he adjusted his baseball cap and gazed at the ripples of heat rising off the land. "I just don't understand why he's doing this," he called back to Suzanne. "He's got to know we're worried sick."

"Of course he knows." During the night, that certainty had led Suzanne to a conclusion she'd tried hard to steel herself against. If she didn't say the word out loud, giving it a reality, a substance, she might be able deny it as a possibility.

"Except, he's still a child, Suzanne. He doesn't have the ability to see how hurtful his actions could be to the people who love him. I figure they've got to come home sooner or later. They'll get hungry, or just plain sick and tired of being on the run. Kids that age talk big, but they're not about to give up the comforts of home for long just to make some stupid point."

Suzanne closed her eyes, willing herself to believe he was right.

Branch stood a few more seconds by the side of the road, then returned to the front seat. Instead of starting the engine, he pulled off his sunglasses and wiped tears from his eyes. Suzanne loved that about him. Big, strapping, six-foot-five-inch jocks were supposed to be the tough, silent types. Branch had never been like that.

"I am so freakin' *frustrated*," he said. "I don't know what to do, where to go. Jack thinks he's the poster boy for street-smart. What a joke. He doesn't know shit about the real world. Sorry," he said, ducking his head. "Didn't mean to swear."

"You think I care about that?"

"No, but . . . you know."

"In the middle of the night, I started wondering," said Suzanne. "If Gabriel did run away, maybe it was the genetic testing that upset him. I should have left well enough alone."

"Oh, baby," said Branch, pulling her hand up to his lips, kissing her fingers. "He said he was okay with it. We made sure he talked to a counselor. What else could we do?"

"He saw his father die of ALS. It was a terrible thing to watch. If he thinks he'll die the same way—" The results of the test wouldn't be back for a couple more days. Until then, they were all holding their breath.

"Okay, let's say Gabriel *was* upset. Why wouldn't he talk to us? Why run off? Makes no sense."

"Like you said, kids that age don't think logically."

Branch took off his baseball cap and ran his hand back and forth over his spiky hair.

She sensed that he was holding something back. "What is it?"

"Nothing."

"No, please. Whatever you're thinking, tell me."

"It's just . . . you know. Maybe it's me. While you were tossing and turning last night, I started thinking. Maybe I shouldn't have adopted him. I've never been a father before. I probably suck at it."

"Oh, honey, you're great with him. You taught him how to water-ski, how to fish. You take him hiking in the woods, got him interested in Little League baseball. Sam was never like that.

Before he got sick, he was working seventy hours a week. He lived his life in his head, and that's what he taught Gabriel. You've helped him become so much more balanced."

"My father was like that with me," said Branch, staring off into the distance. "I guess I take after him. But *work*," he repeated. "I wish I could be more like your first husband. If that job I applied for would only come through." He paused, crossing his arms. "If it wasn't for Gabriel and Jack, it's all I'd be thinking about. Three years, Suzanne. I've been looking for a decent job for three freakin' years. I don't want to get my hopes up, but if I get this one, I'd be making great money. I'd feel human again, like I was contributing to the family, not sponging off you."

It was a conversation they'd had many times in the last few years. Nothing Suzanne said or did ever seemed to mitigate his sense of failure. Without a steady job, a way to define himself, a reason to get up in the morning, he'd been cut from his moorings. The few temporary jobs he'd found hadn't added up to much.

Branch had grown up in Ohio. Because of a football scholarship, he'd attended the University of Minnesota, which was where he'd met Andrew and Eric. He'd dreamed of being a star player in the NFL ever since he was a kid. When he was drafted in the ninth round by the Indianapolis Colts, he figured he'd died and gone to heaven. In the last regular season game that year, he received a career-ending neck injury. He'd worked like crazy to make a comeback, though in the end, he'd never played another game. He eventually moved back home to Cleveland to lick his wounds before finally taking a job with a landscape firm.

With nothing else going for him, Branch had made landscaping his career, starting his own company in Winfield a few years later when Andrew began rehabbing houses. At the time, the housing market was booming, with no end in sight. The common wisdom said that homes were the bet that never went bad. Branch had worked closely with an appraiser, a loan officer at the local bank, and Andrew. The four of them were like a mini-company, although they each kept separate books—had separate business cards. Everything had come crashing down when the housing market tanked in 2008. Branch limped along for a couple more years, eventually filing for bankruptcy in 2010.

Suzanne and Branch had become engaged a few months before he'd filed. At the time, he was hoping he wouldn't need to take such a drastic step, but when it became clear that it was necessary, he'd asked Suzanne if she wanted to back out. She remembered the night vividly. They'd gone out on Arbor Lake for a ride on his pontoon. The soft summer breeze, the gorgeous orange-and-peach sunset, and her love for him were all stirred together in an intoxicating mix. She understood that nothing was ever simple, but canceling the wedding was the farthest thing from her mind. When she told him, he seemed almost surprised, as if he'd expected the worst. She hated that he'd been willing to give up on their dream so easily, that he wouldn't fight for her. Sometimes he seemed as if every ounce of fight, of normal self-esteem, had been beaten out of him. Because of that, she wanted this new job for him as much as he did.

Grasping the steering wheel with both hands, Branch said, "I need you to listen to me. You and I both know I'm not a smart man."

"No—"

"Just listen. *Please.* I'm not like you and Gabriel—or your first husband. All I want is a quiet life. A few cold ones after work.

Church on Sunday. The sports page. The chance to get outside and enjoy nature. Sometimes I think you married the wrong guy. I'll never be able to help Gabriel with his honors math, not like his real dad. I believe in God, love the church, but I'm not interested in thinking about all the stuff you do. Asking all those big questions. I just want some peace. A chance to support my family. Is that so much to ask?"

"Whether or not you get that job, we'll be fine," she said, gazing up into eyes.

"No, we won't. It's not like it was for our parents, when one job in a family paid all the bills. The longer I go without work, the deeper the hole we're digging for ourselves. Maybe . . . maybe we should say a prayer. Ask God to help us find the boys—and help me get that job. You're the minister," he said, placing his hand on the back of her neck. "You've got a special relationship with God. You should start."

Suzanne was relieved when her cell phone rang. Checking the caller ID, she saw that it was her brother. "This might be important," she said, clicking it on. "Hi, Eric. Heard anything?"

"Here's the situation," came his anxious voice. "Steinhauser thinks the kids are over in Short Creek."

"Thank you!"

"Just got off the phone with him. A guy called the Winfield police to say he'd seen two boys who matched Jack and Gabriel's description loitering around a 7-Eleven. When he walked over to talk to them, they ran into the bathroom and wouldn't come out. Steinhauser's on his way."

Suzanne relayed the information to Branch. "We're leaving right now."

"Andrew's with me. We're already on the road."

"Don't be angry at the kids," said Suzanne, snapping on her seat belt as the truck jerked forward, kicking dust away from its back tires. "We need to understand why they did it."

"I want to throttle them, but yeah, I hear you. I am so relieved."

"Me, too. See you in a few." She closed the phone and held it tight, a shiver of hope rising in her chest.

6

Jane arrived at Andrew and Eric's farmhouse that night later than she'd expected, having been waylaid by a problem at the Xanadu Club. She was selling it to her ex–business partner, Barry Tune. Barry had taken over the daily management last year. When Jane had time to stop in, which was rarely, she felt that the club was going downhill. She'd trusted Barry because of his experience in the industry. By the time she'd realized she'd made a mistake, it was too late. The old employees at the club were unhappy, the new employees were lowlifes, druggies, and losers, and the food standards had taken a nosedive, and unless she devoted herself to the place exclusively for the next six months—or longer—nothing was going to change.

When Barry had made a lowball offer to buy her out, she'd rejected it out of hand, but then found herself dithering over it. She'd attempted to negotiate a better deal, though in the end had taken his offer. She planned to sign on the dotted line early next week. Unfortunately, her lawyer and Barry's lawyer had nearly gotten into a fistfight today over what Jane considered a minor detail, so she and Barry had met with them to smooth out the issue and move things forward. Jane had to admit that she'd felt more than a few pangs of regret when she stopped by the club for a few minutes after the meeting. Once upon a time the place had been a jewel, a crumbling Art Deco movie theater that she'd turned into a hot, urban, Uptown nightclub. Sure, the food was basic turn-and-burn steakhouse fare, but with the addition of an interesting wine list and some unusual upscale menu items, it had been a classy one. That was all gone now. She'd had a good run, but restaurants didn't last forever. It was time to cut her losses and move on.

Jane pulled her CR-V off the gravel road into the farmhouse's long driveway a few minutes before eight. A BMW and two trucks—one new and expensive looking, the other rusted and old were already parked in the drive. She maneuvered her SUV into the grass next to a long row of thickly blooming spirea.

It was that golden time of evening, when the world—the trees, the bushes, the house, even the RV parked at the back of the yard—looked as if it had been bathed in amber. The house was a newly painted two-story wood structure with a spacious screened front porch and a garage toward the back that looked as if it might once have been a barn. A tall grass meadow ran along the west side of the property, with woods bordering the rear. A green-and-white domed tent had been set up on the lawn in the backyard.

Jane hadn't spoken to Andrew since this morning. He'd left her a message, saying that everyone was planning to gather back at the farmhouse for dinner around seven, and that she should join them. As she got out, hope circled inside her mind that the boys had returned, even if it meant she'd made the trip for no good reason.

Noticing a bunch of cigarette butts in the grass, Jane bent down to take a closer look. She pulled out her cell phone and took a quick picture. They'd been fairly easy to spot, their tan filter tips clearly visible against the green. What surprised her was finding a single roach—the end of a marijuana joint—in the midst of the butts.

"Find something interesting?" came an unfamiliar voice.

Jane cupped her hand around the roach and stood as a man with wavy black hair and a prominent Adam's apple, shirtless, wearing a pair of ripped jeans, ambled toward her. He was loose limbed and lanky, and skinny as a stalk of wheat.

"Who would you be?" he asked.

"Name's Jane," she said. As he came closer, she noticed a gold earring attached to his left earlobe. "I'm a friend of Andrew and Eric's."

"Are you now." The guy had a tattoo of an anchor on one forearm, a naked woman on the other.

"Truman Lindstrom, Eric's uncle," he said, glancing at the cigarette butts on the ground.

"Those yours?" she asked.

"No, ma'am. Can't say that they are."

"I assume you heard about—"

"Jack and Gabriel? Yeah, I know."

"You have any idea who might have been out here smoking?"

"Nope."

"You smoke?" she asked.

"Last I looked it's still a free country."

"Smoke any weed?"

"Matter of fact, I do." He bent over and picked up one of the butts. "But this isn't weed. It also isn't my brand. I smoke Chesterfields. These are Winstons."

She glanced over at the tent.

"Anybody figured out what they're up to?" he asked, shifting his weight from one leg to the other.

"Up to?"

"You know."

"Not sure I do."

"Kids," he muttered. "They're like mice. They mess around where they don't belong."

"Meaning?"

"You always ask this many questions?" He flashed her an amused smile, then headed back across the lawn to his RV, sat down on a folding camp chair, spread his legs wide, and pulled a pack of cigarettes off the table next to him.

"Charming," whispered Jane, trotting up the steps to the porch. She called Andrew's name before she stepped inside. "Anybody home?"

Andrew came dashing out of the back of the house, his face drawn with worry. She hadn't seen him in a few years and was surprised to find that his chestnut hair, once almost the same color as hers, had receded and was shot through with gray. He'd let it grow long, binding it in a ponytail, and had shaved off his beard, revealing a firm jawline and a dimpled chin. He was thickly muscled through his chest and arms, looked strong and fit, though he'd put on weight.

"The kids back yet?" she asked.

"Afraid not." He ushered her into the dining room, where the family was gathered around an old octagonal game table surrounded by folding chairs. The interior of the house was the exact opposite of the exterior, with holes in the walls, peeling paint, water stains, cracks in the ceiling, and an oatmeal-colored carpet that looked like it was flecked with more than color variation.

"We thought for sure we'd found them this afternoon," said Eric, rising and giving Jane a peck on the cheek, then motioning her to a chair. "A man called the police and said he'd spotted them over in Short Creek. When we drove over, we discovered that he'd found two kids, all right, but not Jack and Gabriel. It was such a letdown. We came back here to regroup before we go out searching again this evening. Are you hungry? I took a tray of lasagna out of the freezer and heated it. Suzanne made a salad."

After shaking Suzanne's hand and being introduced to Branch, Jane sat down between Eric and Andrew. The chair was empty, most likely because they didn't want to sit next to each other. While Suzanne made her feel welcome by offering her a glass of lemonade, Branch, the new husband, dished her up a plate of food. He was a big man, with a long face, a high, wide forehead, and narrow cheeks. His manner was appealingly shy; he was the kind of guy who, for whatever reason, never took his baseball cap off, even inside the house. He dwarfed everyone in the room.

Jane ate her dinner while listening to the conversation, attempting to take each person's measure. She sensed that it was a close group. Suzanne was warm and articulate, though behind her outward openness Jane detected a certain wariness—a stiffness that caused many silent assessments before she allowed herself to speak. Jane couldn't help but wonder what this carefulness was hiding.

After dinner, everyone pitched in to clean the kitchen. Once the food was put away and the dishwasher was loaded, they all drifted out to the living room with mugs of coffee.

"I'm glad you agreed to help us, Jane," said Eric, draping an arm around his sister's shoulder. He was a classically handsome man, a kind of fair-haired Lord Byron whose looks still had the power to drive women, and undoubtedly a few men, crazy. He was, however, an older, less pumped version of the guy who'd once picked Andrew up after work and whisked him away in his convertible.

Jane decided that it was time for her to ask a few hard questions. She began with the cigarettes and the roach she'd found out in the grass.

"Where exactly did you find them?" asked Eric.

"By the spirea, a few feet from the driveway. I met your uncle outside while I was examining them. He said he doesn't smoke Winstons."

"Oh, please," said Andrew. "He smokes anything he can bum, and that includes weed."

"When was the last time someone cut the grass?" asked Jane.

"Tuesday afternoon," said Eric. "I know because I did it."

"Anybody else around here smoke? Cigarettes or weed?"

"Nobody," said Andrew.

"Well, actually, I do," said Branch holding up his hand a bit sheepishly. "A cigarette or two a week—when I feel stressed. I'm trying to quit."

"I don't think that counts," said Eric.

"Whoever was out there was smoking in full view of the house," said Jane. "My guess is, it probably happened after dark."

"You think it was the kids?" asked Branch.

"If they're smoking behind your back, I doubt they'd do it in the open, even at night."

"So what's it mean?" asked Andrew, settling into a chair.

Turning to Eric, Jane asked, "Have you had any recent visitors?"

"Not that I know of."

"Somebody was out there," said Andrew, running his knuckles across the scruff on his cheeks. "Whoever it was, he was standing not twenty feet from that tent. If you mowed the grass on Tuesday afternoon, it had to be sometime Tuesday night."

"The night the kids took off," said Jane.

"You think someone was standing out there watching the tent?" asked Andrew.

"Are you suggesting the boys were taken?" demanded Suzanne. "That they didn't run away?"

"I'm not suggesting anything," said Jane. "But we have to explore all the possibilities, look at every piece of potential evidence. There were five cigarette butts out there and one roach."

"If it was one person," said Andrew, "he would have been standing there for quite a while to smoke five cigarettes. Fifteen minutes? Half an hour?"

No one offered a different opinion.

"I better call Steinhauser," said Eric, fishing his cell phone out of his jeans.

"The BCA in St. Paul might be able to pull some DNA off the cigarettes," said Jane. "Problem is, I'm not sure how long it will take them to run tests. We could use this information right now, but that's not how forensic examination works."

"Not like on *CSI: Miami*?" asked Branch.

"Nothing at all like that. You also have to figure that the butts and the roach have been out in the grass for a few days. They may prove to be worthless, even if they are evidence."

Suzanne began to pace in front of the TV. "The police *have* to take this seriously now. No more, 'The boys will be home by bedtime.'"

"Has the cop you talked to last night been out to the house today?" asked Jane.

"He came this morning," said Andrew. "Looked at the tent. I don't think he found anything. He planned to spend part of the day talking to the boys' friends. We've already done that, but he seemed to think he could get more out of them than we could."

"And then he planned to speak with some of their teachers," said Branch. "Lord knows where he thinks that will get him."

A throat cleared.

Everyone turned to find a plump, owlish-looking man with round, dark-rimmed glasses, his arms at his sides, standing in the living room doorway. He had on running shorts and a T-shirt, his running shoes loosely tied. Adjusting his glasses, he glanced tentatively around the room. "The door was open. I thought it might be okay to come in."

"Mr. Eld," said Andrew with a forced smile. "Hi. Sure, it's fine."

"Hi there, Pastor Born," said Eld, nodding to Suzanne, then extending his hand to Branch.

Since everybody knew the guy except for Jane, Andrew introduced him as Aaron Eld, the seventh-grade science teacher at the middle school.

Eric nodded to Eld as he ducked into the kitchen, the cell phone plastered to his ear.

"I'm sorry to intrude at a time like this," said Eld.

"You've obviously heard about our boys," said Andrew.

"That's why I'm here." He removed a small yellow-and-white cell phone from the front pocket of his running shorts. "I sometimes go for a run in the evenings. When I was out tonight, just a few minutes ago, I spied this under a bush. I know Gabriel has one just like it. I confiscated it from him one afternoon before school was out. He was using it to make calls during class. Do you think it's his?"

Everyone gathered around to look.

"It's either broken or out of juice," said Eld, pressing and holding the on button with no result.

"It's Gabriel's," said Branch firmly, taking it from Eld's hand and turning it sideways. "See that nick along the edge? Gabriel dropped it the first night he had it. He was outside in the driveway. It hit one of the brick pavers and made that mark. He was really pissed about it, too. Asked if we could take it back so he could get a new one."

"Where did you say you found it?" asked Jane.

"Under a bush," said Eld. "When I leave my house, I usually head up the hill past the Carnegie library and then cut across Grand Avenue to the joggers' path that hugs Bay Point Lake—you know, by the park? It was under the hedge on the east side of the library. The color made it stand out, otherwise I never would have seen it."

Inside the pocket of Eld's T-shirt, Jane noticed the unmistakable outline of a pack of cigarettes. Unusual for a runner to be a smoker, she thought.

"Once you get it working," said Eld, "you might find something that could help you locate the boys."

"Thank you so much," said Suzanne, watching her husband try to remove the back.

"Yeah. No problem. If there's any other way I can help, my number's in the phone book. Well," he continued, with everyone's attention fixed on the phone, "sorry to barge in. I should get out of here and let you people get back to . . . whatever." He inched toward the door. "I like those boys a lot. They're good kids."

He gave off a distinctly uncomfortable vibe. Since he appeared to be the poster child for bookish introversion, Jane figured that accounted for it.

"Better get home," he said again, raising his hand in a tight, mechanical wave.

"Thanks so much, Aaron," said Suzanne, smiling up at him, then returning her attention to the phone.

7

Eric sat on the front porch and watched the moon cast its weak light on the slope of meadow that stretched from the woods to the county road. Steinhauser had come, looked at the cigarettes and the roach, bagged them, and then gone. He didn't seem to find them as significant as everyone else had, but said that he'd bring them back to the station and talk to his chief. He explained that he hadn't learned anything new from talking to the boys' friends or teachers earlier in the day. He said he'd keep working the case until they were found. Suzanne asked about the possibility of issuing an Amber Alert. She was clearly scared by even the merest hint that the boys might have been abducted.

Steinhauser had hedged his response, saying that since Jack had run away once, it was more than likely that he'd done it again. Amber Alerts were issued only after certain criteria were met, criteria that this situation didn't rise to—at least not yet.

Branch and Suzanne had finally left around nine. Jane had taken off for Minneapolis a few minutes later. Before she left, she'd said that finding the phone might be a positive sign. If someone had abducted the boys, why toss Gabriel's cell carelessly under a bush? Why not throw it in a lake or a Dumpster and erase it completely? The fact that it was found by the library suggested that it might have fallen out of Gabriel's pocket, pointing to a less terrifying conclusion than an abduction. Until the boys were home and safe, however, nobody would know for sure what had happened, and yet it was a piece of hope in an otherwise depressing day, something Eric intended to hold on to.

Tapping his fingers impatiently on the arm of the wicker rocking chair, he refused to get up and go back into the house to look for Andrew. He was probably upstairs packing more of his clothes to bring over to Ingersoll's house. Burl Ingersoll was president of Ingersoll Savings & Loan, the largest bank in Winfield. Andrew had worked with him, and with Garland Friedrich, a home appraiser, during the heyday of Andrew's house-flipping empire.

Garland was long gone, but Burl still owned the bank, and for whatever reason—nefarious or otherwise—was one of the richest men in town. Many residents thought Ingersoll and Friedrich should be in jail for fraud. Nothing had been proved, though the scuttlebutt around town suggested that Friedrich had inflated the price of the properties, and thus, to get people with iffy credit a loan, Ingersoll had been only too happy to offer subprime loans. While Andrew hadn't been involved directly, all of the houses he'd rehabbed had been sold through Ingersoll, with Friedrich serving as the appraiser. The fallout had cast suspicion far and wide, landing on Andrew as well as Branch.

The truth was, both Branch and Andrew had lost a ton of money. In hindsight, it was clear that they'd stayed in the market too long. Made bad investments. Bet on a housing market that seemed like it would never turn sour. Eric had done everything he could to help Andrew through the worst of it. He didn't blame him, and yet Andrew assumed that since he blamed himself, Eric had to feel the same way.

Listening to the jangle of crickets, the house rafters settling after the heat of the day, Eric wondered what the next few days would bring—for the entire family.

"I fixed us cheese and crackers," said Andrew, coming through the screen door with a tray, glasses, and a bottle of wine.

Eric raised his eyebrows.

"Come on. We need to regroup. We can be civil for ten minutes, can't we? Besides, I'm hungry."

Andrew was always hungry. It was something Eric loved about him. "Does it feel weird being back here?"

"Yeah, a little. But it also feels . . . sort of normal."

"I'm not sure what normal is anymore." Eric touched the wedding ring on his finger. "Do you know how many houses we've lived in since we moved back here?"

"Don't start," said Andrew, sinking down on a padded love seat.

"I'm not trying to start a fight. I'm just curious if you remember."

"Five," he answered. "I know how to count."

"I was just thinking about the parties we used to give."

"We had it down to a science. The music. The wine. The food. The cleanup."

"Why haven't we given any parties in the last few years?"

Andrew picked up a slice of cheese. "Maybe there's nothing to celebrate anymore."

"How . . . utterly . . . utterly . . . sad." Eric fingered one of the crackers. "I assumed you were inside packing more of your clothes. You still staying with Ingersoll?"

He shook his head.

"No?"

"No."

"Where then?"

He poured them each a glass of wine. "I work up in Minneapolis. Since I'm not living here anymore, it makes sense to stay up there." Taking a sip, he let the news sink in for a minute, then continued, "You're going to be angry when I tell you."

Eric looked over at him.

"I'm staying with Terrence."

"Terrence Wilson? The guy who used to book your band gigs?"

"He's got a big house in Eden Prairie, with an apartment above his garage. It's actually pretty nice. Bedroom. Living room. Kitchenette."

This was not what Eric wanted to hear. "So tell me, Andrew. Are you sleeping with him?"

"None of your damn business."

"He's been after you for years."

Sucking in a breath, Andrew said, "It's not like that. I'm not interested in him. Besides, I work so damn many hours that when I get home, all I have energy for is sleep. I've got four side jobs going at the moment. What more do you want from me?"

"We're moving into dangerous territory here."

"What isn't dangerous territory for us these days?"

Eric had come to one major conclusion since Andrew had moved out: Running the café, even though he'd made a commitment to his father to take over the place, wasn't bringing in enough money. It also allowed him way too much free time. He was lonely and was therefore constantly frustrated with Andrew for being gone so much. Andrew had the opposite problem. He was crazed

61

by too much work, with no time to think about anything except keeping their heads above water financially. Each silently—and not so silently—blamed the other.

Shifting in his chair, Eric made a stab at changing the subject. "Sometimes I think this town is dying."

Andrew kicked off his athletic shoes. "The Ben Franklin store closed last week. The sporting goods store up on McKinley is hanging on by a thread."

"It's the Walmart up on the highway. It's killing the retail stores. They can't compete."

"This isn't the town we grew up in."

"We agree on that," said Eric. Draining his wineglass, he continued, "Shawn Wainwright called me last week. He wants me to do some speechwriting for him, and for the conservancy."

"You gonna do it?" asked Andrew, grabbing another piece of cheese.

"I'm thinking about it."

They sat silently for a few minutes, looking up at the stars.

"If Jack did run off again," said Eric, pouring himself another glass of wine, "I can't help but think it's because of us—our split."

Andrew exploded. "Absolutely everything is my fault, isn't it?"

"Do you realize how often you respond to something I didn't say?"

"It's subtext. I get it. You're the long-suffering one. The good son and the good father. I'm the screwup because of the houses I couldn't sell, and because I'm gone so much that I'm not around to do my fair share with Jack. Do you really think that I want to live like this?"

They were like dueling phonograph records. The needle—

62

their conversations—might slip and slide around for a while, but eventually they always fell back into the groove. "Can you see that we're in some sort of crazy blame loop that neither of us can climb out of?" The phone in the back pocket of his jeans began to ring. Sighing, he said, "I better take it." He said hello and listened. When he heard nothing but silence on the other end he said, "Is anybody there?"

"I'm calling about your boy," came a man's voice.

Eric felt his pulse heat up. "Do you know where he is?"

"If I did, I wouldn't tell you."

"Excuse me?"

"You've got no business being a parent. That kid of yours doesn't have a chance. He'll grow up just like you. Sick. Twisted. You *gays* make me want to hurl."

"Who is this?"

"You should be run out of the state—out of the country. Maybe I'll get a posse together and come visit you one of these nights. I know where you live. Better keep your doors locked is all I can say." The line disconnected.

"What is it?" asked Andrew, gripping Eric's arm. "Who was that?"

Eric closed the phone and held it to his lips. "The wing nuts are coming out of the woodwork. The guy said he might come by with a bunch of his buddies one night soon. We're gay so we have no business being parents."

"You know, there are times when I wish you'd let me bring my rifle home, instead of leaving it with Branch."

"No guns in the house. Ever."

"You like being a sitting duck?"

The landline in the kitchen rang.

"I'll get it," said Andrew, thrusting himself off the love seat.

Eric followed him inside, standing in the doorway, holding his breath.

Andrew said hello. A moment later, "Oh, hi, Mrs. Knox." He listened. "Thanks. We appreciate that. Yes, I'll tell him. You're very kind." He paused. "Yeah, we're holding up. It hasn't been easy. You're right, having a pastor in the family helps. Sure, we'll let you know. Yeah, you too. Night." As he placed the phone back in its cradle, he said, "Thank God not everyone is a bigot." He paused, then added, "I'm staying here tonight. I'll sleep on the living room couch. Until we get this settled," he said, moving to the back door to check the lock, "I think we should make sure this place is always secure."

Eric was silently grateful. With Andrew in the house, he wouldn't feel so alone. It was something. Not much in the scheme of things. But something.

8

Aaron Eld had lost his faith—not in God, but in experts. His dad had been a military man and had raised him to respect authority. He'd been taught, not always in words though certainly in practice, to trust society's institutions—the church, the government, the school system, hospitals, corporations. He'd also been convinced that the world was a meritocracy. If you worked hard, got a good education, lived as a good citizen, respected authority, your life would be successful.

During the past ten years, as Aaron watched each of these cherished institutions deal with disgrace, scandal, and perfidy of every sort, his faith in the American Dream had been sorely tested. He'd been appalled when the pedophile priest outrage erupted in the Catholic church, although the institution itself still seemed to continue on with nothing but a minimal falter. After the Wall Street implosion, which had nearly tanked the world economy, the men responsible, with few exceptions, were still in charge, still raking in the cash as if nothing had happened. It seemed like forgiveness was the order of the day for the millionaires and billionaires, while the rest of the society lived with the hard hand of accountability.

Obviously, something in the system had gone terribly wrong. Aaron often heard people talking about American exceptionalism as if it were a given. Most seemed to agree that the U.S. was better educated, brighter, more moral, richer, more talented, and harder working than anyone else in the world, and therefore had a right to take charge of the planet.

Unfortunately, Aaron no longer saw it that way because the facts simply didn't support it.

During the presidential election of 2012, Aaron had proudly become a fact-checker. He wrote a small blog, which he updated several times a week, offering details on the research he conducted. Not many people read it, though that wasn't the point. What bothered him most were the powerful voices abroad in the land insisting that one fact was as good as another. That, he'd concluded, was a con job. Absolutes did exist. Opinion wasn't an absolute, no matter who uttered it. Words had intrinsic meaning and shouldn't be bent out of shape to serve a political, religious, or philosophical cause.

With all the empty rhetoric circling the societal drain, the problem seemed to be that governing still had to get done. For a country, a state, a town to be orderly, to move forward on issues that needed to be addressed, a citizen had to *trust*. No individual could know everything, all the ins and outs of an issue, and therefore people picked surrogates—news sources, political parties, magazines, newspapers, radio and TV shows that would filter and package the information for them. Trust was society's currency. Without it the wheels came off.

And thus, for Aaron, trust had become the fundamental problem of his existence. His cynicism appalled him, and yet he could see no way around it. He looked at all authority figures now and wondered what they were hiding—were they malicious, driven by some idiot ideology or greed, or merely incompetent? Because, one way or the other, the average citizen was getting shafted right and left, with no way to change it, sometimes no ability to even understand it, and no end in sight.

That's why Aaron sat in front of the TV night after night, as he was doing now, seething inside, watching Fox News for an hour or two, then changing over to CNN or MSNBC to get a different view on the same general theme. After his wife went to bed, he'd retreat into his study, close the door, and write letters. A few he'd sent, though most he put in a drawer because they betrayed not only anger, but rage. He vented in the only socially acceptable way he knew how. It was a futile exercise. Power to the people. Hilarious. Another slogan that meant nothing in this second decade of the new millennium. The men who owned the country would never allow the *bewildered herd*—the writer and public intellectual Walter Lippmann's name for the American public—to have any real power. For all practical purposes, the world had become George Orwell's *1984*. War was peace. Freedom was slavery. Ignorance was truth. And Aaron's current favorite aphorism to enter the fray: corporations are people.

Feeling the light touch of a hand on his shoulder, he turned and looked up into the face of his wife, Holly. Maybe there was one person in the world he still trusted.

"Are you coming to bed soon?" she asked, playing with the back of his hair.

"I thought I'd watch a little *Letterman*."

"Okay," she said. "Maybe I'll sit with you for a few minutes."

Slipping his arm around her, he saw that the butterfly rash on her cheeks and the bridge of her nose looked worse.

"How are you feeling?" he asked.

"Good. Not to worry."

"It's my job to worry."

She rested her head on his shoulder. "I'm going to be around for a long long time. You better get used to it."

Aaron had met Holly during his second year of teaching. He was living in Minneapolis at the time. Holly worked the morning shift at a restaurant he frequented on the weekends. She was ginger haired and friendly and he was instantly attracted to her. She could make him laugh when he had a hangover, which was no small accomplishment. He eventually asked her out.

Holly had grown up in Siren, Wisconsin, a small town north and a little east of the Twin Cities. Less than a year after they'd met, Aaron was so lost in love that he'd popped the question even before he'd bought a ring. They were married in the spring and spent the summer backpacking across Europe. The following year, he'd been offered a teaching job in Winfield. Holly was happy to get back to a small town. Aaron wasn't so sure he'd like it. Even with his hopeless credit and credit card debt, they were able to buy a nice house and settle in.

It became clear to Aaron almost immediately that he and his new wife were perfectly suited to small-town life. All their pleasures were home centered—the modest though absorbing delights of domesticity. Holly made curtains and painted all the rooms. They went to garage sales to furnish the place. Aaron planted a garden. They made friends with their neighbors and hosted several cookouts that first summer.

Neither of them had ever expected to live in such a beautiful—

and big—home. Their only sorrow during those first few years together had been a miscarriage. It hurt them both deeply because they'd hoped to start a family right away. Holly eventually found a part-time job at a women's clothing store, where she was able to buy all her clothes at a discount. She always looked so pretty, far prettier than a geeky, tubby guy like Aaron deserved. She also had loads of spunk—and a temper. She called it "ginger power." She didn't lose her temper often, but when she did, Aaron usually found something to do outside.

Aaron's mother had died in '09 and left him a small inheritance. It was pretty much gone now, though he'd made sure to keep the worst details of their financial situation to himself. Holly didn't need the added worry.

Sensing his wife's restlessness, and not wanting to go to bed just yet, he said, "Want to play cards?"

She snorted. "You mean like poker? You're hopeless. If we played for real money, I could take you for every dime you have."

His skin felt tight when he smiled. "I should work on my poker face."

"You okay?" she asked, pulling away from him.

"Just a little down."

"Where were you tonight? You got home so late."

"I took a drive. Needed some air."

"Don't you get enough air when you're out running?"

"I wanted to cool off." He could feel her watching him like she wasn't sure she believed him.

"You're still upset by what happened at school at the end of the year," she said.

"No. Yeah. Maybe."

"You want to talk about it?"

69

"Nope."

She blew a lock of hair away from her face. "The principal's a jerk."

"I couldn't agree more."

"Come on," she said, tugging on his arm. "Come to bed."

"It's early."

"I'm offering you my body, asshole."

When he turned, he saw that she was bestowing her best lecherous grin on him. Sometimes he loved her so much it hurt. "You go. I'll turn off the lights and be right up."

How could he ever tell her what he'd done? The truth was, Aaron was every bit as much of a liar as any other man.

9

Cordelia gritted her teeth as the doorbell rang for the third time in the last five minutes. She was seated in a comfy chair in her study, reading through a bunch of applications, trying to come to a decision about what firm to hire to do the theater's marketing. Instead of concentrating on the task at hand, she was deep in reverie, devising ever more drastic schemes to force her sister to move out.

She'd already tried the direct approach. "Did your Realtor show you the perfect condo yet?" Of course, the answer was no. Octavia was an insane perfectionist. Cordelia's next comment was, "Look, you either move out or I buy a Gatling gun. A big one. Civil War era." Or words to that effect. Octavia laughed. Such silliness. Cordelia's final ultimatum was something like, "If you don't leave, and I mean right now, I'm going to haul all your Jimmy Choos up to the roof, douse them with charcoal lighter, and burn them to a crisp." That had caused a momentary narrowing of her sister's eyes, but she'd shrugged it off, saying that it was an empty threat. She threw Cordelia's oft spoken phrase back at her: "Cordelia Thorn does not haul." And that was the end of that.

Less than an hour ago, Octavia had announced that she'd invited a few friends over for cocktails. She'd shouted for Bolger, Hattie's live-in nanny, to dig out Cordelia's most expensive caviar, then go to the grocery store for the rest of the fixings—"Oh, and buy the makings for those little cream cheese and crab creations I adore so much." Bolger, who generally behaved in an adult fashion, had turned into a lapdog under Octavia's command, doing her bidding without grousing while gazing adoringly in her general direction. He was deeply smitten by celebrity.

Frankly, thought Cordelia, as Peter O'Toole had said in *The Lion in Winter,* it was a tangle.

"Deeya," called Hattie, skipping into Cordelia's study. "The mayor is here."

Cordelia cocked an eye. "The mayor of what?"

"Of . . . umm . . . Nottingham?"

"I think you're thinking of the Sheriff of Nottingham."

"Yah."

"The Sheriff of Nottingham is here?"

"Ah . . . yup."

"Anyone else?"

"Another man." She scrunched her eyes shut. "Tom Courtland."

"The *actor,* Tom Courtland?"

"He smells nice."

The doorbell rang for the fourth time.

"Mommy said I can't watch my TV show in the living room because that's where they're having the party."

"Meanie."

"Yah. She told me I had to go somewhere else. That the party was only for grown-ups." She plunked down on the floor and began to pick at the tufts in the rug. "She never wants me around. I don't think she likes me very much."

"Oh, honey," said Cordelia, lifting her into her lap. She refused to tell the little girl that something that didn't feel like love really was love. That kind of message was confusing. "Your mommy isn't . . ." She struggled for the right word.

"Nice?"

"Not always."

"If she doesn't like me, I don't like her."

Cordelia understood the impulse. "She's——"

"Selfish," said Hattie. "I wish she'd go."

Cordelia cuddled her close. "You're the most important part of my life. You know that, right?"

"Yah. I do."

"We're a team. We help each other."

The doorbell rang for the fifth time.

"I have to get out of here," muttered Cordelia, her eyes darting wildly around the room.

"Can I come with? Bolger is ignoring me, too. I wanted to play Clue, but he was too busy in the kitchen." She oozed primal hurt.

"Mean, nasty people."

"Yah." She scowled. "Can we go somewhere with a big TV?"

"I've got the perfect solution."

Hattie threw her arms around Cordelia's neck. "Thank you, Deeya."

"We don't need my booze and my caviar. Right?"

"We can have yummy fluffernutter sandwiches."

That, thought Cordelia, might be going a little too far.

Jane tossed her keys and silver credit card case into a brass dish on the counter in her kitchen and, after crouching down, she rubbed and petted her two dogs, Mouse, a brown lab, and Gimlet, a miniature poodle puppy. Gimlet was so insanely happy whenever Jane returned that she yipped and jumped and twirled and licked and pawed until she got the attention she felt she deserved. Mouse, a more restrained—and perhaps mature—personality, always allowed Gimlet her moment in the sun, sitting down and waiting for Gimlet to get her affection first. Jane adored both of them, but Mouse was a mensch—a noble animal, a kind and decent soul, maybe her best friend next to Cordelia, and also a dog that was thrilled to have the more overtly emotional Gimlet as a companion. After letting them out the screen door into the backyard, she listened at the bottom of the stairs, hearing the steady click of Avi's computer keyboard.

Avi Greenberg was Jane's new girlfriend. Jane never knew what Avi's schedule was because it changed so frequently. She worked as a part-time bartender at a restaurant down on the 494 strip. She'd recently taken over an upstairs bedroom in Jane's house and made it her writing studio, and she was free to use it whether Jane was home or not.

Avi didn't live with Jane. She had an apartment across town, one she shared with a law student and part-time exotic dancer, a woman Jane loathed. Her name was Georgia Dietrich. With her looks and skills, she was cut out to be nothing less than a filthy rich, highly sought after attorney. Jane had nothing against lawyers. Her father happened to be one. Her father, however, was honest, a quality Georgia lacked.

Avi had come into Jane's life suddenly, turning everything

she thought she knew about herself upside down. It was Jane who was always the reticent one in any relationship, the woman who took her time, analyzed the situation from every conceivable angle, resisted the idea of living together because she was a workaholic with loner tendencies, a forty-five-year-old woman who liked her privacy and was set in her ways. In less than a week, Avi had changed all that. Jane still wasn't sure what had happened or how. She wasn't the type to fall in love at the drop of a hat. She didn't believe love at first sight was even possible. People who experienced it were fooling themselves, which was why there were times lately when she wondered if she'd gone quietly and completely mad.

Avi was unlike anyone Jane had dated before. Physically, which was as good a place to start as any, she was androgynous, half Jewish, half Latino, with skin that looked tan even though she rarely spent much time outdoors. With her half-nerdy, half-sultry looks, her dark hair and eyes, her boy clothes, horn-rimmed glasses and red-and-white striped Keds, she did clean up awfully well, which meant that when she chose to go the lipstick-and-eyeshadow route, as she did for her bartending gigs, she looked hot. Then again, Jane thought she looked spectacular in any and every incarnation.

More important, perhaps, there was the matter of Avi's intelligence. She was a writer, a fascinatingly creative woman who'd been struggling for years to write the Great American Novel. Since completing her grad school degree in creative writing, she'd written half a dozen books, none of which had found a publisher.

Jane had been allowed to read only two of the novels, both wonderfully fresh, sexy as well as powerful stories, peopled with

75

crazy, funny, damaged, but always deeply human characters. She had to admit that she was almost as enamored of Avi's writing—and the mind it revealed—as she was of Avi herself. She hadn't said that out loud because she instinctively felt Avi would see it as sucking up—and most likely she wouldn't believe it anyway.

Avi wasn't always easy to be around. Her outward charm masked a vulnerable, occasionally even bitter woman who struggled with depression and a chronic inability to value herself and her work.

Hearing the clicking stop, Jane headed upstairs. The door to the bedroom was open, revealing a darkened room lit only by the light of the computer screen. The bed in the room had been replaced by a sofa. Jane walked in and sat down.

"I got your text," said Avi, swiveling her chair around. "Where's Winfield?"

"Southern part of the state. About an hour away."

"A new case?"

"How come you didn't text me back?"

"I was writing. Didn't want to stop."

She seemed unusually discouraged. "How's it going?"

"I have absolutely no idea. That being said, it's done."

Jane moved to the edge of the couch. "Congratulations."

"Yeah, yippee. Another book in the can, and I do mean the *can*."

"You never know. Maybe this will be the one."

"I'm starving. I'm always hungry when I travel through the Slough of Despond."

"I've never read *Pilgrim's Progress*."

Avi removed her glasses, rose, and dropped down on the couch next to Jane. "I love it that you're literate. If I'd written *that* book, instead of John Bunyan, nobody would have ever heard of the Slough of Despond."

"You say you're hungry." Food was something Jane could work with.

"How about you fix us one of those trays . . . like you do. With the radishes and butter and coarse salt."

"You actually like that?"

Avi kissed her, then stared into Jane's eyes. Jane was ready for more, but Avi stopped her. "Let's have some wine."

"Wine is good."

"Oh, and do you have any of that stuff you make with chicken livers and brandy?"

"Pâté?"

"Yeah, and that nice stinky cheese and garlic sausage. I mean, there should be a few perks when you date a restaurateur, yes?"

"I hope there are more than a few," said Jane, tipping Avi's face toward her and giving her another kiss, one that did start turning into something more. "You're sure you want to eat?"

"I need sustenance to keep up my mental and physical vigor."

"Have you eaten anything today?"

"Does coffee count?"

When Jane stood, Avi stood with her, resting her arms on Jane's shoulders as she reached behind her and removed the pins from Jane's hair. "You leave here every day looking so professional, so spit and polish, hair in a French braid or a tight bun, all buttoned up. I like to unbutton you."

"Works for me."

"I like you best with your hair down, your feet bare, wearing jeans and an old shirt—in other words, when you lower your standards to my level."

On the way down to the kitchen, Jane heard the front doorbell chime. "Will you answer that?" she called back to Avi. "Whoever it is, get rid of them. We need to spend some quality time together. Read anything you want into the word 'quality.'"

"Afraid that's not going to happen tonight."

Jane stopped halfway through the dining room and turned around. "Because?"

"I can't stay. Georgia needs a ride home from the club."

"She has a car."

"It's in a body shop. The right fender's all smashed in. She took a bus to work, but she doesn't like to take the bus late at night."

"Then take a cab."

"Come on. Don't be like that." With a smile forming, she studied Jane's reaction. "You think she did it on purpose, don't you? As a way to make sure I don't spend the night with you."

"Never said that."

"No, but I'm right. You really hate her."

"I don't trust her."

"Or me, obviously."

The doorbell continued to chime.

"Listen to me for a second," said Jane. "What I don't trust is—" She couldn't bring herself to say it.

"What?"

"I guess . . . what it comes down to is that I don't trust that you want to be with me."

Avi blinked a couple of times, giving away nothing.

"I want a chance for us, without Georgia playing her little games in the background. I want a free and clear shot."

Now the doorbell sounded as if someone was leaning on it.

"It's Cordelia." Nobody else would ring a doorbell like that, with the exception of a five-year-old.

"Food," said Avi, grinning, pointing to her mouth. "And just so you know, I'm not interested in Georgia, I'm interested in you." She went to answer the door.

Since Cordelia would soon swoop in, Jane decided to triple what she put on the tray.

"Evening, all," said Cordelia, breezing into the kitchen wearing her current favorite attire, a black and-gold Indian wedding sari. It was not only beautiful, but it covered her length and breadth more than adequately. At nearly six feet tall and weighing in at well over two hundred pounds, she was the embodiment of Mother Earth. Jane was also struck by the physical similarities between Cordelia and Nigella Lawson, the English food writer. There were moments when they looked so much alike—especially during Lawson's more full-figured periods—that they could have been twins separated at birth.

Spying the bottle of Montepulciano Jane had just removed from the wine rack, she said, "Am I interrupting something?"

Hattie bounced into the room. "Can I watch your TV downstairs?"

"Of course you can," said Jane, giving Hattie a hug.

"And can I have some popcorn?"

"Coming right up" said Cordelia, dumping the stack of file folders she was holding on the kitchen table. "I'll bring it down when it's ready."

After the little girl had scurried off, Jane said, "Avi and I were just about to have a bite to eat. I assume you'll join us?"

Cordelia rummaged around inside her sack purse until she came up with a bag of microwave popcorn. "I'd be delighted. Mainly, I need a quiet place to work. Octavia is giving another one of her impromptu soirees. Seems Tom Courtland is in town."

"The actor?" said Avi, opening the microwave and placing the bag inside.

"One of Octavia's Hollywood buddies. The mayor's there, too."

"The mayor of Minneapolis?" asked Jane. "How did Octavia meet him?"

"She knows his wife . . . or something. And then a few of Bolger's theater buddies stopped by to bask. Oh, and a director friend of Courtland's stopped over to lap up my caviar and swill my vodka. Nice of Octavia to be so lavish."

Jane assembled a thick slice of Jarlsberg, the brandied pâté, a box of Breton crackers and set them on the tray, then began to wash and clean the radishes. Once done, she finished by adding to the tray a chunk of fresh unsalted butter, a slice of aged Prima Donna Gouda, a bowl of fat green pistachios, and some lovely fleur de sel. "Am I missing anything?" she asked.

"I don't suppose you've got any of that Day-Glo-green jalapeño jelly?" asked Cordelia.

Jane added that to the mix, set the tray in the center of the kitchen table, grabbed the bottle of wine off the counter, added another wineglass, and sat down. "*Et voilà.*"

"What's with all the work?" asked Avi, nodding to the files as she buttered herself a radish.

"I started the evening working on selecting a marketing firm for the theater. Those"—she pointed—"are scripts. It's absolutely crucial that we pick a winner for the first play."

"Something tried and true?" said Avi, pouring the wine.

"Heavens. That's why I left the Allen Grimby. I'm sick to death of tried and true. I want to *offend*. To shake up the theater world around these parts. We need to aim at a younger audience,

80

at least occasionally, which means a production that's faster paced, entertaining, and preferably written by someone who's still alive."

"Octavia agrees?" asked Jane.

"We can't even agree on what color white to paint the hallways. This theater renovation is sucking me dry—financially. Octavia simply doesn't understand how important certain things are. She won't pay for them, which means I have to."

"Is she really that rich?" asked Avi.

Both Jane and Cordelia gave leaden nods.

"From acting?"

"Heavens, no," said Cordelia, slathering pâté on a cracker. "She inherited the money from Hattie's father—Roland Lester."

"I know that name," said Avi. "But I can't place it."

"He was a famous Golden Age Hollywood film director," said Jane. "Octavia had his child—Hattie—through, shall we say, an act of immaculate conception."

"He'd had his sperm frozen," said Cordelia, "and waited for the woman with the right genetic potential to come along."

"And then he died and left a mansion on the Connecticut shore and the balance of his fortune to Octavia and Hattie." Jane got up to check on the dogs. Mouse was sniffing the peonies near the garage. Gimlet had found herself a chew toy and was lying in the grass, gnawing on it.

"Not to change the subject," said Avi, "but how did Nolan like his new office?"

"He stayed for several hours," said Cordelia between bites. "Shut the door and emoted privately. When he reappeared downstairs a few hours later, waiting for a cab to take him home, he looked almost cheerful."

Jane was glad to hear it. She hadn't talked to him since leaving the theater.

"So give us the down and dirty on what you were doing in Winfield," said Cordelia. "All I got was your text."

Jane spent a few minutes giving them the details on the two missing boys, ending by saying that she would need to drive back first thing in the morning. She hoped the kids would return on their own, although certain things didn't add up.

"Like what?" asked Avi.

"Well, for one thing, I don't understand why the cop in charge of the case isn't being more proactive. The boys are twelve, not exactly small children, but still. Anything could have happened to them. They've been gone almost forty-eight hours. The parents are worried sick. If I were him, I would have covered a lot more bases by now."

"Simply bad at his job?" asked Avi.

"It's possible," said Jane. She didn't want to jump to conclusions, and yet if Steinhauser didn't develop more enthusiasm for the case and soon, she'd be forced to conclude that something else might be in play.

"Poor Andrew and Eric," said Cordelia with a deep, rumbling shiver. "I don't know what I'd do if anything ever happened to Hattie. You need any of my extraordinary investigative expertise, Janey, you know where to find me."

Cordelia drifted downstairs to the rec room a while later. Jane asked if she could concentrate on her work with the TV on.

"I have no problem ignoring shows featuring reptiles."

Shortly after eleven, Avi announced that she had to take off.

Feeling thwarted but keeping it to herself, Jane accompanied her to the front door.

"Ever thought about installing a basketball hoop above your garage door?" asked Avi.

Jane found it an odd question. "Um, not really."

"You should."

"Because?"

"When I need to think, shooting hoops helps focus my mind."

"Really."

"You should try it. So should Cordelia."

"Oh, that's a perfect idea. I'll be sure to pass it on."

"And Jane." Avi leaned back against the front door and grinned. "About Georgia. Give me a little credit, okay? I know who Georgia is. And I know who you are."

"Is that good?"

"Yeah, Jane." She pulled her close. "That's very, *very* good."

10

When Suzanne and Branch returned home that night, Branch stood at the kitchen counter and downed several shots of scotch.

"I don't know what to do," said Suzanne, staring at the empty shot glass. The moment she'd learned that Gabriel and Jack were missing, she felt as if time had stopped. "It's dark out. Gabriel hates the dark. You know him. He always has a night-light on in his bedroom. What if he's in the dark somewhere? He'd be so scared. What if he's scared, Branch? What if he's in pain?" She felt her husband's arms fold around her.

"It'll be okay," he whispered. "We'll find them, bring them back."

"Pour me one of those," she said, nodding to the bottle.

"You sure?"

Downing the bitter liquid, she grimaced. "Awful stuff." Because of her mother's addiction, she hated alcohol on principle.

"It will help."

She doubted it.

Neither of them had slept much the last two nights, which was taking a toll on their moods and their ability to think clearly. After Branch drifted off to bed, Suzanne sat for a while in her study, scrolling through Internet articles on runaway kids and child abductions. By eleven, she'd hit a mental and emotional wall. The only thing she could think to do was get outside and walk.

Finding her keys, she stepped quietly out of the house, glad for the moonlight and the drop in temperature. Ten minutes later she found herself across the street from her church. She hadn't been heading anywhere, at least not consciously, and yet here she was. Since she had her full set of keys with her, she unlocked the side door, noticing, as soon as she entered, that a light glowed in the senior pastor's office at the far end of the hall.

Suzanne had been the interim senior pastor for almost a year while the committee on nominations searched for a replacement for Burton Young, her beloved friend and mentor who was retiring. Suzanne didn't want the job, and yet she'd felt more than a twinge of disappointment when the offer never came. It was clear that the committee was looking for something she obviously didn't bring to the table. So be it, she'd thought. It would have been terrible timing if they had chosen her.

When Vivian Brassart arrived from Alabama in November, Suzanne had felt equally amazed to discover that the committee had chosen a deeply conservative preacher, someone they hoped would, to quote the chairman of the committee, put the "fear of God" back into the life of the congregation.

During the intervening months, the selection had begun to cause a rift in the church, a potential disaster that was barely averted with a promise from Vivian to make changes more slowly. The very fact of her presence, and of the religious philosophy she brought with her, made the entire point moot, in Suzanne's opinion, as her initial amazement began to morph into outright shock.

In early July, the congregation was scheduled to vote on whether or not to open the church's doors to the LGBT community. Both Burton and Suzanne had lobbied strongly for it. With Vivian's arrival, Suzanne had noticed a change come over many of the members. People who had once seemed supportive of the idea were now voicing opposition. A new—or perhaps an old—harsher, sin-centric conservatism seemed to be gaining ground.

For the first time in her pastoral life, Suzanne began to hear negative comments from members of the congregation about "blacks," "feminists," "liberals," and "Muslims." She even heard the words "socialist" and "communist" chucked into a few heated conversations. Vivian's inflexibility, the black-and-white way she saw the world, stunned Suzanne. Her reading of the Scriptures was equally fundamentalist, as every Sunday she referred to the Bible as the "inherent, unalterable Word of God."

Suzanne's path to the ministry had first led her to Greek scholarship. In divinity school, she'd studied the New Testament, not simply from the more common devotional standpoint, but from a critical-historical point of view, as virtually all seminarians did. Suzanne went even farther, thinking that to understand what God was trying to say to the world, she needed to learn the language in which the books were originally written. That took her an extra five years. She came to see what every biblical scholar already knew: The Bible was full of factual errors, discrepancies, and even outright forgeries. For some, it didn't change their faith, while for others, it did alter the way they viewed not only

Scripture, but God. Most seminarians left this information behind closed seminary doors as they received their diplomas and entered into congregations, rarely to ever speak about it again. Thus, those sitting in pews on Sunday mornings never heard about historical-critical scholarship. Vivian had graduated from Boston University School of Theology. She'd learned the same things Suzanne had, and that's why her simple answers outraged Suzanne so deeply.

The devil, the wages of sin, and the ultimate depravity of human beings filled Vivian's Sunday sermons. She spoke down to the parishioners and at the same time seemed amazingly skillful at whipping up their emotions. She practiced doublespeak— preaching the importance of love, while concentrating on messages of exclusion and hate. It was the righteous versus the damned. Good, God-fearing Christians against every other creed on Earth. As the national election grew close, politics began to creep into her sermons, something Suzanne vehemently opposed. Many in the congregation were able see the change for what it was, but most seemed willing to give Vivian the benefit of the doubt.

Entering the softly lit sanctuary, Suzanne sat down in a back pew to think. With these issues on the table, problems that had occupied her so totally that, for months, she'd barely looked up, she wondered if she'd missed something with Gabriel. Thinking about him now, remembering how sad his eyes had looked when she'd dropped him off at her brother's home on Tuesday afternoon, she realized he no longer talked to her the way he used to. When had that happened? She must have brushed it away thinking that it was his age, his move toward his teenage years. If it was Gabriel's decision not to communicate, not her decision to stop listening, then she figured she was off the hook. Except that now she saw that small piece of self-serving analysis for what it truly was—a rationalization. She'd been too preoccupied, too overwhelmed by a contradiction she'd found in her own life— specifically, the disparity between who she wanted to be, who she thought she was, and who, when it came right down to it, she really was—that she'd stopped reaching out to him, failed to ask questions, failed to listen, failed to be fully present with him during those rare moments this past year when she was home. In all the heaviness of her own work and spiritual life, Gabriel and his needs had gotten lost.

"Suzanne?" came a soft, delicate voice, heavy with a southern accent.

She turned to find Vivian, wearing what she always wore in church—an oddly formal Geneva gown and cassock—gazing down at her. Suzanne had the distinct sense of looking up at a hawk, with its hard, sharp, intensely cold eyes. She could easily imagine Vivian swooping down from a height, attacking in a slow, controlled dive, feet outstretched, ready to grab her—the small vole—in her talons.

"I just heard the news," she said, sitting down one pew in front of Suzanne and turning around. "Your son. It was a kidnapping?"

Suzanne had always loved southern accents. Vivian had changed that view almost overnight. "We don't know," she replied, wishing Vivian would go away.

"Have you heard from . . . anyone? A ransom note?"

"No."

"It's a horror when these things occur. Proof that we live in a sick society, Suzanne, that the human heart is indeed deceitful above all things and desperately wicked. I quote Jeremiah seventeen:nine. If we need proof, here it is. Men who do things like that deserve to burn for eternity in the hottest, darkest, deepest reaches of hell."

The fact that Suzanne didn't believe *anyone* should burn in hell—or that a loving God would even think of such a punishment—was hardly the conversation she wanted right now.

"Anything I can do—"

"Thanks, Vivian. There's nothing."

"Will we see you at choir practice tomorrow?"

"I've already spoken to Seneca White. She'll take it for me this week."

"That's probably wise." Once more, she stood looking down at Suzanne with her dark hawk eyes. "God's ways are inscrutable. Just know that this is happening to you for a reason."

"To *me*?" she said, her voice rising. "What about Gabriel and Jack?"

"His will be done."

"You think God had something to do with those boys being taken?"

"He knows when a sparrow falls. He allows it. You might even say He ordains it."

Suzanne stood to face Vivian. "I don't think *God* had anything to do with my boy being taken—unless He's a sadist. Is God a sadist, Vivian?"

She reacted as if she'd been slapped. "I know you don't mean that."

"I do," she said. "If God isn't love, than I'm not interested in being His representative."

"You're upset."

"You're damn right I am."

"Good night, Suzanne. I'll pray for you."

Not wanting to wake her sleeping husband, Suzanne slipped quietly in the front door a little after midnight. She was met by the sound of the coffeepot gurgling in the kitchen and the shower on in the upstairs bathroom. Climbing the stairs to the second floor, she entered the bedroom and sat down on the rumpled bedsheets to wait.

"What's going on?" she asked when Branch emerged naked, towel-drying his hair. As he started to pull on some clothes, the digital clock on the nightstand glowed 12:14 A.M.

"Where were you?" he asked.

"I went for a walk."

"At this hour? You should have left me a note."

"I'm sorry. I ended up over at the church. Ran into Vivian."

"Oh. That's good. You probably needed to talk to someone besides me about what's going on."

She stuffed a pillow behind her back and leaned against the headboard, watching him grab his jeans off the back of a chair, pull them on, then start searching for his boots. "Are you going somewhere?"

"You bet I am. This may seem like a long shot, but I think I may know where the boys are."

Her heart skipped a beat.

"That old hunting shack I use in the fall. Gabriel's been there with me. More than once."

During deer-hunting season, Branch and an occasional hunting buddy would spend weekends at a cabin in the woods. Sometimes Andrew went along, though once he'd shot himself a deer, he didn't go again. Suzanne had seen the place only once. It was so run-down and dingy that she'd never had any desire to go back. The men would bring up cots and sleeping bags. The cabin didn't have any electricity or running water. There was a wood-stove in one corner to heat the place when the weather turned cold. They hauled up coolers for their beer and food, peed in the woods, and generally had a high old time. Suzanne hadn't been thrilled when Gabriel insisted that he be allowed to go along last fall. He'd driven up with Branch twice, even been allowed to fire a rifle a few times, a big deal in Gabriel's youthful opinion.

"I can't believe he'd know how to find it," said Suzanne. It was a good fifteen miles away, and then another mile or so off the county road, with nothing but a dirt path through the woods to the cabin.

"He could find it," said Branch. "I know he could. If nothing else, it would get them out of the elements. If he and Jack were intent on running away, it would be a perfect place to hole up. Nobody but me and Andrew and maybe one other guy ever goes out there, and then only during hunting season. It's totally re-mote." Yanking a sweatshirt over his head, he added, "I'm gonna check it out."

"Now?"

"I have to. What do you say? You coming?"

She could hardly let him go without her. "I'll fill a Thermos with coffee."

On the ride to the cabin, they were uncharacteristically quiet, wrapped in thought, each nursing a silent hope. Once they'd turned off the main road and headed into the brush, Branch cut the lights on his truck and used the moonlight to navigate. He came to a full stop about twenty yards from the cabin door. Everything looked dark and quiet, with no signs of life inside. The sound of crickets engulfed them as they approached.

Branch gave the door a sharp rap. "Hey," he called. "Gabriel? Jack? It's me. Open up."

Suzanne stood back and scanned the property. "I don't think they're here."

Branch turned the handle and pushed the door inward. Removing a flashlight from his back pocket, he turned it on and pointed it inside. "Duck," he called, dropping into a crouch as a bat flew directly over his head.

Suzanne hit the dirt and watched it flutter away into the night.

Still crouched, Branch washed the beam over the interior. "Nothing," he said, his voice full of dejection. "Damn it all. I was so sure." He sank down on the ground. "The cabin's got two doors. This one, and one that leads out to a small deck off the back. I suppose they could have heard the truck engine and taken off."

They scrambled around the side of the cabin. Suzanne stood next to Branch as he directed the beam of light at the woods. "Just a sec," he said, trotting up the steps to the deck and darting inside. Coming back out a few seconds later, he said, "There's no sign of them. No food, no candles, nothing that tells me anyone's been here."

In the moonlight, Suzanne could read the defeat in his face. "Like you said, it was a long shot."

Slamming his fist against the railing, Branch's eyes rose to the starry night sky. "Where the hell are they?"

Run away or taken, thought Suzanne. Either way, she felt as if someone had sunk a knife deep into the core of her. Seeing the tears stream from Branch's eyes, she felt her own eyes well.

"What do we do now?" he asked, walking back down the steps to take her in his arms.

She had no idea.

Sinking to his knees, he reached up for her hands. "Pray with me."

She knelt down, feeling the heat of his body next to her, yearning deep in her soul to be able to offer some easy, uncomplicated, comfort. As much as she wanted it, as hard as she searched for the right words, indeed, any words, they refused to come. In their place she recognized more fully than ever before the magnitude of her grief, not only for the loss of her child, but for the loss of her childlike image of God.

11

FRIDAY

The sun had just begun to burn through the mist when Jane rolled
her CR-V into Andrew and Eric's drive the following morning.
Truman, wearing a sleeveless T-shirt that was more holes than
shirt, head down, ignoring her arrival, was working a section of
grass with a rake, a large black plastic garbage bag on the ground
next to him. Instead of going inside, Jane walked over to find out
what he was up to.

"Morning," she called, seeing and then smelling the foul patch
of rotting fruit and vegetables that had been dumped in the yard.
"Jeez, what happened?"

He shrugged, pulling on some plastic gloves, then bending down
to pick up several particularly slimy potatoes.

In Jane's opinion, having worked in commercial kitchens for
most of her adult life, there were few worse vegetal smells. "You
have any idea who did this?"

"Saw a car pull up before I went to bed last night. Maybe they did it. Maybe they didn't."

"What time?"

"After one. Can't be precise."

"Did you recognize anybody?" She backed up a few paces to get away from the stink.

"You think I got night-vision goggles permanently attached to my face?"

Andrew stepped out on the front porch and called her name.

She turned and smiled, repositioning her sunglasses as he strode out to greet her.

"Didn't expect you so early."

Jane had a lot she wanted to accomplish today.

"Just so you know, we started getting a lot of phone calls late last night." He tucked his hands into the pockets of his cargo shorts, motioned for her to walk back to the house with him. "Some were nasty, but a few were from neighbors and friends wishing us well. Life is sure a mixed bag." He glanced back at the rotting mess in the yard. "Truman was kind enough to offer to take care of it for us." Lowering his voice, he added, "I don't much like the guy, and then he goes and does something unexpectedly decent. Makes me feel like a shit."

"Was he friendly with the boys?"

"Between you and me, I think he scared them. He can be gruff."

"That's what scared them? His gruffness?"

"Jack never said anything directly, it was just a feeling I got."

"Truman ever been married, or have any kids himself?"

"I honestly don't know. He's generally against anything that would cramp his freedom. Eric thinks he may be a survivalist."

"How does he support himself?"

"No idea. Never says much about himself."

As they were about to head inside, Suzanne's gray Prius turned into the drive and came to a stop next to Eric's BMW.

Andrew waved. "Morning. Where's Branch?"

Suzanne eased out of the front seat, then ducked back inside to retrieve a leather briefcase. "He had a second interview up in Prior Lake this morning. I told him to go. If he gets that job, it would mean the world to him. To both of us. I told him we'd hold down the fort until he gets back." She hugged both Andrew and Jane. "Maybe this will be the day the boys come home. I've decided to keep a positive attitude."

Jane walked behind them as they moved up the steps into the house.

Coming around the corner into the living room, she found Eric seated on the living room couch, a cup of coffee in his hand, his laptop open in front of him on the coffee table. Several folded blankets and a stack of bed pillows rested on the arm of the couch. If she had to guess, she'd say that Andrew had spent the night. She wasn't sure what it meant, but hoped it signaled a lessening of tensions, if not something more significant.

"Quick request," said Jane, stepping over to the stairway off the dining room. "I'd like to take a look at Jack's bedroom. When I'm done, I'm hoping we could drive into town so I could do the same with Gabriel's. I assume the police have already examined both rooms."

Eric leaned back, spread his arms wide across the back of the sofa. "Steinhauser never asked."

Jane didn't even try to hide her surprise.

"You think that's poor police work?" asked Suzanne. She'd gone into the kitchen to get herself a glass of orange juice and was coming back through the dining room when she stopped to take in Jane's reaction.

"Yeah, I do. It's one of the first things he should have done."

"I spent some time looking around Jack's room yesterday," said Eric. "Didn't find anything out of the ordinary."

"And I didn't sleep much last night, so I spent a few hours in Gabriel's room," said Suzanne. "Unlike Jack, Gabriel's neat. Eric thinks he's ridiculously fussy about his stuff. Maybe he is."

"I'm going to take a quick look," said Jane.

"Take a right at the top of the stairs," said Andrew. "It's the room with the dark blue walls. Not exactly what Eric and I wanted," he added. "It was a compromise."

The dark blue was hardly visible, thought Jane, since the walls were almost entirely covered with posters. She spent a few minutes going through Jack's drawers, finding nothing out of the ordinary. Suzanne's comment about Jack's lack of organization had been an understatement. Clothes, athletic shoes, towels, candy wrappers, books, notebooks, and an avalanche of assorted boy junk littered every surface. When she sat down on the bed to take a look at the drawer in the nightstand, she sat on something lumpy. Digging under the sheets, she found a beat-up old teddy bear. Kids at his age were at that weird in-between stage when they were still children, though struggling to appear more grown up—to *be* more grown up—and angry when the adults in their lives didn't treat them with adult respect.

After searching through the closet, Jane was about to admit that nothing in the room suggested anything unusual or untoward when she spotted a digital camera sitting on top of a bookcase. She picked it up and turned it on. Four photos popped up. The first showed a group of dead animals—or pieces of dead animals. She couldn't identify every one of them, but was pretty sure she recognized a rabbit, several squirrel bodies, all missing their heads, a crow wing, a skunk, and a raccoon, all lined up in a precise row. The second photo was of a deer, most of its lower body missing. The third shot captured a close-up of molding chipmunk carcasses. The final shot showed a pile of assorted bones, with a few pulled from the stack and arranged in circular patterns in the foreground.

On the face of it, the shots didn't mean much. A boy could easily develop an interest in animals he might find in the woods, and yet, taken as a whole, with all the manipulations, the pictures struck Jane as grotesque.

Carrying the camera downstairs, she was about to show it around when Andrew flew in the front door holding a piece of paper. His face had turned ashen.

Suzanne was so startled by his expression that she dropped her half-drunk glass of juice. The glass hit the floor and sent a spray of liquid across the carpet and the bottom of her tan cotton slacks.

"I . . . I—" said Andrew, unable to get the words out.

"You went out to get the mail," said Eric.

"I . . . I should have known," said Andrew, appearing dazed, his eyes unable to focus. "The mail never comes this early. I saw that the red flag was up and thought—"

Suzanne snatched the paper from his hand.

"Out loud," said Eric. "Read it."

" 'Your boys,' " she began, " 'are safe. You have twenty-four hours to come up with a hundred thousand dollars in hundred-dollar bills. If you go to the police I WILL KNOW. *If you go to the police you will never see your sons again.* THIS I PROMISE YOU. I'm watching. Be smart. I will call at nine tomorrow morning with more instructions. Be ready with the cash or prepare for the consequences.'" With a trembling hand, she passed the note on to Eric.

Jane moved up closer so that she could read it. The words had been typed on a sheet of white typing paper. "Was there an envelope?" she asked.

Andrew shook his head. "Just this." He held up a cheap Samsung flip phone. "It was in the mailbox along with the note."

"Jesus," said Eric, covering his mouth with his hand.

"Did Truman see it?" asked Jane.

"He was the one who pulled it out of the mailbox. He read it first, then gave it to me."

All eyes turned to Jane.

"What do we do?" asked Andrew.

The words in the note had passed like an electric shock through everyone in the room. Jane's first thought was to caution everyone about making a quick decision, one they might come to regret. "We have to think this through very carefully."

"Do we contact Steinhauser?" asked Eric.

"No," said Andrew, his voice adamant. "We do what the note says."

"But how on earth are we supposed to come up with a hundred thousand dollars?" said Eric. "We can hardly pay the light bill."

Jane absently slipped Jack's camera into her pocket, her mind racing. The facts she'd learned while earning her PI license argued against an actual kidnapping. Of the seventy some million kids in the U.S., less than a hundred were provably abducted by strangers each year. The chance that a child would have a heart attack was vastly greater than that he would be the subject of an abduction *by a stranger*. And child heart attacks were so rare that most parents never even considered worrying about them. And yet Jane couldn't dismiss the possibility, especially since her niece had been one of those abductees.

"People think we're rich because of the cars we drive," said Eric. "The way the outside of our house looks. I've heard comments, haven't you?"

"Right," said Andrew, drawing his arms rigidly across his chest. "One more thing that's my fault because, once upon a time, I earned some big bucks. What's *not* my fault, Eric? Was I responsible for 9/11? The bridge collapse up in Minneapolis? Hurricane Sandy?"

"Stop it," ordered Jane. "This isn't the time to work out your personal problems. It's vital that we all work together."

Eric dumped himself onto the couch. Andrew stayed put in the dining room.

Stepping up to the front window and looking out at the yard, Suzanne gave herself a moment and then said, "We're looking at it the wrong way. This is actually good news. They're alive. That's more than we knew five minutes ago. We can work with this."

"But the money," said Eric.

"I'll rob a bank if I have to," said Suzanne, spinning around. "I'll do anything to get those boys back. You think I'm kidding?" she asked, her eyes flashing.

"Suzanne, be reasonable," said Eric. "We can't become bank robbers."

"Reason went out the window when my son was taken."

"She's right about one thing," said Jane. "This gives us information we didn't have before. We know what the motive is."

"Money," said Andrew.

"So?" said Eric. "I don't know anywhere we could get that amount of cash. When you add in the time element, it's completely impossible."

"If I could get the money," said Jane, "is that your decision? You want to keep the cops out of it? You need to be sure."

"I'm sure," said Andrew.

"Yeah, me, too," said Eric.

"Suzanne?" asked Jane. "What are your thoughts?"

"I'm with the guys," she said. "No police."

Jane wished she had the money to give them. Cordelia might be an option, except that after what she'd said last night, Jane assumed that she was stretched thin. That left two other possibilities. "I may have a solution," she said.

They all turned to stare at her.

"What?" asked Eric.

"I'll explain later." However she did it, she had to piece together the money by the end of business today. Heading for the door, she said, "I'll call as soon as I know anything."

On the way out to her SUV, she could hear Nolan's voice in her head telling her to take the note to the police and let them handle it, that if she didn't, no one would see the boys again. Since Nolan had spent his life as a cop, he trusted the police. She always listened to him and gave his opinions extra weight. Through him she'd met a number of cops in the last couple of years. A few had even become friends, so it wasn't that she had anything against the police. On the other hand, she didn't have the knee-jerk respect for them that Nolan did—especially not the local guy handling this case. Which meant there was no real point in calling Nolan to ask for his advice. For good or ill, this decision would belong to her and the boys' families.

12

Julia Martinsen was a doctor of oncology, an honored humanitarian who'd spent years helping the poor in third-world countries gain access to health care. Three years ago she'd created the People's Clinic in downtown Minneapolis, where low- or no-cost health care was administered to the poor of the Twin Cities, mainly by retired doctors donating their time.

Julia was a wealthy woman. She was also Jane's ex, which gave Jane access to a darker side of the good doctor, a face Julia never willingly revealed to the world. For many years, Jane had worked to excise Julia from her life. She had no desire to invite her back in. And yet here she was, standing in the foyer of a low-rise condo on Lake Calhoun, using the in-house phone to call up to her loft.

Closing her eyes, Jane listened to the phone ring several times. It was possible she wasn't home. Last Jane had heard, Julia was in Japan to offer whatever help she could to the earthquake and tsunami victims.

Five rings.

"Hello?" came a cultured female voice.

"Julia?"

"Yes?"

"It's Jane. Jane Lawless."

There was a pause, during which Jane castigated herself for slipping in her last name. Of course Julia had recognized her voice.

Then, teasingly, "Lawless? Can I take that at face value? Are you, indeed, *lawless?*"

"I need to talk to you."

"About?"

"Can I come up?"

"Do you ever recall a time when I said no to you?"

The buzzer sounded and Jane was in. She took the elevator up to the fourth floor—the penthouse. Instead of opening her front door and making it easy, it appeared Julia was going to make her knock. Typical.

Jane knocked. Almost a minute went by before her ex appeared, dressed in a powder-blue silk bathrobe, her feet bare. She'd been fighting some sort of illness the last time Jane had seen her. By the healthy flush on her cheeks and the weight she'd put on, she was no longer the thin stick figure that had tugged so hard at Jane's heart. Cordelia thought Jane was a sap for retaining any feelings at all for a woman who was an undisputed liar, who saw the world as a chessboard and herself as a grand master, and yet Jane found that most people, Cordelia included, were an irrational mixture of qualities. She might have no desire to ever be with Julia again, and yet she had to admit that she still cared—a little—about her.

"You must have an oil painting of yourself in your attic," said Julia. "You don't look an hour older than the day I first met you."

Julia threw out compliments and praise as easily as a clown

104

tossed candy to children at a parade. Everyone loved her for it and yet it was essentially empty. "Can I come in?"

"Of course," she said, sweeping her arm. "Take off your coat. Take off your clothes." She laughed at the joke that wasn't a joke and backed up. "I'm kidding. Have you had breakfast?"

"I could use some coffee."

"Lucky for you I was just about to make some." She moved into the open kitchen and poured hot water from an electric kettle into a press pot. "If I didn't know better, it almost seems like I was expecting you."

The comment gave Jane a queasy feeling. It also made her realize how much she didn't want to be here.

"Go sit down and I'll bring this in."

She'd only been in the loft once before, a summer night when Julia had offered to make her dinner. In a weak moment, Jane had accepted. The loft sat at the corner of Lake Street and East Lake Calhoun Parkway, with a wall of windows overlooking Lake Calhoun on one side, and downtown Minneapolis on the other. Julia had managed to sublet it and eventually buy it, one of the hottest properties in town.

"How've you been?" asked Jane, taking a seat on one of the buttery leather couches.

"If you really want to know, I've never been better. And you?" She came in with a tray of coffee and biscotti and set it down on the square glass and steel coffee table.

"Good."

"I hear you're selling the Xanadu Club."

"You still follow what I do?"

She smiled as she poured them each a cup. "Not really. But I do read the local rags. Never thought you'd let it go."

"Restaurants have life cycles. That one's on its way out."

"Really? I was there the other night and it was packed."

Jane allowed the comment to pass.

"Since you asked," she said with another sardonic smile, "I'm just back from Haiti. I've been doing some charity work down there." She turned the cream pitcher around and picked it up. "You might as well cut to the chase and tell me why you're here. You obviously didn't stop by to catch up. And don't give me that wounded look. If I can cease playing games, so can you."

Jane appreciated the candor. "Two boys were abducted from their home a few nights ago. I'm working with the parents."

"Still a wannabe PI?"

"I have my license now."

She stopped stirring the cream in her cup. "You're working with that friend of yours?"

Jane pulled a business card out of her billfold and pushed it across the coffee table.

"Impressive. Okay, so back to these boys. How old?"

"Twelve. The parents received a ransom note this morning."

"How much?"

"One hundred thousand."

Julia held the cup to her lips. "And you came to me because you know I have it."

"Well, actually . . . yes."

"Can you promise I'd get it back?"

"I wish I could, but no."

"Then why should I?"

It was a cold comment and it threw Jane. "Because you can. Because the parents are desperate. Because it's the right thing to do."

"I don't always do the right thing," said Julia, setting the cup down. "You know that. You can hardly say I haven't paid my dues to society. I've devoted my life—"

"You think that gives you a pass for all the other crap you pull?"

"Are we talking about the money now or us?"

Jane looked down, shifted in her seat. "The money."

"If I give it to you, what's in it for me?"

"What do you want?"

"I'd have to think about it."

"Well, think fast: I need the cash before the banks close today."

Tapping a finger against the side of her cheek, Julia leaned back against the couch and crossed her legs. "This is delicious. I have you at my mercy."

"You're not the only rich person I know."

"A date."

"Excuse me? You mean . . . the fruit?"

"Don't be obtuse."

"A date with me?"

"No, with Cordelia." She gave a dramatic shiver.

"We were done with that a long time ago."

"Were we?"

"What do you anticipate happening on this date?"

"Whatever I want. Remember, you came to me. Or do your tender scruples prevent you from bartering? The lives of two boys for, shall we say, a little human warmth?"

"Are you actually suggesting—"

"Would you expect anything less from me?"

"I'm with someone, Julia. It's not negotiable."

107

That stopped her. "I hadn't heard. Who is she?"

"None of your business."

"You two living together?"

"Not that it's any concern of yours, but no. She *has* taken over one of my bedrooms to use as a study."

"She's an artist?"

"A writer."

"Fascinating. What sort of writing?"

"She's a novelist."

"Published?"

"Not yet."

"Is she beautiful, Jane? Is she better in bed than me? Don't lie. We both know what we had together."

"Okay," said Jane, standing up. "It's official now. This was a bad idea." She started for the door.

"Let me give your question a tad more thought."

"Don't bother." Julia wasn't her only option.

"Don't go away mad. You never know. I could change my mind."

Jane slammed the door on her way out.

13

The air in Gabriel's bedroom was clammy with air-conditioning. Suzanne lay on her son's bed, staring up at the ceiling fan, feeling as if she'd forgotten how to breathe. She heard a scrape and a thud, then Branch's voice called from the living room. "Suzanne? You here?"

"I'm upstairs," she called back. Her body felt like it was encased in cement. She listened to his quick footsteps on the stairs, stealing herself for more bad news. With her focus still on the fan, she sensed his presence in the room.

"I got it," he said.

She could tell he wanted to whoop for joy but checked himself because of the boys. "Oh, honey, I'm so proud of you." This man who meant everything to her, a guy who had struggled with all his might to keep his self-esteem alive, couldn't even allow himself to celebrate his good news. It wasn't fair. "Come here," she said, holding out her hands.

He threw himself into her arms. "I shouldn't feel this happy," he whispered. "Not now. It's wrong."

"Feel it," she said. "Enjoy every minute of it."

He held her tighter. "I love you."

"You deserve this."

Backing up, his eyes full of excitement, he said, "I start in two weeks. They really want me. Offered me all kinds of perks. I'll get a new truck. Health and dental insurance for all of us. Profit sharing. After the probation period is up, they're giving me a five percent raise, and we'll revisit my salary again in January. I'll be in charge of two landscaping crews to begin with." Kissing her fiercely, he held her close. "I got it. Can you believe it? The guy with no luck finally got lucky."

"It's that rainbow trout tie clip I told you to wear. Can I pick a lucky tie clip or can I pick a lucky tie clip?"

He leaned back and laughed, full throated, a sound she hadn't heard in years.

"I know how hard you must have prayed about this," he said. "Me, too."

He was sunburned and, without his baseball cap, the cowlicks in his short, spiky hair twisted in every direction. But she had to tell him. As much as she didn't want to bring him down, he had to know about the ransom note.

By the time she'd finished, he was sitting across the room, head in his hands. "You think Jane can come up with the money?" he asked.

"It's our only hope."

"What about Steinhauser?"

"We're leaving him out of it."

"Good. I don't like him."

"Because he's a cop."

"Has nothing to do with that."

"Then what? There has to be a reason."

He removed the tie clip. Next came the tie and then his light blue dress shirt. He walked across the hall to their bedroom and came back wearing his Twins cap and a clean T-shirt. "I promised Gabriel I wouldn't say anything. But . . . hell, guess it doesn't matter now."

"Say what?"

"You know Gabriel's on Steinhauser's Little League baseball team. Well, they got into it last week. I mean, really got into it. I been trying to make all his games this summer. I missed the first few, and only got to see the final four innings of the one last week. You were supposed to come, but—"

"Vivian called a council meeting."

"Yeah. Anyway, Steinhauser had Gabriel playing right field instead of third base. It was a lame call. Gabriel doesn't have the arm strength to be an outfielder. And then, when he dropped an easy catch, Steinhauser got super hot under the collar. Gabriel made a couple other knuckleheaded moves. I mean, right when I got there, I could tell something was wrong. I waited around for him afterward so I could give him a lift home. When he didn't show, I went into the park building and found Steinhauser screaming at the kid about his lack of focus. He accused Gabriel of not being serious about his play, said that he'd have to decide whether he wanted to keep him on the team or kick him off. I thought he was being way too rough and told him so. Gabriel got between us and, I'm sorry to admit, had to drag me off him. He made me promise not to tell anyone about it, like . . . I don't know . . . like he was ashamed of me for trying to deck the guy. I told him what Steinhauser said to him was total bullshit. He begged me to let it drop. So that's what I did. It's got nothing to do with what happened to the boys, but it still burns me."

Suzanne was appalled to think something like that had happened and she knew nothing about it.

"Look," said Branch, kicking off his dress loafers. "I'm gonna change into my jeans and put the pontoon in the lake so I can take photos of it. If I can get them up on Craigslist right away and underprice the thing, maybe I can sell it fast. Just in case Jane can't get us all the money we need."

Suzanne's first instinct was to tell him to wait, to argue that he wouldn't get much for it anyway, so why try. And yet, seeing his determination, she knew he had to do it, had to contribute something. He couldn't just sit around and act like a victim any more than she could. Selling the boat was better than robbing a bank, though neither would be the solution they so desperately needed.

Holly Eld stood at the sink staring silently out the kitchen window as Aaron walked up behind her and put his hand on her shoulder. "What are you looking at?"

"My Corolla," she said, her voice oddly flat. "It's official. The motor's toast."

She'd just come back from Hoffman Automotive, where they always took their cars for repair.

"Sorry," said Aaron. A second car was something they could ill afford, though he was smart enough not to jump for joy at its demise. "It's not the end of the world."

"No, I know. Except, now that I'm feeling better, I wanted to look for another part-time job. If I find one, how will I get around without a car?"

"I'll take you. It will save on insurance money and gas."

"Sometimes it feels like everything is about money. I hate it.

Hate all this scrimping." She moved over to the refrigerator to get out the fixings for their lunch. "I bought it when I started waitressing, took almost every dime I had. It was old even then, but it was special. It was mine." Swiveling around to look at him, she said, "You know I'm not all that interested in material things. We're so rich by so many people's standards. It's just . . . it hurts to lose that car. I can't explain it."

Aaron understood that it was some sort of symbol to her. At times like this, he felt keenly that he was living inside the maws of a vice—their financial problems on one side and the life he wanted to provide for Holly on the other.

After making them two turkey sandwiches, she removed two cans of soda from the refrigerator and sat down at the kitchen table. "Join me," she said, holding out her hand to him. "Honestly, I didn't mean to whine. I have you. I'm a lucky woman." She opened up her Sprite, took a sip, then held the sweating can against her forehead.

He sat down at the table, pressed his hand over a gouge in the wood. "I start teaching summer school next week."

"I'll miss you. I like having you home."

Bitterness dripped inside him like a leaky faucet.

"We're going to be just fine," she said, getting up to search through the cupboard until she came up with a bag of chips.

Aaron thought about the saying: "If you're in a hole and you keep on digging, that's the definition of insanity." Maybe that was his problem.

When they were done eating, Holly said, a gleam in her eye, "Let's go to the Dairy Queen. What we need are two big Blizzards."

"Huh?"

"Stop being so freakin' grim, okay?"

"Was I?"

"Strawberry Cheesecake Blizzard for you and a Midnight Truffle Blizzard for me," she said, adding, "If we can afford it."

He stiffened. Before he could form a response, she said, "That was a joke."

14

After striking out with Julia, and kicking herself for wasting precious time, Jane sat in her car and phoned Cordelia. She needed to wheedle information out of her without appearing to do so. "Hey, where are you?" she asked when Cordelia finally picked up.

"Hatts and I are crossing the street to my architect's office. I was hoping they could come over to the theater, but they want me at their place so they can show me the model they built."

"For what?"

"I've decided to turn part of the first floor into a small, seventy-five-seat experimental stage. Octavia wanted to rent it out to a retail store, but I nixed that. We've already got a coffee shop going in, and a New York–style deli. That pretty much covers my periodic espresso crises and my lunch debates."

"Is Octavia meeting with you and Hattie at the architect's office?"

"Nah. As usual, she has more important fish to fry. She's over at the theater as we speak. They're putting the finishing touches on her office today."

"I thought she was moving into the broom closet."

"Very occasionally I *may* exaggerate. She said she has to be there to make sure everything is perfection itself. What are you up to?"

"Still working with Andrew and Eric."

"I have to say, I'm having a hard time letting Hattie out of my sight."

"I don't suppose you've got a hundred thousand dollars lying around that you'd like to donate to a good cause?"

"They received a ransom note?" she cried. "When do you need the money by?"

"The end of business today. I'm going to call my dad, see what he can do." Jane had no intention of calling her father. He'd been having his own financial problems and she wasn't about to burden him with something else to worry about.

"Good idea, Janey. Wish I could help. I might be able to put together part of the cash, but it would take way longer than that."

"I'll figure it out."

"You call if you need me. Cordelia Thorn may not provide drive-through financial services, but she has many other fine qualities. I'm taking Hattie for a haircut when we're done here, and then I'll be back at the theater."

"I'll be in touch." Jane rang off, delighted that she'd been able to find the information she'd been looking for without tipping her hand.

After a short drive downtown, she parked in the lot behind the theater and took the elevator up to the second floor. She found a workman in the hallway and asked him where Octavia's office was located. Trying to settle herself, to mute the festering in her stomach, she approached the door. If Octavia said no, Jane had nowhere else to turn. The lives of two children were riding on this conversation. She had to get it right.

Knocking on the open door, Jane scanned the room. Seeing Octavia's blond head pop out of the door in the back, she plastered on a quick smile.

"Jane, hi. Come in and see my new digs."

She stepped across the threshold, breathing in the smell of new carpet, new furniture, and fresh paint. Unlike Cordelia's office, which was being decorated in Gilded Age elegance straight out of an Edith Wharton novel, Octavia's was sleek and modern. Neither sister was a minimalist, although they treated their grandeur requirements in different ways.

"Do you have a minute to talk?" asked Jane.

"Why so serious?" She smirked. "Love that line. Don't get a chance to use it as often as I'd like."

Jane nodded to a couple of metal chairs that looked like modern art exhibits. "Let's sit."

"You really are in a black mood. Can I offer you anything? A brandy? A coffee? A few minutes of free Freudian—or I should say Octavian—therapy?"

Patience had never been one of Jane's saving graces. Cordelia was her best friend, which meant Jane generally had no problem putting up with her lame wisecracks. She was even charmed by some of them. Cordelia's little sister, however, was a another matter entirely.

"I need one hundred thousand dollars," said Jane.

Octavia blinked. "Don't we all, darling."

"I'm not joking. Two boys were kidnapped on Tuesday night from a small town in southern Minnesota. A few hours ago the parents received a ransom note. If they can't produce one hundred thousand dollars in hundred-dollar bills by tomorrow morning, they'll never see those kids again."

"And this is my problem . . . why?"

"Because I'm making it your problem."

Her finely plucked eyebrows arched.

"Look, Octavia. You're the only person I know who could give me that money and never even miss it."

She digested that a moment, rearranging herself in the chair, brushing her fingertips across her short, razor-cut bangs. "And?"

"And what?"

"Forgive me, Jane, but you failed to explain the most important part. What's in it for me?"

Jane's first thought was that Octavia and Julia had been separated at birth. Her second thought was even less charitable. "What do you want?"

Her eyes flashed. "I'd think that would be obvious."

Jane had no idea what she was talking about. "I guess you're going to have to spell it out for me."

"A simple act of kindness." She smiled. It wasn't a friendly smile.

"Meaning?"

"Cordelia and I put you on the board of this theater, a ten percent voting share. We did it for a reason, one you're quite aware of. If the two of us come to an impasse over an issue, you would be the tiebreaker." She held Jane's eyes. "I'll give you the money gladly. I'm always interested in helping a good cause. In return, the next time I need it, you will agree to cast your vote with me."

Jane felt like she was in a foxhole watching a grenade drop next to her feet. "You'll give me the money if I agree to betray my best friend."

"I wouldn't put it in such Faustian terms. I'm merely asking for a favor."

"What if I give you the money back? That way, you're not out a penny."

"Ah, there's the rub. For that to happen, you'd need me to give it to you in the first place. My offer stands. If you manage to retrieve the cash, consider it yours. Give it to your favorite charity. Take a trip to Tahiti. Frankly, Jane, I'd happily pay you for your vote, but you wouldn't take it."

Jane couldn't help herself. "You suck, Octavia. You really, *really* suck."

She laughed. "Sticks and stones."

Two boys' lives trumped just about anything Jane could think of, even her loyalty to Cordelia. She didn't see that she had a choice.

"Do we have a deal?"

Looking away, Jane said, "We do."

"Wonderful," said Octavia. "I'll call my banker. You'll have the money by this afternoon. I'll give you a call when it's ready for you to pick up. This feels good, Jane. Friends helping friends. I hope we can find a way to do it more often."

Walking down the hall to her new office, praying that Nolan was a hundred miles away, Jane unlocked the door and then ducked inside, feeling like a gallon bucket of movie slime had been dumped all over her. How was it possible that she knew so many narcissists? They were falling out of trees, clogging the rivers and streams, eating up the ozone layer. They seemed like the twenty-first century's equivalent of the living dead, except that they smiled a lot, and instead of finding their way through the world with

119

their arms outstretched, they used sarcasm to navigate, bouncing it off the foreheads of unsuspecting humanoids like a bat wielding its sonar.

Easing down on the couch in the waiting room, Jane took out her cell phone and punched in Andrew's number. She reached his voice mail. "I've got it," she said. "I'll be down later in the day with the cash. Stay strong, okay? We'll do everything in our power to get those boys back." That finished, she typed a text message to her niece, Mia—the one who'd been abducted two years ago. Jane needed to see her, to spend some time with her.

"Hey," she texted. "Let's get together. Horseback riding? Lunch? New art exhibit at Walker? U name it. Hugs and love, J." Mia was deaf. Their preferred method of communication these days was e-mail or texts. It had been over a month since Jane had seen her. Much too long.

Finally, searching the extensive contact list on her iPhone, she located the other number she needed. A few minutes later, as she was about to say good-bye, the door opened and Nolan wheeled himself in. He nodded to her as he rolled into his office.

Stuffing the phone back into her pocket, Jane stood at his door and watched him remove a briefcase from his lap. Underneath were the two local papers. He set those on the desktop and then turned to open the blinds. "Afternoon," he said, a bit too casually.

"How'd you get here?" she asked.

"Cab."

"Want some coffee?" She'd smelled some brewing in the break room.

"I could be persuaded." He looked good, dressed more comfortably today in jeans and a red polo shirt. His forehead was beaded with sweat, which he patted off with a white handker-chief.

Jane ran down the hall and came back carrying two mugs. "Cream, two sugars," she said, setting his down in front of him. Pulling up a chair, she continued, "So how do you like this place?"

He took a sip before responding. "It'll do."

"Oh, come on. You can only push these miserly comments so far before it seems like a pose."

He laughed. "Okay, you got me. I like it. In fact, I more than like it."

She was relieved by the declaration.

"So, what have you been up to?" he asked, glancing through one of the newspapers.

"I've got a case."

"Want to talk about it?"

Actually, she did, though she didn't want to go into detail. "What do you do when a client wants to act in a way that might be against his best interests?" She was having second thoughts about not letting the local police know about the ransom note.

"Try to talk them out of it."

"Yes, but what if *you're* not sure what the right move is? I mean, maybe they made the right call. I can't act against their wishes, can I? They've confided in me. I have proprietary information that I'm obligated to keep private."

"Like a therapist and a patient. Sure, I look at it that way, too. Thing is, you can't let them walk into a situation that's way over their heads. That's what you're there for."

"What if it's over my head?"

"What kind of case?"

"Involves a couple of kids. They're missing."

121

"And?"

"They received a ransom note."

He hesitated a moment. "They don't want to go to the police because they were threatened, told they'd never see the kids again if they called the cops. Listen to me, Jane: Everyone's out of his depth on a case like that. The outcome rides on too many details you can't control."

"But, if it were you, you'd try to convince the family to talk to the police."

He stretched his arms high over his head. "Believe it or not, I've never worked an abduction. I know a few cops who have. One made a total mess of it. Hurts even to think about it. Another one did everything right and the little girl was never seen again. To answer your question: Yes, I always think it's best to go to the police."

"Even in a small town? Even when they don't know what they're doing?"

"Was an Amber Alert issued?"

"Everyone thought the boys had run away because one of them had tried it before. The thing is, the cop in charge never even looked at the boys' bedrooms."

"Not smart. I'll bet you did."

"Only one. So far."

"You find anything?"

"Maybe. I'm not sure because I haven't had time to pursue it."

Leaning into the desk, Nolan made a bridge of his fingers. "It's the parents' call. That being said, let me give you a piece of advice. First, do they have the money?"

She nodded.

"How much?"

"A hundred thousand."

He winced. "Okay, listen carefully: Up until now, the kidnapper's held all the cards. As soon as he knows you have the cash, *he* begins to have a dog in the fight. He can feel that money in his hand, taste it, smell it. You could say he wants that money almost as much as you want those kids back home. So work with that. You hear what I'm saying?"

"I think so."

He folded his hands on the desk and tried again. "Now that you've got a card to play, stand up to him if he asks you to do something you know is flat-out stupid. Chances are, he'll give you some latitude. I can't predict when or how this might take shape, or why you'd need to make a demand of your own, but remember, you've got some leverage now that you've got the cash."

"I get it. Thanks."

"What I'm here for. You believe in prayer?"

"Not really."

"Well, I do. I'll send up a few smoke signals on your behalf. You're gonna need them."

Shortly before two, Jane stood outside Avi's apartment in the saunalike heat and buzzed her apartment. She'd given Avi a key to her house, but because of her roommate, Avi hadn't felt comfortable doing the same.

"Yes?" came a woman's voice over the speaker.

"I'm freezing out here," said Jane. "Let me in, let me in."

"Who is this?"

"Georgia?" Jane had thought the voice belonged to Avi.

"Oh, Lawless. Yeah, you better join us in front of the fire."

When the buzzer sounded, Jane bounded up the stairs to the second floor. She'd been hoping Georgia would be out—or had suddenly moved to Pittsburgh—though she was always around these days, studying for the bar exam.

Avi opened the door, dressed in her usual bartending drag. Black everything.

"On your way to work, I take it," said Jane, glancing at Georgia, who was seated at the dining room table, her work spread out in front of her. Georgia gave Jane a smile and a prom queen wave.

"Afraid so," said Avi.

"Do you have a minute?"

"For you, more than a minute."

Jane nodded to the hallway. Personal conversations while seated in the stairwell weren't exactly the height of comfort or privacy, but with Georgia able to eavesdrop on virtually anywhere in the apartment from her perch in the dining room, it was their destination of necessity. As always, Jane's first impulse was to grouse about Georgia. Knowing it did nothing but frustrate Avi, she did her best to rein in the choice comments she was devising and instead get to the point, her reason for coming. First, she gave Avi a long, slow kiss.

"That was nice," said Avi. "You've come bearing news?"

Jane pulled away, tilted her head. "How could you possibly know that?"

"The way you're fidgeting. You're pumping one leg. Rubbing your palms together. You always fidget when you've got something important to say."

Jane didn't like being so transparent.

"Come on, out with it. Otherwise I'll be late for work."

She stopped rubbing her hands and instead, sat on them. "You said last night that you'd completed the final draft of your new novel."

"I said I wasn't happy with it."

"I know, but you're never happy with anything you've written."

"You have a point."

Jane started again. "A few years back, I authored a cookbook based on the food we serve at the Lyme House. I used an agent in New York to make the deal. Her name is Constance Riley, part-owner of Riley Moreland Literary Agency. I got to know her pretty well. She's a real foodie, even flew out to Minneapolis to eat at the restaurant. Anyway, I called her a little while ago."

Avi turned and gave Jane a heavy-lidded stare.

"She represents all kinds of writing, although I wasn't sure if she did fiction. Turns out, that's her major interest. I told her about you, that I'd read a couple of your unpublished novels and thought they were wonderful. She agreed to look at the new one. Couldn't say exactly when she'd get to it, but soon."

Avi's eyes darted right, then left. "I don't know what to say."

"Don't say anything. Just send it as a Word doc, that way she can download it onto her iPad. She reads on the train going to and from work."

"I am . . . utterly speechless."

Jane removed a slip of paper from her pocket and handed it to her. "That's all the info you'll need."

"But it's not ready."

"Are any of your books ready?"

"Well—"

"Send the manuscript, Avi. You'll regret it if you don't."

She hesitated. Then, suddenly, she stood up and whooped.

"Does that mean you'll do it?"

"You are a freakin' miracle worker."

"I got you a read. It's the book that will make or break the deal. I'm betting on the former."

Avi gave Jane a quick peck on the cheek and then dashed back to her apartment, calling, "I'll thank you properly later."

"I'm counting on it," whispered Jane, unable to suppress a self-congratulatory grin.

15

That evening Jane drove back down to Winfield, the briefcase with the money tucked safely into the backseat. She'd been looking forward to spending some relaxing time alone on the road, and yet as she sailed down Highway 52, she couldn't stop herself from worrying—about the boys, about Eric and Andrew, about Avi, and about the urge she felt to spend time with her niece, Mia. She knew worrying was a pointless exercise. It made you feel as if you were doing something when in reality, you were doing nothing. Getting together with Mia would be the fix, especially if she wanted to drive out to Henderson Stables. Jane loved riding, as did Mia. On one of their first trips, Jane had invited Cordelia and Hattie to come along. Cordelia, alas, had nixed the idea before Hattie even learned of it, mainly because she'd already done the "horse thing" with one particularly outdoorsy girlfriend and had needed a full week at a private spa to recover.

When Jane came through the door and into the front room of the farmhouse an hour later, she saw immediately that she'd walked in on the aftermath of a fight. Eric was in the kitchen with his sister, heads together at the kitchen table, while Andrew had taken refuge in the living room, talking, or rather not talking, to Branch.

Jane set the briefcase down next to a rocking chair. Branch glanced up at her with helpless eyes. "We all okay?" she asked, shifting her gaze from Andrew to Branch, and then back again to Andrew.

"He blames me for everything," said Andrew, his voice still raw with emotion. "I mean, does he think I wanted this to happen? He's the one who kicked *me* out. All I'm trying to do is dig us out of the mess, but he never gives me credit for anything I do."

"That's not true," shouted Eric, charging out of the kitchen, his face red with outrage. "It's like you've forgotten how to listen. I'm *not* saying that at all."

Jane hardly felt comfortable inserting herself into their problems, and yet if they ever needed to be on the same page, it was now. Before she could come up with way to nudge them toward détente, Cordelia, wearing a bright yellow-and-red-striped sundress, sort of an homage to a beach umbrella, sailed into the room carrying several long, covered aluminum trays. The pungent smell of garlic and lemon wafted into the negatively charged air.

"There are more goodies in my car," she said to Andrew, motioning with her eyes for him to go get them.

"Cordelia?" said Eric, his mouth dropping in surprise. "What are you doing here?"

"Bringing sustenance to the downtrodden," she said, swooping into the dining room and setting the trays down on the table. "You wouldn't think Greek food could weigh so much."

"Dinner?" said Jane, as surprised as everyone else by her friend's sudden appearance. Somehow Cordelia had managed to perform a minor miracle. She'd broken the tension in the room.

"Moussaka. Gyros. Pita. Hummus. Souvlaki. Tzatziki. Spanikopita. Am I missing anything?"

Suzanne came out of the kitchen, her thin fingers curled around a sweating glass of iced tea.

As background noise, the window air conditioners wheezed out semicooled, though far from dehumidified, air.

"I have to say that really does smell good," said Eric, a shock of blond hair falling across his eyes.

"Maybe if we eat something, we'll all feel better," offered Branch. He squeezed out a weak smile, trying his best to interject a positive note into the conversation, such as it was.

"You brought the money?" asked Eric.

Jane nodded to the briefcase.

"Terrific," said Cordelia. "I was beginning to wonder if your father could come up with that on such short notice."

Jane tried to swallow her sense of betrayal, with little success. "Yeah," was all she managed to say.

"Maybe someone should get Truman," said Eric, prying back the heavy aluminum cover on one of the trays. His enthusiasm to include his uncle wasn't overwhelming.

"I'll go," said Jane. She grabbed a pita wedge and dipped it into the hummus. The food was more than welcome, as was Cordelia.

Striding across the backyard, she stopped in front of the old RV and rapped on the door. When nobody answered, she knocked again. Twice. Figuring she'd done her bit to include him, she crossed around to the other side of trailer, more out of curiosity than anything else. She stood on tiptoes and tried to see in a window, but found she wasn't tall enough. As she was about to leave, a worn section of grass, one that led into the woods, caught her attention. Since she didn't exactly want to head back right away, and curious where the path led, she followed it through a section of low brush into the woods. About thirty yards in, she came to a clearing. Hearing twigs snap behind her, she turned to find Cordelia pushing her way past a large pine bough while waving a swarm of gnats away from her face.

"Lord in heaven, what have you found now?" she said, slapping her arm and flicking off a dead mosquito. "What's that? Some sort of Native American . . . ritual . . . thingie?"

Deep in the shadows at the edge of a slope was a grouping of animal carcasses. "Yuck" was the first word that leaped to mind. "I wonder if Truman set that up," said Jane.

"Heavens. Have you met this Truman person?"

"Can't say it was a pleasure."

Like the photos Jack had taken, the assembled critters were numerous and diverse. What Jack hadn't shown in his snapshots was the way they were positioned in a circle. The spectacle, for want of a better term, was not only startling, but disturbing. Most of the carcasses were in various stages of decomposition.

"Roadkill?" asked Jane.

They both stood for a moment and gaped.

"Not all of them," replied Cordelia, lifting an eyebrow and nodding to the head of a bear placed directly in the center of the circle. "If I'm not mistaken, that's a bullet hole. Is this Truman person some sort of sadist?"

It was as good a guess as any. "How come you followed me out here?"

"Because I wanted to know if you planned to spend the night in Winfield."

"I think so," said Jane.

"I'll join you."

"Really? Then we should call the motor inn in town, get ourselves a room."

"Already done." Moving backward a couple of steps, she said, "You need me, Janey. You may be the one with the PI license, but I've always been the intuitive genius behind your brawn. And besides . . . I want to help. I need to. What if something ever happened to Hattie? Just the idea—"

"May I repeat—nothing's going to happen to Hattie."

"No, of course you're right. But . . . I mean—"

"I get it," said Jane. "You don't have to explain."

As they made their way back to the RV, Truman roared up on a motorcycle. Strapped to the back by bungee cords were several long cardboard cylinders.

Removing his helmet, he set the kickstand and then swung his leg free. "Hey," he said, trying but failing to look nonchalant. "What's up? Why all the cars in the drive?"

"Why all the animal bones and carcasses in the woods?" asked Jane.

His expression betrayed nothing but mild interest.

"They belong to you?"

Scratching his chest through his T-shirt, he gave a shrug and said, "No more than the rocks and the trees."

"Did you arrange them?"

"I'd say that's a need to know kind of thing—and you don't."

"What do you do with them?" asked Cordelia.

"If I wasn't clear enough the first time, let me try again: None of your goddamn business. Now your turn. Why all the cars in the drive?"

Jane wanted to simply walk away, but her instinct told her to keep it civil. "We came out to invite you to dinner. Cordelia brought some Greek food."

"That right," he said, brushing off his pants. "Cordelia who?"

"Thorn," she said.

He looked her up and down.

She looked him up and down.

Neither seemed to come to any conclusion.

Switching his attention back to Jane, Truman said, "Did you get the money?"

"Money?"

"For the ransom."

"It's been handled."

"A hundred thousand dollars? You must be a real fat cat."

"I must be."

"Well. Anything to get those boys back, right?"

"You coming up to the house?" asked Cordelia.

"Think I just might do that, Cornelia."

"Cor*delia*."

Jane had the sense that he'd mispronounced her name on purpose.

Nodding to her dress, he said, "Spanish flag, right?"

"Formula One, Grand Prix."

He grunted.

She matched his grunt and upped it one louder.

On their way back to the house, with Truman striding ahead of them, Jane whispered, "He look familiar to you?"

"You mean his resemblance to Popeye?"

Jane hadn't noticed that, but could see it now that it was pointed out.

"I don't usually run around with seedy looking Merchant Marine types," she whispered back. "Did you see that anchor on his bicep? Talk about a walking cliché."

"What about the naked woman on the other arm?"

"Well, that one's more understandable." She winked.

Jane wasn't sure *what* Truman was. The bones in the woods suggested, at the very least, a bizarre personality, and at the other extreme, someone who might be dangerous.

"He'll probably ask me for a date," said Cordelia, rolling her eyes.

Later that night, as Jane stood at the motel room window, Cordelia sat on her bed saying good night to Hattie over the phone. It was going on ten and the temperature was still over a hundred. Tomorrow was supposed to be another hundred-plus day.

"Tomorrow," Jane whispered, a heavy sense of unease settling over her.

Moving back to her bed, she stretched out, stuffed a pillow behind her head, and picked up a plastic glass half filled with wine, setting it on her stomach. She listened through all the "good nights and night nights and sweet dreams." Cordelia loved that kid like nothing else in her life. All parents understood the primal fear of losing a child. Would the boys be home tomorrow night, safe with their families? Could Jane actually pull it off?

"More wine?" asked Cordelia, flipping her phone closed. She picked up the bottle of Pinotage, something she'd brought with her. South African wine was likely not a hot seller in Winfield.

"I'm good," said Jane.

"Are we all set for tomorrow?"

"Ready as we'll ever be."

"You as worried about Eric and Andrew as I am?"

"Pretty much." Anyone could see that they were barely holding it together.

"What do you make of Suzanne and Branch?" asked Cordelia, stepping over to her suitcase to retrieve her nightie, sleep mask, and bag of assorted creams and potions.

"I think they're a better bet to pass the money to the kidnapper than the guys." She hesitated, her gaze roaming the room. "I feel like I'm really out of my depth on this one."

"If it's any consolation, I'm scared, too."

Picking up a photo of Jack and Gabriel off the nightstand, Jane examined the faces. Both boys looked so incredibly young. Jack's brown hair was longish and shaggy. His eyes were dark, deep set, his smile toothy and full of mischief. Gabriel was bigger, his features more blunt, his sandy hair short, not quite a crew cut, but not far from it. His expression was more direct and serious, lacking Jack's warmth. "Do you remember Jack and Gabriel at the wedding?"

"That was pre-Hattie, back when I thought all children were noisy, sticky, and rude."

"I know more than a few adults who fit that category," said Jane.

"Too true." Cordelia edged around the bed and sailed into the bathroom. "It's my turn to shower. The AC in here isn't exactly up to Ritz-Carlton standards."

As the water snapped on, Jane turned off the light above her bed. If she ever needed to be fresh and rested, it was tomorrow morning. Taking one last swallow of wine, she set the glass on the nightstand, then turned on her side, faced the wall, closed her eyes, and waited for the sleep she knew wouldn't come.

16

An oppressive heat hung over the meadow in front of Andrew and Eric's house when Jane and Cordelia arrived the following morning. Jane had been right to predict a sleepless night, although Cordelia had slept, as always, like a log, dead to the world long past the time when Jane was up and out of the room searching for coffee. The tall grass rippled in the breeze as they approached the front porch. Andrew was seated on a rocker, a glass of orange juice in his hand. He looked up at them as they moved past, offering nothing, not even a smile.

While Cordelia sat down on the couch in the living room to talk to Branch, Jane found Eric and his sister in the kitchen, once again huddled together over the table, talking softly.

"Morning," said Jane. The clock on the wall above the stove said it was a quarter to nine. Fifteen minutes and the call would come. "Who's got the cell?" she asked.

"Andrew has it," said Eric. "I think I should be the one to talk. He, of course, disagrees."

"Help yourself to some coffee," said Suzanne.

Jane had already eaten breakfast while Cordelia was back at the motel, snoozing. "Anybody get any sleep?" she asked.

Suzanne shook her head. "Branch and I stayed here. Andrew slept on the couch. We brought over our sleeping bags and slept in Jack's room."

While they were talking, the landline rang.

Eric jumped up to answer it. "Oh, hi, Matt," he said, slumping back down on his chair. *Steinhauser*, he mouthed to Jane. "This morning? No, that's not good for us. What?" He listened. "No, sorry. Doesn't work. Did you learn something new?" He listened a bit longer this time. "Well, that's just peachy, Matt. What question? Ask it now." He pressed a couple fingers to his forehead. "Jesus. No, Jack wasn't suicidal. Neither was Gabriel. Where did you even come up with that idea?" He looked over at Jane. "We're in the dark, I realize that. You should know, the family has hired a PI. No, I don't think you're incompetent, but it's my right. Yeah, talk to you later. Okay, bye." He clicked the phone off and dropped it on the table. "That guy thinks the boys might have made a suicide pact. And I think *I'm* the one who always jumps to the most radical conclusion first. I mean, fuck him." Then, realizing he'd sworn in front of his sister, he apologized.

"Don't," she said, clearly irritated. "Why do people think they need to protect me from strong language? Do you think I've never heard it before? Do you think it burns my skin or something? That I'm so delicate I can't handle it?" She'd overreacted and seemed to know it. "Sorry. I'm not in the best mood. You ask

137

me, if any situation called for a little swearing, this does." Pouring more coffee into her mug, she said, "Branch and I counted the money last night before we went to bed. Just to be on the safe side. It was all there."

"This waiting is driving me nuts," said Andrew, coming into the kitchen, followed by Branch and Cordelia. "That would be perfect timing, wouldn't it? If Steinhauser drove over. You're sure he understood you? He's not going to just show up?"

"I assume he understands English," said Eric testily.

"As long as you were clear," said Andrew, equally testily.

"Come on, guys," said Cordelia. "Let's bury the snark for the duration."

They all pulled up chairs and sat down.

At 9:00 A.M. sharp, the small cell phone in the center of the table rang.

Both Andrew and Eric lunged for it, inadvertently knocking it to the floor.

"Will you two grow up?" demanded Suzanne.

Cordelia reached for it at the same time Branch did, their heads colliding.

"That's it," said Jane, standing and holding out her hand. "Give it to me."

Grudgingly, Branch handed it over.

Jane flipped it open and said hello.

"Who are *you*?" came a metallic-sounding voice.

"My name is Jane. Who's this?"

"Put Eric on. Do it now or I'm ending the call."

Jane remembered the advice Nolan had given her. She hoped like hell he'd been right. "I've got your money. Since I'm the moneylender, you're going to have to work with me."

"No police. I told him that."

"I'm not a cop. I'm a friend of the family. I own a restaurant up in the Twin Cities. The family doesn't have that kind of money, which is why they called me. Tell me how you want this to work."

The caller didn't respond. Then, "One hundred thousand in hundred-dollar bills?"

"Exactly what you asked for."

"I will only talk to Eric, Suzanne, or Andrew."

"No," said Jane. Her voice was firm even though her heart was hammering. "You want the money, you talk to me."

"I have the boys. You do what *I* say."

"I'm happy to do what you say," said Jane, trying to be conciliatory without giving away any ground. "Where should we meet you?"

"We? What the hell are you trying to pull?"

"My coowner is with me. We're not cops. We have no guns, no weapons of any kind. We're simply conduits. We have the money, which we're not letting out of our sight until we give it to you. A hundred thousand dollars," she repeated. "If you don't want it, that's your call."

The comment was met with silence.

Then, "I don't like this. It's not what I asked for in the note."

"You asked for one hundred thousand dollars in hundred-dollar bills. I have it. It's all yours. It's in a briefcase right next to my feet. I'm willing to give it to you in exchange for the boys. A simple transaction. But if you want it, you have to deal with me and my partner. You have my word. We don't want any violence. We just want to make the exchange and bring Jack and Gabriel home safely."

More silence. Jane bit the inside of her lip, looked down, looked up, looked out the window.

"I'll call you back," came the metallic voice. The line disconnected.

"What happened?" demanded Suzanne.

"He's thinking about it," said Jane.

"You should have let me talk," cried Eric. "You're ruining everything."

"Give it a chance," said Branch.

"I think he's right," said Andrew. "She's the professional. Let her do what she thinks is best."

"*I'm* the father," said Eric.

"Who do you think I am?" demanded Andrew.

The cell phone rang.

Jane held it to her ear. "Yes?"

"Listen carefully. I'm only going to say this once."

With everyone standing mutely on the porch, Jane and Cordelia jumped into Cordelia's red convertible, the top up for this occasion, the gas tank full, and tore out of the driveway. Jane had asked Cordelia to drive so that she could monitor what was happening around them. The first order of business was to tap their destination into the GPS: 18405 County Road H. According to the information she received back, it was 7.4 miles away. The voice on the cell phone had instructed her to pull off onto a dirt road next to a mailbox that said THE RUTHERFORDS.

"It's going to be a simple exchange, right?" asked Cordelia, her voice rising above the wind buffeting the ragtop. "The kids will be there?"

"He didn't say."

140

"You sure it was a he?"

"For all I know it could have been a space alien."

"Oh, that's good. Always nice to know who you're dealing with."

Looking back over her shoulder, Jane scanned the road, trying to determine if they were being watched or followed. As they moved from open cornfields to a more wooded area, rural mailboxes began to appear on their right. She squinted to read the numbers. "Slow down. I think we're close." Another quarter mile and Jane said, "See that redwood sign? Pull off there."

Cordelia braked and took a hard right, coming to a stop in the middle of the one-lane dirt and gravel path. "This is it?"

"That's what he said."

She turned off the engine. "I don't see anyone."

"Then I guess we wait." She pushed the car door open with her foot and got out. Off in the distance two crows called to each other. Above them on the telephone wires, even the sparrows seemed to be waiting and watching.

For one brief moment back at the house, when she'd demanded the kidnapper deal with her, she'd felt a frisson of power. That was all gone now. Whoever was behind the robot voice held every card that counted.

Cordelia slid out and moved up next to her. "Maybe we should try to find the house the address is attached to."

"No, he said to stay by the mailbox."

"Because?"

Jane felt her pulse quicken as a white truck rumbled over a rise in the distance coming from the direction of Winfield. As quickly as it appeared, it had zoomed past. Jane recognized the make because she'd been thinking about buying a truck before she found her used C-RV. This one was a late-model Chevy Avalanche. The gold Chevrolet insignia was prominent on both the front and rear.

"Couldn't tell if that was a man or woman driving," said Cordelia, taking off her sunglasses and using the edge of her black tank top to clean the lenses. "Whoever it was, they were wearing a baseball cap and dark glasses."

A tan baseball cap, thought Jane. If it was the robotic voice, it wasn't much to go on.

A few seconds later, another car came roaring past, this one a gray Nissan sedan. It appeared to be traveling faster than the first, no doubt speeding. All Jane could make out was a man with a dark beard.

"Are you sure we've got the address right?" asked Cordelia, sitting down on the back bumper.

Jane pulled a piece of paper out of the pocket of her jeans. "Yes. Stop asking questions, okay? You're driving me crazy." Suzanne wasn't the only one in a bad mood.

"What was that?" asked Cordelia, standing up and whirling around.

Jane had heard it, too. Whatever it was, it was coming from the mailbox. She rushed over and pulled the front cover down. Sure enough, another cheap cell—just like the one that had been stuffed in Andrew and Eric's mailbox—was vibrating and buzzing. Jane grabbed it and flipped it open. "Hello?"

"So far so good," came the metallic voice.

"Where are you? Where are the boys?"

"You got a pen and a piece of paper? I want you to write this down."

Jane pulled out the small notebook she always kept with her. "Okay."

"Drive west on County Road H, away from Winfield. You need to go about twenty miles. You're looking for Lamb Avenue. Take that north. It turns into Dundee Trail and then takes a westerly jog. Just before it jogs west, turn right onto Weaver Road. You'll see a small sign that says 'Crowne Rock Estates Model Home.' If you pass the sign for Northfield, you've gone too far. Once you're on Weaver Road, it's about two miles to the model. If you see a car—any car or truck, or any person—leave immediately. Are we clear?"

"I don't understand—"

"You don't need to. Do you have the directions?"

She repeated them back.

"Good. Make sure you have the money. Oh, and one more thing. Put your cell phones in the mailbox. Not the cheap one I gave you, your personal cell phones. Do it now or the deal is off."

Jane looked around. Was it possible someone was actually watching them?

Once their phones were stowed, Jane returned the cheap cell to her ear. "This isn't necessary," she began. "Hello?" Looking up at Cordelia, she said, "He's gone."

Half an hour later, after getting stuck behind a slow-moving tractor, Jane spied the sign for Weaver Road. "There," she said, touching Cordelia's arm and pointing.

Cordelia eased her car onto the newly laid asphalt. Pressing the pedal almost to the floor, she sped for the model home in the distance. Clusters of trees dotted the flat landscape. It felt like the middle of nowhere. Jane wondered how many model homes had been sold.

"No cars around," she said, twisting in every direction. Without realizing it, she'd been holding her breath.

Cordelia blasted past a bunch of excavating machinery and pulled into the circular drive in front of a new two story house. "I don't see anyone."

Jane did a quick visual sweep of the property. Everything seemed quiet. Trotting up the steps to the front door, she used the brass knocker. "Hello?" she called, trying to make out what was behind the frosted glass.

"Try the doorbell," called Cordelia.

Jane located a lighted switch and pressed it. She waited almost a minute before she turned and found her friend leaning against the passenger's door, arms folded. "Nobody home?"

"Now what?"

"Maybe he's here, he's just being coy."

"I don't see a car. How would he have gotten way out here without one?"

Jane did another three-sixty survey of the area, her gaze coming to rest on one particularly dense clump of pine.

"See something?"

"I'm not sure."

"I'll bet everyone back at the house is wondering what the hell's taking us so long."

"We can't call them."

"We could use the cheap cell?"

Jane dug it out of her jeans, jerking with surprise as it started to ring. "Hello?" she said, walking back out to the car.

"These are my final instructions," came the metallic voice. "Leave the money behind the arborvitae in front of the house."

"Wait. No. What about the boys?"

"If the money is all there—"

"I told you," said Jane. "It is."

"Then we're good. The boys will be home by midafternoon."

"No way," said Jane. "This is an exchange. No kids, no cash."

"It's not going down that way," came the cold reply. "This is a deal breaker. Leave the money and go. If you don't, then our communication is over."

"Then it's over."

"I'm counting," said the voice. "If you don't agree to my terms by the time I get to ten, I hang up. You can take the money and burn it for all I care." He paused. Then, "One. Two."

It had come down to a game of chicken. Whoever blinked first, lost. If neither blinked, everybody lost. Jane knew that if she handed over the money, she gave away all her leverage. And yet if she didn't—

"Three. Four. Five."

"Half the money now and half after the kids come home."

"Six. Seven."

Jane's eyes skirted back to the dense section of pines. "How do I know you'll live up to your end of the bargain?"

"Eight. Nine."

She hesitated, feeling like Columbus sailing toward the ends of the earth. "Okay. You win."

"Good. Nice doing business with you."

She pulled the phone away from her ear and saw that the caller had disconnected.

"What did he say?" demanded Cordelia. "Janey, say something."

"We leave the briefcase. He delivers the kids this afternoon." The look of revulsion on Cordelia's face nearly dissolved her.

"But I thought—"

"I know," said Jane. "I don't see any choice but to do what he says." She hit a button under the dash and popped open the trunk. After lifting the briefcase out and making sure it wasn't locked, she stashed it behind the bush.

"What if he takes the money and the kids never come home?"

Jane erupted. "You think that hasn't occurred to me?"

"Calm down."

"How can I calm down? I've made a mess of this. I don't know what to do. If you do, this would be a good time to share."

Cordelia's gaze roamed the horizon. "I don't have a clue."

In a tightly compressed voice, Jane said, "Then get back in the car and drive."

17

"It's six," announced Suzanne, holding up her arm and tapping her watch. "Officially evening. I'd say that ends our hope that the boys would be back this afternoon."

They'd all gathered to wait it out on the porch. The atmosphere had seemed hopeful at first. The money had been paid. It was only a matter of time. Yet as the minutes ticked by, with no word from the kidnapper, no boys racing across the grass and up the front steps into their parents' outstretched arms, anxiety had seized everyone by the throat and talk had pretty much died. Every so often Eric would leave his chair, enter the house, and return with a fresh pitcher of lemonade. Glasses would be filled. Jane offered encouraging nods and smiles, but it was meaningless and they all knew it.

By late afternoon, even without Suzanne's announcement, Jane's hope had vanished. She'd drifted off into her own private hell, sitting alone on the front steps. She couldn't bear to look at her friends' faces another minute. She should have handled everything differently, though for the life of her, she couldn't figure out what that might have looked like. Nobody had accused her, or said the words they were undoubtedly thinking. They couldn't attack her for complete incompetence because, if nothing else, she'd been the one to come up with the money. Still, the terrible burden of all those unspoken judgments weighed on her.

What had she missed? Should she have refused to give the guy the briefcase? There were too many questions and not a good answer in sight. Glancing over at Cordelia, seeing her usually ebullient friend sitting with her arms at her sides, looking helpless and morose, the knife sunk in deeper.

Each time one of the group's many phones rang, as they had all afternoon, Jane jumped, feeling as if she'd touched a bare wall socket. Occasionally, someone phoned with a tip—a boy sighted here or there who looked like Gabriel or Jack. Three calls could legitimately be considered prank or hate calls, dumping vitriol on Andrew or Eric for having the nerve to raise a child. A psychic called from Duluth, saying that the boys' bodies would be found near a quarry. If someone would pay her expenses, she'd drive down to Winfield to help the police with their search. At one point, Branch suggested that they all toss their phones in the garbage. The comment had been met with stony silence.

Rising to her feet after Suzanne's announcement, Jane dug in the pocket of her jeans for her keys.

"Going somewhere?" asked Andrew. He'd switched his position and was now sitting on the porch floor, his back resting against the love seat.

"I'll be back," said Jane.

"You want me to come with you?" Cordelia called after her.

Jane gave her head a stiff shake as she jumped into the front

148

seat of her CR-V. On her way out of the drive, she felt momentarily nauseous. The acid in the lemonade seemed to be eating its way into her stomach. She should have eaten more today, not that she'd had the time, the opportunity, or the interest. Popping open the glove compartment, she dug out a package of peanuts, ripping open the top with her teeth.

She looked both ways on the county road, then turned right, heading toward their first destination. Pulling up next to the redwood sign a few minutes later, she jumped out to check the mailbox. Sure enough, the cell phones were right where she'd left them.

On her way to the model home for the second time that day, she punched in Nolan's number.

"Hey," she said when he answered. "It's me. I need to talk." She briefly explained what had happened, answering his questions, which were surprisingly specific. "What are you thinking?" she asked finally.

"How far are you from the model?"

Jane checked the odometer. "Maybe a mile to the turnoff."

"Okay, we've got a few minutes, so listen up: You did nothing wrong, Jane. Do you hear me? Nothing."

It was exactly what she wanted to hear and yet she wasn't sure she believed him.

"You can't control a situation like that. You did everything you could to make it work. Frankly, I think you showed a lot of guts."

"Thanks. I think." Up ahead she saw the sign for Crowne Rock Estates. Moving from the cement highway to the black asphalt utility road made the ride feel much smoother and quieter. "I can see the model from here."

"Good. Any cars around?"

"No, just like before. None."

"Tell me what else you see?"

Pulling into the circular drive, she could tell without getting out that the briefcase was gone. Okay, she thought. It was what she'd expected. Maybe there was still hope the boys would be returned. "The money's gone."

"What about that section of trees that caught your eye?"

She put the car in park, twisted her head, and turned to look. "Maybe I saw movement. What else could it have been?"

"Think. Close your eyes. Imagine it."

"Maybe . . . maybe it was the sun glinting off . . . a mirror?"

"Possible. What else?"

"I saw something that looked flat. I figured it was light coming through the trees."

"Did you notice a color?"

She struggled to remember. "Not really. Just white. As I think about it, I'm not sure what it could have been."

"A car?"

She recalled the truck she'd seen on the highway coming out of Winfield.

"The sun's in a different spot now than it was six or seven hours ago," said Nolan. "Can you drive over to the spot to get a closer look?"

"Sure. Why not?"

The CR-V rumbled slowly across the new sod. She maneuvered it down an embankment onto some flat, raked dirt, and then headed straight for the small grove a few hundred feet away. Stopping a short distance from the trees, she got out and crossed the final few feet on foot.

"Anything strike you?" asked Nolan.

She stood and looked at the clearing behind the pines.

"Any tire tracks?"

Bending down, she said, "Not that I can see. The ground's all covered with pine needles. Wait." Walking back to the edge of the tree line, she saw what she'd failed to see on the way out. She'd been moving too fast and not looking down. "Bingo. Tire tracks in the dirt. Big ones. There was a white Chevy Avalanche on the highway, one that passed us the first time we stopped."

"What direction was it headed?"

"West. Toward the model home."

"My guess is, that's your kidnapper. Find that truck and you've found the boys. Unless."

"Unless what?"

"I'm sure this has already occurred to you. The fact that the kidnapper wouldn't let you talk to the kids. That could be significant."

She had wondered about that. "What are you saying?"

"Could be a ruse. He doesn't have them. He never did. Or—"

"You don't have to spell it out."

"With signs up all over town, lots of people knew they were missing. But here's the trick: You have to proceed as if he does have them, though you can't discount that fact that he might not."

"What kind of sick human being would try to make money on someone else's tragedy?" Anger heated up inside her. "I'm going to find that SOB if it's the last thing I do."

"Be smart. Work your way through the possibilities."

She counted them up. "The boys were either abducted or they took off for their own reasons. If the latter, we're back to square one. If the former, then the kidnapper may still return them, or maybe he never planned to." That seemed to be the least favorable outcome. "Or he never had them in the first place and this whole thing was a way to extort money, which means I just gave some SOB a hundred thousand dollars for nothing."

Nolan sighed. "Money, or the lack of it, makes people do terrible things."

"Tell me about it," said Jane, looking up. Instead of the sky, she saw Octavia's face leering back at her.

18

It was later that night, curled up in an armchair, that Suzanne realized what she had to do. Branch was across the room, sprawled on the couch, a baseball game on TV, his eyes glazed, a million miles away. "Honey," she said.

"Yeah?" he responded, unmoving.

"I need to go out."

"Okay."

"I have to talk to Burton Young."

"That's probably good. Talking to another minister will help you."

"Will you be okay while I'm gone?"

His head dipped.

"Branch?"

"I keep running it over in my mind, trying to understand what happened. They were fine. Both boys were fine. Last time I talked to them, they were laughing, giggling . . . you know, just . . . normal. So, I mean, I don't believe they ran off. Not for a second.

Who took them? What sort of sick, twisted——" He pressed his fists against his eyes.

Her heart ached for him. For all of them. "Maybe I should stay."

"No. Go talk to Burton. Makes sense. I think . . . I can't stand being cooped up in this house either," he said, repositioning his baseball cap. "How long will you be gone?"

"An hour. No more."

"Let's take a pontoon ride. We've got cell phones, so it's not like we can't be reached. What do you say? Won't get dark for hours. This might be one of the last times I get to ride on that boat."

"Because?"

"I put it up on Craigslist last night. Will you come? You can meet me at the boat launch at Arbor Lake."

Suzanne didn't feel much like it, but she could see by the eagerness in her husband's eyes that it was what he wanted. Maybe even needed. "Sure."

Suzanne called Burton from the kitchen phone, relieved to find him home. She suggested that they meet at Amanda's Pie Shack near his house in Bridger. When she got there, he was seated in one of the booths, a cup of coffee on the cracked Formica tabletop in front of him. He stood as she approached, held out his hands to her.

"The boys?" he asked, his eyebrows arched expectantly.

She shook her head.

"But the ransom——"

"We paid it. They never came home." She felt herself begin to crumble.

"Sit," he said. Holding up his hand, he ordered another coffee. "Have you had anything to eat?"

"I'm not hungry."

He sat back down and watched her. "I appreciated your call yesterday, keeping me in the loop. Tell me how you are?"

She spoke slowly, explained what had happened, and ended by saying that she'd never felt so lost in her entire life.

Burton was a frail, bookish man, so unlike Branch. His best feature was his eyes—clear, kind, full of warmth. He listened with his eyes, spoke with them, touched and even embraced people with them—if any of that was even possible. Suzanne had liked him from the moment they first met.

She leaned back as a waitress set the coffee in front of her.

"How's Branch taking all this?"

"I haven't told you the good news. He found a job. He'll be on probation for six months. After that, he'll get a raise and even some profit sharing. It's a good salary, more than he expected."

"Such great news. I'm so happy for you both."

"Thanks."

"And how's everything at the church? Vivian still being . . . Vivian?"

She wanted to tell him, ached to explain what was going on inside her, but something always stopped her. She thought tonight might be different. All her normal defenses were down. Nothing felt real.

"Something you want to say?" he asked.

Could she? Guilt was combustible. As long as her lies went unchallenged, the guilt only increased. She wanted Burton's serenity, though she understood she would never have it—not now. The past still tugged at her. Sometimes she tried to slip back into the old verities, try them on like a pair of old shoes. They didn't fit anymore. The soles were all worn away and the toes felt too tight. Burton had helped start her on a spiritual journey she assumed would bring her great happiness and fulfillment. Instead, she'd taken dynamite to that road, blowing away chunks until it had become impassible. She was at a crossroads, a crisis point, one that Burton, for all his kindness and ability to listen, might not be able to understand. She loved him for so many reasons. The idea that her choices would hurt him was almost too much to bear.

"What can I do?" asked Burton, his hand reaching across the table for hers.

"Talk to God. Tell Him to bring the boys back."

His eyes were immensely sad.

"What good are we if God won't reach down into the world and act when we ask Him to? We're His priests. His intercessors. How can He stand to watch all this pain and not do something about it?" She couldn't help herself. The words had simply fallen out of her mouth.

"It doesn't work like that. The pain is what teaches us."

"What did the Holocaust teach us? Biafra? Six thousand years of war and rape, hunger and ravaged lives. Children dying before they even have a chance at life. I feel so alone, Burton. Why does God seem so cold, so indifferent?"

"I'm sorry this is happening to you."

"It's not just Gabriel. This has been growing in me for a long time. Even before my first husband died, I was questioning my beliefs. What the church teaches—it doesn't make sense to me anymore."

"I see." Still holding her hand, he said, "And Vivian didn't help matters."

"I hate the way she uses God as a weapon. But, again, it's more than that. How can any human being ever say they know the mind of God?"

"You still believe in God?"

"I believe in a consciousness beyond ourselves, but not the gods we've created in our own image, for our own purposes, to serve our needs, our fear of death."

"Then you have to find a new path."

She gazed up into his eyes. "You don't condemn me?"

"Condemn you? Why would I do that? You're struggling, just like the rest of us. The Christian path works for me. I find great meaning in it, but that's not to say it should be everyone's path. The world is a very big place. We all have a lot to learn. There's room for all of us, Suzanne. Room for different opinions. Change. Growth. Perhaps even a spirituality that isn't tethered to a specific religion. I don't know. But I learn more every day. That's what I love about life. It's always evolving, always teaching me something."

She felt tears of gratitude burn her eyes.

"I believe that God does act in our lives, does help," said Burton.

"You *believe*. You have faith."

"I do."

"That's what I've lost," she said. "Maybe that seems sad to you. But for me, it's liberating. The only thing is, I'm finding this new direction painfully lonely. What do I do with my life after I leave the church?"

"I'm sure you've thought about it. And I'm also sure you have some ideas."

She looked down into her coffee cup. "You're going to think I'm crazy."

"Tell me."

"I want to get a law degree, eventually work with people who've been sent to jail for crimes they didn't commit."

"You'd have to leave Winfield."

"I've already checked into the University of Minnesota and William Mitchell. Branch could work in Prior Lake, we could even live there. It might be a good thing to get out of here. I mean, how do I tell my family what's going on with me? My congregation?"

"You'll find a way," said Burton.

"You're sure."

"I'm sure of one thing. You're a good woman. You'll work it out."

"Will you help me?"

He squeezed her hand. "In any way I can."

Driving down the path to the boat launch a while later, she found Branch hunched on the dock, his hands covering his face, the pontoon tied to a post. "Problems?" she shouted, getting out of her Prius and approaching the dock on foot.

He raised his head. In a tightly compressed voice, he said, "When I pulled the canvas cover off, I found something I didn't expect."

She moved up behind him, seeing the word "Satan," the numbers "666," and several pentagrams scrawled across the pontoon's carpet and seats. Most of the seats had also been slit, foam spilling out onto the deck. "Oh, honey, this is awful."

"That about covers it."

"Why? Who?"

"Must have happened during the night. I'm thinking it's a curse. Somebody's trying to put a curse on me. Those are powerful satanic symbols."

"No, they're not." It sometimes amazed her what he believed. She crouched down behind him, put a hand on his shoulder.

Shaking it off, he jumped into the water and began to pull the pontoon toward the trailer. "Let's go home."

"This was just some stupid prank."

"No, Suzanne. It wasn't. It was a message."

19

"I feel like the proverbial rat," said Cordelia, the last words of the cliché left unspoken as she held the trunk of her car open while Jane lifted in her overnight bag.

"Nothing proverbial about you," said Jane with a smirk.

"I am *not* saying I think this situation is a sinking ship. It's just, I have to get back to the Cities because of the infestation."

Cordelia had been on the horn earlier with Bolger, who informed her that Hattie's bug collection, the one she hid in her closet—the one nobody knew about—had somehow made a jailbreak. Centipedes, spiders, flies, silverfish, and a veritable flotilla of other tiny insects were roaming the loft at will.

"Thank God Bolger was there to take charge. He's calling a pest control company."

"Is Hattie okay with all the potential destruction of life?" asked Jane.

"She's not the least bit bothered—as long as she gets to do the autopsies."

"Excuse me?"

"Don't you remember when Blanche came inside with two huge, horribilious june bugs attached to her fur?"

"Not really." Blanche was the matriarch of Cordelia's cat colony.

"Bolger and I were both scared to death that their demise would send Hatts into a paroxysm of grief. Turned out, she was fascinated. She used a magnifying glass to dissect the carcasses."

"Maybe you're raising a medical examiner."

Cordelia shivered. "Hattie's a strange child. Sometimes I wish she could be strange in a normal way. You know, like have a crush on Bette Davis—"

"Or Natalie Portman."

"Right. Or insist on viewing Alfred Hitchcock's complete oeuvre in one sitting."

"Like you did when you were a kid."

"Exactly."

Jane shrugged. "Different strokes."

"How lovely, Jane, that you can so concisely sum up Hattie's psychological depths."

They were standing outside the motel, sweating in the oppressive evening heat. Jane looked up at the cloudless twilight sky and said, "We need a storm to break this weather."

"We need something all right," said Cordelia, sliding in. She had a red bandana tied around her head, more as a fashion statement than a sweatband, though it would serve both purposes. She loved to drive with the top down, the wind providing the air-conditioning. "I wish you luck. Are you going back to the farmhouse tonight?"

"Not unless something happens."

"Well, be safe. Text me with updates. And don't do anything

I wouldn't do—and I wouldn't do anything dangerous." She saluted and then backed the car up and eased out onto the street, waving as she sped away into the night.

Feeling at loose ends, Jane decided to walk into town and look for a place to have dinner and a glass of wine. After the day she'd put in, she figured she deserved it. She washed up in the bathroom, then locked the motel room and headed toward Main.

Passing Lindstrom's Bar & Café on her way to the spot where she'd eaten breakfast, she stopped to look in the window. It was just after nine. The café was dark, but continuing on a few steps, she found the bar still open, with half a dozen people gathered at a single table, and others sitting alone on stools watching a baseball game on the flat-screen TV over the bar. Curious to see what Eric and his family had built, she stepped into the cool, dimly lit interior. A door along the side wall led into the restaurant. A sign on a rope strung across the doorway said, CLOSED.

The bartender looked up as Jane approached. He was a middle-aged guy with a shaved head and a tattoo spreading from his shirt collar up the side of his neck.

"Help you?" he asked.

"Whatever you've got on tap is fine."

"Blue Moon, Pabst, or Rolling Rock."

"Give me the Rolling Rock." The group at the table was making so much noise that she turned around, finding a bunch of angry faces. "Something wrong?" she asked, returning her attention to the bartender.

"We found out last week that our post office is being closed. It's got a lot of people around here pretty pissed off, me included. Won't be good for business, I can tell you that much."

"Sorry to hear it."

"Yeah, well. I don't know who makes these decisions, but the ripples are gonna last. Anyway, can I get you anything else?"

"You serve food?"

He pushed a plastic menu card across to her. She took a quick look, saw the usual bar fare, and ordered a cheeseburger. Checking her phone for messages, she saw that she had a text from Mia.

"J—Hi. All of the above. Esp. horses. Am at a cabin on north shore with Mom. Dad in Atlanta. All home next Sunday. Got braces. Hate them!!!!!! Excited to C U. Love, M."

Jane was relieved to finally hear from her. She would make a firm horseback riding date with Mia when she returned—and offer sympathy about the braces.

As the bartender pulled her beer, making sure it had a nice creamy cap, Jane made herself more comfortable on the stool.

"You new in town?" he asked, setting the glass down in front of her, then pushing over a bowl of popcorn. "Don't think I've seen you in here before."

"Just visiting. I'm a friend of Eric Lindstrom's."

"Ah. The boss."

He nodded and was about to move away when Jane said, "I'm curious. Do you know anybody around here who drives a newer model white Chevy Avalanche? Four-door cab."

Leaning his elbows on the battered oak counter, he thought for a few seconds. "No, can't say that I do. How come you're interested?"

"One passed me on the highway just outside of town. Came so close to my car that it nearly drove me off the road."

"Huh. You get a license plate?"

"Happened too fast."

He shrugged. "Sorry."

She ate her burger and watched the game, all the while making mental notes about what she wanted to accomplish tomorrow. She figured she'd give herself the morning to nose around before driving back to Minneapolis. Avi had offered to stay at the house to take care of the dogs while she was away.

"Another brew?" asked the bartender as he removed her empty plate.

"Just the check. And one other thing: Do you have a Winfield phone directory?"

"Sure do," he said, reaching under the bar. "This thing covers Winfield, Short Creek, and Bridger."

She thanked him. After he'd walked off with her credit card, she looked up the address of the science teacher she'd met at Eric and Andrew's house—the owlish-looking jogger who carried a pack of cigarettes in his pocket. That and the fact that he'd found Gabriel's cell phone made him a person of interest, to use a phrase from the current cop cliché manual. Passing her finger down the row of Es, she finally came to Aaron Eld, 631 Tyler Street. When the bartender returned with her receipt, she asked him for directions.

"The bar's on Main. When you get outside, turn right and go two blocks. That's Tyler. Take another right and it should be maybe another two or three blocks."

She thanked him, signed the receipt, and gave him a tip he'd remember. She'd never met anyone who worked in a restaurant or bar who didn't tip well.

Once she was back out on the street, the heavy heat and even heavier humidity dropped on her like a wool blanket. This was the hottest June in memory. All the way to the Eld house she alternated thoughts of moving to someplace like Greenland, which was melting fast but had to be cooler than Minnesota, with thoughts of the conversation she hoped to have with Avi later tonight, when she got back to the motel.

Eld's house was easy to find because a light was on over the front door, which allowed Jane to see the numbers clearly even from across the street. It was a large, two-story, white clabbered structure, with a white picket fence around the front yard. Very Frank Capra. Since it was after ten, knocking on the front door wasn't an option. Luck, however, appeared to be with her. Eld, wearing dark sweatpants, a sweatband around his head, and a dark T-shirt, had come out the front door.

Jane ducked behind a hedge.

He looked around for a few seconds, adjusted the earbuds in his ear and the volume on his MP3 player, then took off running. In this heat, a jog, especially after a greasy burger and a beer, was the last thing Jane felt like. Waiting for him to get half a block ahead, she followed on the opposite side of the street, ready to dart behind a tree or a car if he should look behind him.

He never did. He ran steadily down Tyler and then up a hill toward the library. One block past it he stopped. Bending over, he put hands on his thighs and breathed heavily.

Jane was a periodic runner, thus even after the dinner she'd packed away, she was nowhere near as winded as he looked. She hid behind a van and watched him pull a pack of cigarettes out of his pocket and light up, clearly strange behavior for a health enthusiast. He leaned against a cement retaining wall for a few minutes, smoking calmly, flicking ash onto the sidewalk, and then tossed the cigarette in the grass and cut across two front lawns to the third house on the next block over, where he knocked on the front door. He stood there, adjusting his round, dark-rimmed glasses, looking nervously over each shoulder, until the door was answered.

Jane assumed that in the darkness he wouldn't recognize her as the woman he'd met at the farmhouse. She crossed at the intersection and headed down the sidewalk, keeping her pace leisurely. As she came past the house, an attractive woman in a Hawaiian print dress opened the front door. Jane could hear Eld say hi. The woman responded with something that sounded like, "You're late." She touched his arm and then stepped back, allowing Eld to enter. The door was quickly shut.

Jane took note of the address—718 Morgan—and studied the house. It was much bigger and older than Eld's, a stately mock-Tudor two-story with lots of timbering on the second floor and a large sunroom off the east side. It was also bigger than the other houses on the block, and set farther back.

Everywhere Jane looked in this small town she found houses for sale, houses with foreclosure notices tacked to the side of the door. This was the most prosperous looking street she'd seen.

The light in the living room snapped off. A few seconds later, a light come on in the basement. Eld had come out onto his front steps, giving the impression of a man going for his nightly jog, and yet that had obviously not been his intent. Was he trying to fool his wife about his true destination? Was he having an affair with the woman who'd answered the door? Nothing particularly unusual about that. People slept around all the time. Still, there could be other reasons for the visit.

Darting across the grass, she crept up to one of the lighted basement windows. Through a crack in the curtain, she was able to see Eld seated at a desk in front of a desktop computer. The woman entered carrying a filled wineglass and sat down across the room on a sofa. She looked uncomfortable, fidgeting with her collar, taking regular sips of wine. She kept looking over her shoulder toward the doorway as Eld tapped away at the keyboard. Jane mentally crossed off the possibility of an affair.

Eld kept checking his watch. Half an hour after he'd arrived, he rose from the desk chair and said something to the woman. She waited for him to walk in front of her, then turned off the overhead light and closed the door behind her. Jane took it as her cue to trot back across the street, where she crouched down behind a car and waited for Eld to come out. She assumed his reason for the visit was to use the computer, although when he didn't come out immediately, Jane began to reassess what might be going on inside. It took another fifteen minutes before he reappeared. The woman wasn't with him this time. He looked both ways down the street, then took off, running in earnest.

It was late. Jane had no desire to follow him back to his house, and no way to get into the home he'd just left. She was tired. Mentally burned out. All she wanted was a shower, a brandy, and a chance to talk to Avi.

20

SUNDAY

As the bells of a nearby church rang out the hymn "Faith of Our Fathers," Jane walked up the steps to the Eld house and knocked on the front door. When it opened, instead of Eld, a young woman with lush copper-colored hair and a nasty-looking rash on her cheeks appeared.

"Can I help you?" she asked, her smile crooked and friendly.

"Mrs. Eld?"

"Holly."

"My name's Jane. I was hoping to talk to your husband."

"He's not here right now."

Standing back, Jane took off her sunglasses and gazed up at the second floor. "You've got a beautiful home. Have you lived here long?"

"Seven years. We love it."

"I've been driving around. Seems like a nice town—except for all the for sale and foreclosure signs."

The woman leaned against the doorjamb. "You're not from around here?"

"No. You know, there's a house up on Morgan. It's a two-story Tudor. Larger than the other homes around it. Sits further back from the street. Do you know who owns it?"

Holly glanced over Jane's shoulder at the CR-V parked by the curb. "The woman's name is Myra Taft."

"She a friend?"

"Yes, a good friend. Her husband died a couple of years ago. She teaches up at the middle school with Aaron. How come you're interested?"

"Actually," said Jane, handing Holly one of her cards, "I'm here on business."

Holly read the front, then flipped it over. "You're a private investigator?"

"Andrew Waltz and Eric Lindstrom hired me to help them find their son, Jack. And Gabriel Born. You know them?"

She hesitated. "I saw the signs around town."

"I was hoping to talk to Aaron about them."

"About those boys? He doesn't know anything."

"He found Gabriel's cell phone the day after he went missing."

"He did?"

"He didn't mention it?"

She examined the card. "Are you suggesting that my husband had something to do with their disappearance? Because if you are, I'm here to tell you you're wrong."

Jane thought it was odd that Holly would immediately jump to such a dark conclusion. "It's nothing like that. I just wanted to talk to him for a couple of minutes."

169

"So, like, you think someone in Winfield took those boys? They could have run away, you know."

"We have evidence that it was an abduction."

"I'm sorry. How awful."

"We don't know who did it," said Jane, "but we know why. Money."

"Doesn't seem like that would eliminate many people. I mean, who doesn't need money?"

"Your husband's a jogger, right?"

"Yeah?" she said warily.

"He sure must be dedicated to jog in this heat."

She shrugged. "He hasn't been doing it long. Just the last couple of weeks—since school let out for the year. He runs in the morning and in the evening. It's cooler then."

"Is he trying to quit smoking?"

"Smoking?"

"Well, I mean, the two don't really mix."

Holly's reaction suggested she hadn't thought about it. "No, I suppose that's true."

"I hear he's very well thought of at the middle school. A popular teacher."

"Depends on who you talk to."

"Your husband's had some problems?" Jane could tell by the look in Holly's eyes that she'd asked one question too many. Holly was done talking.

"Look, Aaron should be back later. If you want to speak with him, you can come back. I should really go."

Jane was about to thank her for her time, but before she could get the words out, Holly had shut the door.

．　　　．　　　．

In the sweltering morning sun, Jane stood with Eric by the side of the farmhouse garage as he let fly with a stream of invective.

"All I can say is, if I didn't know it before, I do now. This town has *more* than its share of slimeballs."

On the west side of the garage, someone had sprayed the word "FAG" in huge black letters. On the east side, the word "DIE" had been scrawled in equally huge letters.

"I called Andrew," said Eric, walking back toward the house. "He said he'd pick up some paint at the Walmart on the way over."

They stopped before they reached the front porch.

"Have you heard from Suzanne and Branch today?" asked Jane.

"I called but nobody answered."

Pushing her hands deep into the pockets of her jeans, she said, "This is hard for me to admit, Eric, but I feel like I failed you. Badly." Probably not the smartest statement ever made by a professional investigator, but it was how she felt. She couldn't hide it.

"No," he said quickly. "You did everything you could. Hell, I don't know how we'll ever pay you back the money you lost."

"Don't give it another thought. It wasn't my money."

"It was your father's. Cordelia mentioned that."

"She's mistaken. The person who gave it to me—who asked to remain anonymous—won't even miss it." She'd already made a deal with the devil. Nothing could change that now. "I'm not done," she added. "I just wanted you to know that I'm following up some leads. I can't promise they'll get us anywhere—"

171

As they were talking, a police cruiser pulled into the yard.

"It's Steinhauser," said Eric.

"What the fuck is going on?" demanded the officer, bursting out of the front seat and heading straight for them.

Eric glanced at Jane. " 'Going on'?"

"I just talked to my chief. I've been taken off the case."

"I don't——"

"Your sister and her husband were in his office when I got to the station this morning. An hour or so after they left, I was called in and ordered to drop my investigation. No explanation. It was given to Bill Jennings. Bill freakin' Jennings. I've been a police officer twice as long as he has."

"I don't know anything about it," said Eric.

Steinhauser turned to Jane.

Eric introduced her as a friend of the family, leaving out the fact that she was a PI. Since it was his call, she went with it.

Steinhauser was older than Jane had expected—gray haired, bowlegged, gut spilling over his belt. With prominent dark circles around his eyes and a body that sagged in the heat, he struck her as a man who was bone weary.

"I don't know what you folks are trying to pull," he said. "I'm good at my job. I don't expect people to go behind my back and make problems for me."

"You better talk to my sister," said Eric.

"I tried. I stopped by her house on the way over here. Nobody was home. You can't expect miracles, you know. I been busting my ass trying to figure out what happened to those kids. They aren't just names to me. I know them. I care about them."

"I believe that."

"What happened back at the station is absolute bullshit. You

172

hear me?" His face looked blistering hot. "You see your sister, you tell her to call me. She's got my number."

With that, he got back in his cruiser and backed out of the drive.

"Boy," said Jane, watching the squad car roar off onto the county highway, "that guy's got one hair trigger temper. I don't think I'd want him around my kid."

When Jane stopped by Suzanne and Branch's house later in the morning, she was relieved to see Suzanne's Prius out front. She didn't want to drive back to Minneapolis before she'd had a chance to check out Gabriel's bedroom.

Suzanne answered the door, ushering Jane into the living room and asking if she'd like something cold to drink.

"No thanks," said Jane. As they walked out to a flagstone patio in the back, Jane explained that she was at the farmhouse with Eric earlier when Steinhauser had arrived, mad as hell that he'd been taken off the case. "He said you and Branch had been in to talk to his chief, that it was all your doing."

Suzanne sat down in the shade. "It was."

"Can I ask why?" Jane sat down across form her.

Taking a deep breath, she said, "Have you ever had a bad feeling about someone? That something wasn't right about them?"

"Sure."

"That's how I feel about Steinhauser." She explained about an altercation between Branch and the cop after one of Gabriel's Little League games. "That's why we had him taken off the case."

"Sounds like the right call," said Jane.

"Yeah. You're sure I can't get you something to drink?"

"Actually, I'm here because I want to look at Gabriel's bedroom."

"I don't know what you think you'll find," said Suzanne. "I've searched every inch of it and haven't found anything out of the ordinary."

"Did Gabriel have a computer?"

"Not one that was connected to the Internet. I use the computer at the church. Branch didn't need one anymore after his landscaping business died. We felt the dial-up modem was an expense we couldn't afford." Running a hand through her hair, she continued, "I've looked all over his computer. So did Branch. There isn't much on it."

"He's not on Facebook."

She laughed. "That's the last thing Gabriel would be interested in. I'm sad to say that he doesn't have a lot of friends. Since his dad's death, it's been hard for him. Branch has really helped him develop some of his athletic and outdoor skills, but mostly he's a quiet kid. He likes to spend his free time reading—when he isn't with Jack at the farmhouse. I've been working so much overtime this past year that I was surprised by how many books he had in his room."

"Books about?"

"Everything. Fiction. Nonfiction. He especially likes fantasy. I think most kids do. Go ahead upstairs and take a look for yourself." Checking her watch, she added, "I've got a meeting at church in half an hour. Something I can't miss. Is that enough time?"

"I'll make it work," said Jane.

Suzanne offered to walk her upstairs, but Jane said she could find her way. She left Suzanne sitting at the table, seemingly lost in thought even before Jane had gone inside.

Gabriel's bedroom was unusually neat for a boy his age. The closet was organized, as were all the dresser drawers. A twin bed with a brightly colored bedspread hugged one wall. Directly across from it, under the only window in the room, was a low bookshelf half filled with books. Stacks of magazines, a couple of board games, a football, a few framed photographs, boxes of CDs, a mini remote-controlled race car, and a new-looking CD player with fairly large speakers filled up the rest. On the wall by the door was a *Hobbit* map of Middle Earth. Next to that was a black-and-white poster of the band Boys Like Girls. The juxtaposition seemed like an apt assessment of the inner life of a boy Gabriel's age. One spoke loudly of childhood, the other of young male sexual angst.

The only part of the room that showed even the slightest disorder was Gabriel's desk. Jane sat down and began to search the desk drawers. She found the usual. Pens and pencils. Markers. A measuring tape. A road map of Minnesota and one of Wisconsin. A stapler. The bottom drawer had room for file folders, though there were only two. One was filled with school papers, the other with pictures Gabriel had cut out of magazines. Mostly pictures of pretty girls. A few of cars. A couple famous athletes.

Crouching down by the bookcase, Jane saw that he had a boxed set of J.R.R. Tolkien's works and the complete Harry Potter series. Most of the books looked new. Pressing her finger on the spines as she moved down the row, she did see evidence of an eclectic mind. Gabriel was not only drawn to fantasy, he also seemed to be interested in archeology, geology, karate, botany, photography, ESP, extraterrestrials, and cooking.

Most of the magazines were sports related. At the bottom of the largest stack she found a magazine stuffed inside another magazine. Pulling it free, she found a well-thumbed copy of *Guns & Ammo* inside a copy of *Sports Illustrated*. She paged through it, seeing large, dark checks next to various rifles.

"Jane," came Suzanne's voice from downstairs. "I need to leave in a few minutes. Are you almost done?"

Jane took one last look around the room, then, still holding the gun magazine, she trotted down the stairs.

"Did you find anything?" asked Suzanne, her briefcase strap slung over one shoulder, car keys in her hand.

"I'm not sure," said Jane. She showed her the magazine. "Is Gabriel interested in guns?"

"No," said Suzanne, paging through it and seeing the same checks Jane had. "Branch let him fire a hunting rifle last fall. Maybe that got him interested. It's not something I was particularly comfortable with. I talked to him about it—and to Branch. I wouldn't allow a gun in this house if it weren't for my husband. He keeps everything locked up. I've never had any worries about that. But boys and guns—they don't mix."

"What kind of firearms does Branch own?"

"A shotgun. A rifle. And a handgun. I can't be more specific because I've never really paid any attention to them. Listen, Jane, if I haven't said this before, let me say it now. I'm so glad you're helping us."

Jane dropped the magazine on a table by the stairs. "Maybe you should wait on that until we see what my investigation turns up."

21

Later that day, as Jane drove up Highway 52 on her way back to Minneapolis, she watched a bank of dark clouds approach the Cities from the west. When she turned on the radio to get the forecast, she was informed that most of the southern part of the state was under a tornado watch until midnight. She'd been expecting a storm. All the heat and humidity pretty much guaranteed it. By the time she turned onto her street, the wind had picked up and the sky had turned that shade of yellow-gray she knew meant trouble. An instant later, the city sirens started wailing.

Up ahead, Georgia Dietrich, Avi's detestable roommate, had just emerged from the front door of Jane's house. "Screw that," she whispered, indulging in the inevitable moment of teeth grinding.

As Georgia backed her way down the sidewalk, she blew kisses until she reached her car. To Jane's knowledge, Georgia had never come over before, although what happened when she was away was anybody's guess. Jane wanted to trust Avi—desperately wanted to—but something inside her always fought the idea. It was probably her own insecurity talking, which upset her because she'd never thought of herself as insecure before. Until now, she'd assumed that Avi spent her days upstairs writing. It annoyed Jane—no, it downright infuriated her—to see Georgia on her property. Okay, so she was jealous. She was human. She was insecure and she was pissed.

Waiting until Georgia had driven away, she parked in the drive and entered the house through the back door. The dogs, tails wagging like turbo-charged metronomes, raced into the kitchen to greet her. "Hey, babes," she said, crouching down. Mouse nuzzled her hand with his chilly nose, while Gimlet jumped up and down trying to lick her face. She spun around so many times in her utter glee that she fell over. Dogs were so obvious. No subtlety at all. Which was why she loved them. She scratched their backs, rubbed their ears—everything she knew they loved. "Where's Avi?" she asked, straightening up.

Walking to the bottom of the stairs, she called, "I'm home. You up there?"

"Just a sec," came Avi's voice.

"The sirens are going off. We better get to the basement."

Avi appeared at the top of the steps wearing a football helmet and holding a fifth of Jack Daniel's. "God, I'm glad you're home," she said, trotting down the steps. "Just so you know, I'm terrified of thunderstorms."

This was news to Jane. "Thus the helmet?"

"Brain protection. If you want, I'll get you one. When I was a kid, I used to hide under my bed every time there was a storm. Sometimes I'd throw up. It was disgusting."

"Is that still . . . a problem?"

"Not so much."

Once ensconced on the edge of the bathtub in the basement bathroom, with the dogs snugged together on a dog bed Jane had dragged into the room, Avi ripped the plastic off the cap of the whiskey bottle and took a swig. She held it up. "You?"

"Think I'll pass."

"Steadies the nerves," she said, ducking at a crack of thunder.

As the storm raged outside, Jane approached the subject of Georgia. "Hey, you know I, ah . . . saw Georgia leave as I was driving up."

"Yeah." Avi adjusted the strap on the helmet. "She came because of the good news."

"Good news?"

She took another swig of whiskey. "That agent you told me about? I sent her the new book yesterday, just like I promised. I stopped obsessing and just did it. This morning, I had an e-mail from her saying she'd read it last night. She had several other books scheduled first, but had forgotten to load them onto her iPad. Since she had my e-mail with the attachment, she opened it. Jane, believe it or not, she loved it. Once she'd started reading, she said she couldn't put it down. She saw the wholeness in my characters, not just the weirdness, the fractures. She seems to really *get* what I'm trying to do. She wants to represent me. Asked if I had other books she could look at. I'm in, Jane! Thanks to you." She tried to give Jane a kiss, but the face mask clunked against Jane's chin.

And *Georgia* was the one she called, thought Jane. Not her. Great. Just superb.

"Then," said Avi, taking another swig.

"Slow down with that stuff."

"Huh? Oh, sure. Anyway, this afternoon, I get a call from a woman—Elaine Ducasse. From Ducasse & Ducasse—it's a very classy small press in Chicago. She wanted to see the entire manuscript. So, I mean, I said, hell. Sure. I e-mailed it to her. I suppose the agent must have contacted her right away. Can you believe it? I've already got a read at a publishing house. It's not New York, but it's not Podunk & Sons Press either."

"That's incredible."

"Boy howdy."

The house shook as more thunder rolled over them.

Avi slid closer to Jane. "Put your arms around me."

Jane had no trouble handling that request.

"You're not frightened of thunderstorms?" asked Avi.

"Well, I don't exactly love them. We'll be okay."

"Sure we will."

Waiting a beat, Jane said, "Why did you tell Georgia your good news and not me?"

"What? Oh, now don't get all bent out of shape. I was on the phone with her when I got the e-mail. Then I got busy looking at other manuscripts, deciding what I should or shouldn't send. Out of the blue, she stopped by a few minutes later to congratulate me." Nuzzling closer to Jane, she added, "Come on, I knew I'd see you tonight."

Jane didn't say anything, mainly because she wasn't sure how she felt.

"Georgia's restful to be around," said Avi. "She's predictable. I like that."

"I'm not restful?"

Tipping Jane's face toward her, she said, "Anything but. On the other hand, you are midwestern."

"Is that good or bad?"

"I used to think it was bad, but now I see it differently."

"Care to elaborate?"

"For one thing, you say what you mean. You don't do double entendres. You're not a cynic about everything in the universe. You don't strike poses for effect. That isn't to say you aren't hard to read sometimes."

"No harder than you are."

She took another swallow. "Here's the thing. I have to be sure this time. I create people for a living—or, for what I hope will be a living one day. The problem is, I don't just do it in my books. I've always fallen in love way too easily. When I do, I stop seeing who the person really is and instead, I make them fit what I need."

"Wish I'd met you before you reformed."

"No, this is better. I think you could be the real thing, Jane. The one who lasts. But I have to make sure I'm not simply seeing what I want to see. I want the same things you do—to love and be loved, a love given freely. Honestly. What I don't want is more neurotic need that comes from chronic dissatisfaction with my screwed-up life."

"Okay."

"Okay?"

"I can wait. I wish you'd move in with me." Jettison Georgia forever, she might have added, but didn't.

"Nope. I need to be able to get away. That's a bottom line for me right now."

"You look ridiculous in that football helmet."

"I know. You'll get used to it."

The house rattled through another clap of thunder.

Avi all but jumped into Jane's lap. So did Gimlet.

"Take my mind off this storm," said Avi, drawing Gimlet into her arms and cuddling her close. "Anything new on the Winfield front?"

Jane brought her up to speed, ending with Matt Steinhauser. "When I was at the farmhouse this morning, he roared up in his squad car looking totally frazzled. I mean, red-faced, dark circles under his eyes, like he hadn't slept in a decade. He's been removed from the case." She explained about Steinhauser screaming at Gabriel after a Little League game. "He's got a bad temper. In fact, he got so hot under the collar about being taken off the case that his first thought was to drive out to the farm to take it out on Eric."

"Not exactly professional."

Not at all, thought Jane as the lights flickered. "Here we go," she said, knowing what would happen next.

A moment later, all electricity to the house died.

"There's a flashlight in that drawer next to you," said Jane.

Removing her helmet, Avi let it drop to the floor. Taking one last swig from the bottle of Jack Daniel's, she said, "I have achieved mellow. Let's enjoy the dark, what do you say?" She ran a finger down the front of Jane's shirt. "And say hello properly."

Jane didn't need to be coaxed.

22

As the wind gusted through the trees, Eric ran toward the garage, shouting, "Come in the house, you idiot, before you blow away."

For the last hour, Andrew had been painting over the words scrawled on the garage walls. Eric had been watching from the kitchen window, dithering, stewing, so angry at himself, at Andrew, at their bottomless self-pity, the thick defensive walls they'd built up until communication was no longer possible, that he felt like a bomb with a lit fuse just millimeters from ignition.

"I'm not done," Andrew yelled back.

"Look up." In the distance, a hook cloud had dropped out of the sky and was swirling its way toward the ground. Eric grabbed the ladder Andrew was perched on and shook it. "Get down."

"Stop it. You're going to make me fall."

"For once, you need listen to me."

Andrew threw the paintbrush at the grass and climbed off the ladder. "I can take care of myself."

"Really?"

"Yes, *really.*"

"Fine. Blow away. What's it to me if they find parts of you scattered over six counties?"

"That's it exactly," said Andrew. "That's the problem." He stood eye to eye with Eric, yelling over the wind. "You don't care. Maybe you never did."

Eric was horrified. "I have loved you so hard, so deeply, for so long—"

"You threw me out."

"You were never here anyway."

Andrew grabbed Eric's shirt.

Eric slammed him back against the garage wall.

"You blame me for all our problems," yelled Andrew.

"Not only do you not listen, you put words in my mouth."

Andrew spun Eric around and pinned him against the garage.

"I still love you," roared Eric, fighting him off. "Do you hear that?"

"I don't believe you."

"You're an asshole."

They wrestled each other to the ground.

"I hate you," yelled Andrew. "You've ruined my life."

Eric tried to respond, but they were kissing now, rolling in the grass, grabbing at each other's bodies.

"We have to get inside," cried Eric.

Instead, they stayed right there, locked in an embrace neither was willing to break. As the wind whipped around them, over them, past them, they held on tight, the storm outside and the storm inside raging in perfect balance. It could have been hours, or perhaps just seconds, but eventually, with a fine mist settling over the land and the sky above turning a deep cobalt blue, Eric and Andrew found themselves staring into each other's eyes.

"What just happened?" asked Andrew, pulling back, a stunned expression on his face.

"I think," said Eric, hearing the faint sound of wind chimes coming from the front porch, "that we just forgave each other."

Eric stood on the front porch and waved as Andrew drove off in his truck. Knowing that the town would be covered in downed trees, Andrew had called Branch. Together they would use their chain saws to help people dig out. It was what Andrew and Branch always did after a storm. What neighbors did for each other.

Walking around the side of the house carrying a large plastic sack, Eric began to clean up the debris. The air was cooler now. Andrew would be back tonight to stay. Neither one of them was naïve enough to think that all their problems had been blown away by a thunderstorm, and yet they'd made their way back to each other, if only for a while. It was progress, and at this point, Eric was happy to take anything he could get.

Hearing a whimpering noise coming from behind the porch, Eric wondered if an animal had become trapped in the redwood lattice. He approached cautiously.

"Dad?" came a soft voice.

Eric felt a shiver roll through him.

"Dad?" the voice came again.

Lunging forward, Eric fell to his knees. "Oh, God," he cried, crushing Jack in his arms. He said the words over and over until the reality sank in. "We were so worried. But you're home. I can't believe it. You're home." He held on for dear life, tears streaming down his cheeks.

"Dad, it's okay."

Holding his son at arm's length, Eric asked, "Are you hurt?"

"No."

"You're sure?" He looked him over. "How did you get here? Did they let you go? I've got so many questions. What's important is that you're back. Safe. I won't let anything happen to you ever again."

Jack was shivering.

"Are you cold?"

"Yeah."

"Come inside." He led his son up the steps and into the house, ordering him to sit on the couch. He wrapped him in a cotton blanket and then sat down on the coffee table in front of him. His relief was so immense that he wanted to shout for joy. Instead, he said, "You're sure you're not hurt?"

"No, I'm okay."

"Did you know we paid a ransom?"

"Huh?"

"Who took you? Can you identify them? Him? Her?"

He shook his head.

"Where did they take you?"

"I don't know where."

"Was it a man?"

"Yeah."

"But you never saw his face?"

He shook his head. "He had on a mask."

"Could you identify his voice?"

"Maybe." He seemed numb, his reactions flat.

"Are you sure you're okay? He didn't hurt you in any way?"

"I'm okay."

"No bruises?" He began to examine Jack's arm, but Jack pulled it back under the blanket. "I told you, I'm fine."

Eric studied his son, not quite sure what to think. "Papa and I were worried sick. What about Gabriel? Did they let him go, too? Is he home?"

"I don't know."

"You don't know?"

His eyes roamed the room. "We were separated."

"Who? How? When were you taken? How did it happen?"

"Can I have something to eat?"

"Oh, Lord. Of course you're hungry."

"And something to drink?"

Eric was appalled that he hadn't thought of it himself. "Come in the kitchen. I'll make you a sandwich."

"Can't I stay here?"

"No," said Eric. He wasn't letting Jack out of his sight. "Bring the blanket."

"Can I have two sandwiches? Or even three. And a monster glass of milk."

"I'm going to call Papa, tell him you're home. And your aunt Suzanne."

Jack nodded, pulling the blanket up under his chin.

"God, I'm so glad you're back."

"Me, too," whispered Jack. "Dad?" His head dipped. "I . . . I love you."

The words, and the sight of his boy so tired and pale, would have broken Eric's heart if he hadn't been so relieved, so over-the-moon with pure joy.

187

23

Suzanne hung back by the doorway into the living room and watched Jack wolf down a grilled cheese sandwich while concentrating all his attention on a TV show. Eric was in the kitchen. By the sounds of pans and dishes clinking, he was cooking. Turning at the sound of the screen door opening behind her, she found Andrew and Branch, their faces eager and full of relief, charging into the living room. Branch kissed her as he brushed past, reached for her hand and pulled her with him. He smelled like cigarette smoke, which didn't surprise her.

As Eric came into the room with another grilled cheese sandwich, Jack looked up, his eyes traveling from face to face. He didn't smile or jump up to hug any of them, which Suzanne found odd, although what was normal under circumstances like this was anybody's guess.

Truman emerged into the dining room from the kitchen, one hand sunk in a package of potato chips. When he saw what was happening, he seemed curious and came in and stood next to Eric.

Andrew threw himself onto the couch next to Jack and buried him in his arms, rubbing his son's hair and kissing his cheeks, filling every part of his soul with his son's seemingly miraculous return. "You had us so worried," he said, brushing Jack's hair back from his forehead. "Eric says you're not hurt. God in heaven, what happened? Some guy with a mask took you?"

Jack nodded, continuing to look around at all the people peering at him. "I wanted to fight him, but he was really big."

"You did the right thing," said Suzanne, snapping off the TV and then sitting down on the couch on the other side of the boy. Branch perched on the arm of a chair. They were all holding their collective breath, hanging on Jack's every word. "Can you tell me about Gabriel?" she asked. "Do you know where he is?" She tried to sound calm, to keep the fear out of her voice. This was what she'd been waiting for. It was hard not to push.

Jack nibbled the edge of his sandwich before finally putting it down. "I haven't seen him since the night we were taken."

"You never even heard his voice," said Suzanne, feeling desperate for more information. "Or, I mean, did the man who took you say anything about him?"

"Nothing."

"One man?" asked Andrew. "Two? More?"

"One," said Jack. "He came into the tent with a gun. Ordered us to go with him. He walked us out to the highway, where we climbed in the trunk of his car."

"You must have been terrified," said Suzanne.

"Yeah, pretty much."

"What kind of car?" asked Branch.

Jack eyed him warily and didn't immediately reply.

"Something wrong?" asked Branch.

189

Jack gave his head a tight shake.

"So what kind of car?"

"It was the middle of the night. I don't know. A Ford, maybe. Something silver."

"A sedan," asked Andrew. "Four doors?"

"Yeah, I think so."

"Did the man threaten you?" asked Suzanne.

"He put duct tape over our mouths. Told us to keep quiet and do what he said."

"Was he wearing a ring? A watch?" asked Eric.

"A ring, I think. A band. Maybe gold."

"Like a wedding ring?"

Rubbing his eyes, he nodded.

Lots of men wore wedding bands, thought Suzanne. It wasn't much to go on.

"And then what?" asked Andrew.

"Well, he, like, drove for a while. When he finally stopped, he grabbed Gabriel first. Shut the trunk and left me behind. And then he came back for me a few minutes later."

"Where did he take Gabriel?" asked Branch.

"I don't know."

"You don't *know*?"

"I never saw him again. I'm not lying. The guy pushed me inside this basement door, stuck me in a room with a mattress on the floor and a really small lamp."

"It was a house?" asked Andrew.

"Yeah."

"Did you recognize it?"

"No."

"Do you think it was in Winfield?"

"Don't know. He told me to keep my mouth shut, that he'd be back later, and then he locked the door. I tried to figure out a way to get out, but without a window, and with the door locked, I gave up. When it got light, he came back with some food."

"He still had on the mask?"

"All I could see of his face was his mouth and his eyes."

"His hair?"

"It was covered by a cap."

"Describe him," said Branch.

"Big. He had on jeans. A white T-shirt."

"What kind of shoes?" asked Branch.

"Shoes? I never noticed."

"His voice?" asked Suzanne.

"I don't know." He seemed frustrated by the questions. "Just a man's voice. He sort of whispered. Louder than a whisper, but not loud. I don't know how to describe it."

"What did he say to you?" asked Eric. "Did he tell you why he took you?"

"He just said that if I didn't give him any trouble, he'd let me go. He told me the same thing every time he brought me something to eat. I got awful hungry, 'cause I think he forgot sometimes."

Andrew glanced up at Eric.

"He never tried to hurt you?" asked Suzanne.

"He never touched me. I hardly ever saw him. He left me a bunch of magazines to read. Crap stuff."

"Was there a name and address on the magazines?" asked Branch.

"I think he maybe bought them to give me something to do."

"Think you'd recognize him if you saw him again?" asked Andrew.

"Maybe. I'm not sure."

"Where do you think Gabriel is?" asked Eric.

He shrugged, looked down at his half-eaten sandwich. "The guy with the mask's probably still got him."

"Why would he let you go and not Gabriel?" asked Branch.

"If I knew I'd tell you. I'm afraid for him. Some guys, they seem normal, you know? But they're not." He flicked his eyes to Truman.

"Meaning what?" said Truman.

"People lie."

"This man lied to you?" asked Eric.

"He's a liar, yeah. I hate him. I wish he was dead." His mouth drew together angrily and his face flushed. He refused to look up.

Everyone exchanged worried glances. For the first time, Suzanne had the sense that Jack might be holding something back.

"How did it work—when he let you go?" asked Branch.

Pressing the heel of his hand to his eye, he said, "He put me back in the trunk. Drove me to a field along the county highway and let me go. Told me which way to head to get back to Winfield. And then he drove off."

"Was it daylight?"

"No. Night. Last night. I ran as fast as I could, but I got really winded and had to stop. I crawled behind a tree. I didn't mean to fall asleep. When I woke up, it was light, so I started walking again. My ankle hurt for a while because I sort of twisted it, but then it went away. I saw the storm coming as I was getting close to the house. I hid next to the porch. I thought . . . I mean I wasn't sure—"

"What?" asked Eric.

"I guess I figured that . . . you and Papa would be mad at me."

"Mad?" repeated Andrew, clearly aghast. "Why?"

"Because."

"You have to explain," said Eric. "We need to understand."

"Just . . . I mean, because Gabriel wasn't with me. Because I wasn't brave."

"Oh, sweetheart," said Suzanne, squeezing his arm. "Nobody blames you for anything."

"I do," said Jack. "I shoulda been braver."

"Listen," said Eric, his hand slipping into the back pocket of his jeans, "I think this is enough for now. Jack's pretty raw from all that's happened." He leaned over, rubbed his son's hair. "You've got to understand that we have a lot of questions. We need to figure out who did this to you and make sure he pays for what he's done. And even more importantly, we have to find Gabriel."

"I'd help you if I could," said Jack, his eyes swelling with tears.

"I know you would, son," said Eric. "And maybe you still can. But right now, I think you're tired. You should finish your sandwiches and your milk." Turning to his sister, he added, "We better call the police. Let them know what's going on."

Jack poked the grilled cheese. "Can I watch TV? For a little while longer?"

"Sure," said Branch. He leaned over and snapped it on. "That the right channel?"

Jack gave a tight nod.

"We're glad you're back," came Truman's voice.

Jack stared straight ahead. "Right," he said under his breath.

24

Aaron found his wife sitting at their desktop computer next to the stairway when he came in that night. He'd been thinking that maybe this was the time to tell her. He had to come clean at some point—sooner rather than later. When he saw the stack of opened mail next to her—containing more than one bill, no doubt—his courage failed him. Context was everything and if she was worried about money, his news could wait.

When she looked up and gave him a full, happy smile, he was surprised. He couldn't find a single trace of tension or concern in her face. "How come you're in such a good mood?" he asked.

"I don't know," she said. "I just am."

They hugged, kissed. "How are you feeling?"

"Good," she said. "The usual joint aches. Nothing terrible."

"Anything new?" he asked, jingling some change in his pocket. Aaron hadn't been home since early morning. After breakfast, he'd driven up to his sister's home in Burnsville to help his nephew fill out college entrance forms.

"No. Well, actually, yes," said Holly. "A woman stopped by this morning. Her name's Lawless. She's a PI."

"Lawless?" He turned the name over in his mind, remembering, though only vaguely, that he'd met her a few nights ago.

"Andrew Waltz and Eric Lindstrom hired her to find their son."

"What was she doing here?"

"I'm not really sure. She wanted to talk to you."

"Me? About what? I don't know anything about that."

"Honey, there's no reason to get upset."

"I'm not upset." He pushed his glasses higher up on his nose.

"Tell me how your day was."

With his eyes darting around the room, he said, "It's a long drive. I think I helped my nephew, though. I'm glad I went."

"Why don't we crawl in bed and you can tell me all about it."

"I'm kind of keyed up," he answered. "Think I'll spend a little time in my study. I'll be up soon."

She seemed disappointed.

"Won't be more than half an hour. Promise."

He kissed her, then picked up the mail. After removing a beer from the fridge, he headed down the hall to his study, the one area of the house that was off limits to his wife. Holly said she understood his need for a private space—it was the way she felt about her small room in the attic. They both trusted each other, and yet Aaron couldn't help himself. From the first, he'd set up little booby traps to catch her in the act of trespass. He hated himself for his suspicion, but there it was.

Sitting down behind the desk, he was astonished to find that the tiny piece of tape he'd spread across the edge of his left bottom drawer had come loose. The shock caused him to sit bolt upright.

The right bottom drawer, where he kept his private letters, remained locked. Unless she'd forced it open, which thankfully she hadn't, the information inside was safe. It took a moment for the full impact of her treachery to sink in. If she'd read through his papers, then much of what he'd been trying to hide from her was no longer a secret. This was a disaster.

Aaron couldn't remember the last time he'd checked the tape. Maybe a week? If she knew what was really going on, why hadn't she said anything? She'd allowed him to make a perfect fool of himself as he lied repeatedly about teaching summer school, when, in fact, his contract had been canceled. He'd been trying so hard to keep the worst from her—not to hurt her, but to protect her. Then, of course, there was that little business about how deeply ashamed he was for the mess he'd made of everything. Okay, so maybe his silence had as much to do with shame as it did with altruism, but that was understandable. Wasn't it?

Since April, Aaron had been unable to pay the monthly mortgage, a balloon payment that was about to sink them financially. With Holly unable to work for so long, and now with Aaron's summer job canceled, it didn't take a clairvoyant to see their future. It wouldn't be long until the bank would begin foreclosure proceedings. What made no sense was Holly's happy smile tonight. If she'd been in his drawer, she knew. Had the smile, the kiss, the hug been an act?

Remembering his beer, Aaron drank it down. Better, he thought. At least he could still afford a drink. He would need to have a talk with Holly. All he knew was that it wouldn't be tonight. He simply didn't have the courage.

Unlocking the right bottom drawer, he found the folder for Craig Gilkey, the principal of the middle school. Fifteen letters.

Some just beginnings. Some twenty pages long. He opened a notebook and began a new page, writing the first thing to come into his mind.

Craig Gilkey
Winfield Middle School
Winfield, Minnesota

Dear Principal Freakin' Douche:
I used to be a nice guy. Even tempered. A
live and let live sort of person. I loved
my job. Loved my students. Loved my
life. What you did to me last spring was the
final straw in a year filled with last straws.
Not sure what I'm going to do, but I've
been giving my options some serious thought.
When I decide on a course of action, rest
assured, buddy, you'll be the first to know.

With sincere malice aforethought,
Aaron Eld

25

MONDAY

Jane was pruning red geraniums in the window box under one of her front windows when a black limo pulled up to the curb and four people—three adults and one child—got out. All were dressed in yellow hazmat suits. The limo driver opened the rear door for them, then removed several large suitcases from the trunk and walked behind them up the front walk.

"Cordelia?" asked Jane, as the four varying-sized yellow earthlings moved past her into the front hall.

"Thanks for the tip," said the driver, setting the luggage in the foyer and giving a friendly nod before scurrying out.

Cordelia had arrived at Jane's door wearing many unusual costumes over the years, but this was by far the strangest.

"We've had an infestation," said Cordelia flatly, removing the elastic hood and unzipping the front of her suit.

Octavia removed her hood as well. Bolger helped Hattie with hers and then removed his.

"You mentioned something about that," said Jane.

"That's when I thought it was merely Hattie's bug collection."

"Bedbugs," said Octavia. "Linden Lofts is lousy with them."

Jane grimaced.

"We're clean," said Bolger, matching Jane's grimace with one of his own. "The luggage is new, as is all of our clothing."

"But . . . why are you wearing hazmat suits to my house? I don't have an infestation."

"We liked the way they looked," said Octavia, as if the comment made complete sense.

"Melodrama," added Bolger. "It's hard not to be melodramatic when you're dealing with bedbugs."

"For obvious reasons," continued Cordelia, "we didn't want to go to a hotel."

"Hotels are breeding grounds," said Hattie, sitting down on the tile to cuddle with the dogs.

Trying not to panic at the thought of having four houseguests, all potentially harboring a stray bug, Jane asked, "How long will you be out of your loft?"

"A week," said Octavia, sauntering into the living room and making herself comfortable on the couch. "Maybe two. Hard to say. Bedbugs are hell on wheels to get rid of."

"Ah," said Jane. "Fascinating."

"It's all right," said Bolger, patting Jane on the back as he walked past. "We forgive you if you need to go throw up."

She forced a laugh.

"You've got four bedrooms," said Cordelia. "You only use one of them. And you also have that third-floor apartment. I thought perhaps Octavia could take that." Speaking to her sister, she added, "It has its own deck, kitchen, such as it is, and living room."

"I like this living room," said Octavia, stretching out on the couch as Bolger sat down on one of the chairs. "I've always admired your home, Jane. You won't mind us camping out with you for a few weeks."

"Janey?" said Cordelia, her face a question mark. "Are we welcome?"

"Um, sure. Of course."

"I knew you wouldn't let us twist in the wind during our time of need." She chucked Jane under the chin.

"I'm famished," called Octavia, raising her arm, her hand swirling languidly. "What's in the larder?"

Cordelia accompanied Jane into the kitchen. "You're really okay with this?"

What could Jane say? Cordelia was her best friend. She smiled, nodded, turned away before she swallowed hard.

"Take a look at my new T-shirt," said Cordelia, opening the front of her suit to reveal the message, ALWAYS GIVE 100 PERCENT—UNLESS YOU'RE GIVING BLOOD. "I almost bought one that said, 'There's Nothing to Fear but Fear Itself—and Spiders,' but it seemed a little too close for comfort."

"What about your cats?" asked Jane, opening the refrigerator.

"I'm boarding them for the duration. Didn't think my cat colony would mix well with your dogs." She sat down at the table and watched Jane take out several packages of sliced meats and cheeses, mayo, mustard, pickles, and lettuce.

"Sandwiches."

"That's the idea."

She rubbed her hands together in anticipation. "FYI, Hatts and I had a little Come to Jesus meeting this morning. I told her that her bug fixation—she calls it a hobby—has to cease. If she wants to pursue scientific inquiry, as opposed to a career in the arts, that's fine with me, as long as it doesn't disrupt my life. Geology. Paleontology. Archeology. She can take her pick."

Jane smiled to herself. Virtually any of the sciences could disrupt Cordelia's peace and quiet very easily. What if Hattie became fixated on chemistry next? The possibilities for negative outcomes were endless.

"Once this bedbug issue is over, we'll have no more creepy crawlies."

"I think the Linden building would need to be hermetically sealed in plastic for that to happen."

"Time will tell. Perhaps Octavia won't be the only person looking for new digs." She peered over the chopping block at Jane's sandwich making. "Extra mayo, no mustard on mine, thanks."

At the sound of the back door opening, Jane turned to find Avi coming into the kitchen through the screened porch.

"Oh," said Avi, clearly surprised to find anyone home. Jane was usually gone for the day by the time she arrived.

"Hey, sweetheart," said Jane, giving her quick kiss.

"Food? Looks like I timed this perfectly." She pulled out a chair and sat down next to Cordelia. "Interesting costume," she said, nodding to that hazmat suit.

"I like it."

"That woman from Ducasse & Ducasse called this morning," continued Avi. "She wants to meet with me, but because she's in Chicago and I'm in Minneapolis, the actual owner of the press is meeting me here at ten."

"Here?" repeated Jane.

"I thought it would be nice and quiet. Georgia scheduled a

study group for our apartment this morning, so it's crawling with law students."

"What's Ducasse & Ducasse?" asked Cordelia.

"You didn't tell her?" said Avi.

"Haven't had time. They just arrived."

"They?"

Cordelia explained about the bedbugs. About Octavia, Hattie, and Hattie's nanny, Bolger Aspenwall III, moving in for the next week or two.

When Avi heard about the bedbugs, she pushed away from the table, moved behind the wood-block island, and leaned back against the kitchen counter.

"I'm deloused," said Cordelia. "Nothing to fear."

"Bedbugs are awfully tiny," said Avi. "How do you know for sure you're not carrying them around in your clothing? Your hair?"

Hattie chose that moment to skip into the room. "Those little suckers are really smart," she said.

"Don't get her started," groaned Cordelia.

"They can go for months without eating. And they have this cool chemical in their spit that makes blood flow really fast when they bite."

"Boggles the mind," said Cordelia. "That I should know something about bug spit."

Avi checked her watch again.

"So explain about this person you're meeting?" said Cordelia, hoisting Hattie into her lap.

"A publisher."

"Are you nervous?" asked Jane.

She seemed unusually reticent. "I don't know this for sure, but I think the owner is going to offer to publish my novel."

202

"You probably shouldn't jump at the first offer," said Cordelia. "There might not be others."

"You'll discuss it with your agent," said Jane.

"I know most of the literati in town," said Cordelia, checking through Hattie's hair. "What's this woman's name?"

"Martinsen," said Avi, nibbling a piece of cheese.

Both Jane and Cordelia looked up sharply.

"First name?" asked Jane.

"Julia. I guess she's a doctor of some sort."

"Dr. Julia Martinsen," said Cordelia. "Well, I guess you could say it's hard to keep an evil genie in her bottle."

"You know her?" asked Avi.

"My stars and garters, yes," said Cordelia. "As it happens, so does Jane."

"Is she easy to work with?" asked Avi.

The doorbell rang.

"I'll get it," called Hattie. Both dogs trotted behind her as she hustled out of the room.

"Wish me luck," said Avi, her face flushed with excitement. "I know this is a totally trite expression, but this could be the first day of the rest of my life."

Jane's wariness was as palpable as Avi's eagerness.

A few minutes later, as Jane, Avi, and Julia made themselves comfortable on the screen porch, Cordelia appeared in the doorway.

"Cordelia Thorn," said Julia with a restrained nod.

"Why Julia Martinsen, as I live and breathe," said Cordelia, in her best Scarlett O'Hara accent.

"Why are you wearing that . . . that—?"

"Oh, I don't know," said Cordelia. "Seemed like a wise choice under the circumstances."

Bolger and Octavia bumped past her to get a firsthand look at what was going on. There were now three people on the porch in yellow hazmat suits.

"Cordelia clones?" asked Julia. "Or are you all part of some new cult?"

"Bedbugs," said Cordelia.

"Pardon me?"

"I'm curious," said Jane, unwilling to let Cordelia monopolize the conversation. "When did you buy Ducasse & Ducasse?"

"Several years ago," Julia responded casually. She seemed to be enjoying herself. "As you well know, I have lots of irons in the financial fires."

"Such as?" asked Cordelia.

"Well, I own a string of movie theaters. A winery in Napa and one in Oregon. A restaurant in Houston, and one in Tokyo. A mining company in Montana. And I'm heavily invested in alternative-energy projects all over the country."

"Why don't we get down to business?" suggested Avi, flashing her eyes at Cordelia.

"Of course," said Julia, reaching for her briefcase. "Cordelia—et al—be dears. Give us a few minutes of privacy."

Looking annoyed, Cordelia said, "If anybody needs us, we'll be in the living room scratching our bites."

"Their what?" asked Julia as they shoved out of the room.

"Nothing," said Avi. "Just ignore them."

"Always good advice." Julia was professionalism personified in her sleek gray business suit and heels. Her blond hair was swept back over her ears, her nails carefully done, her jewelry understated. Avi, by contrast, in her clunky horn-rimmed glasses, boyish clothes, and plaid athletic shoes, was Julia's antithesis. Jane couldn't believe she'd ever fallen for Julia's outward perfection.

Focusing all her warmth on Avi, Julia began, "I want you to know how much I loved your book. Elaine Ducasse sent me a digital copy shortly after she received the manuscript from you. We think this could be a huge book for us, something that will put you on the literary map. I realize that Ducasse & Ducasse isn't New York, but we give our authors far more attention than any New York press would, and I can promise you a promotional budget that will exceed anything any of the big five will offer."

"What exactly did you like about my book?" asked Avi, a certain skepticism creeping into her voice.

Jane's cell phone vibrated in her pocket. Excusing herself, she went back into the kitchen to take the call.

"Jane, hi, it's Eric."

She'd planned to call down to the farmhouse this morning, but so far she hadn't had a chance. "You sound excited."

"Jack's home. Whoever was holding him finally let him go."

She could hardly believe what she was hearing. "Gabriel, too?"

"Afraid not. Jack hasn't seen him since the night they were taken."

"I don't understand."

"Suzanne and I would like to talk to you. Andrew's with Jack. He and Branch decided to spend more time helping people clean away downed trees after the storm last night. Winfield was hit hard. He thought it would be good for Jack to do a little physical work, get his mind off what happened to him. Suzanne and I are in the car, on our way up to the Cities. What if we met you at your house in say, half an hour?"

Jane wanted to talk to them, too, but not here. "Listen, it's kind of a zoo at my place. Why don't we meet at Cordelia's new theater. My partner and I have an office on the second floor, front of the building. Corner of Harvard Place and 12th. You know where that is?"

Eric said he did. "I did something I'm not proud of. I'll tell you about it when we see you."

Jane's emotions were deeply mixed. She was elated about Jack, though her concern for Gabriel pretty much quashed the good feelings. Why would one boy be released and not the other? As she came back through the door into the screened porch, she heard Julia say:

"So, the bottom line is, even if you get a better offer from another press, we'll meet or exceed it. That's a firm promise from me to you. If you've written other novels, we'd like to look at those, too."

All the skepticism in Avi's face had been replaced by an expression that was nothing short of rapt. "I'll need to talk to my agent first," she said.

"You have an agent?"

"Isn't that how you found out about my book?"

Glancing up at Jane with a Cheshire cat smile, she said, "Actually, I had some inside information. But of course, go ahead and talk to him."

"Her."

"She can call Elaine and they can work out the particulars."

Avi paged through the contract Julia had handed her. "This looks intense."

"Which is why you need a good agent," said Julia, turning her high-beam smile on Avi. "She *is* a good agent, right? Reputable. Successful. Knows the fiction market?"

"That's what I'm told."

"Well, if you find you need help in that department, too, just say the word." She rose and extended her hand. "I won't take any more of your time. I hope you'll consider Ducasse & Ducasse. I look forward to talking to you again."

"Why don't I walk you out?" said Jane, wanting to have a word with Julia before she flew off on her broom.

Once outside, she said, "What are you up to?"

"Up to?" repeated Julia. "Exactly what I said. I laid all my cards on the table. I came to offer your friend a book contract."

"She's not just my friend. She's my girlfriend."

"I'm well aware of the distinction."

"If you're trying to hurt her—"

"Why would I do that?"

"To hurt me. To get back at me for ending our relationship."

"Jane, Jane, Jane." She opened the trunk of her Lexus and placed her briefcase inside. "You should really think about seeing someone for your narcissistic tendencies. Not everything is about you."

"I'm not letting you play with Avi's life—with her career."

"I'm hardly playing," said Julia, all the amusement draining from her face. "I think," she added, sliding into the front seat, "that you'd best let Avi decide what she wants. I made her an offer. It was a good one. I doubt she'll find anything better, especially in this book market. If you try to insert yourself into the negotiations, I think you'll find that you come out on the short end. Then again, she's your girlfriend, as you're so quick to point out. You know her far better than I do. Just a word to the wise: I'm offering her the brass ring, Jane. What she's dreamed about. If you make it a choice between Ducasse & Ducasse—otherwise known as *me*—and you, who do you think will win? It's a fascinating question, don't you agree? Can't wait to see how it all turns out."

Jane stood in the street seething inside as Julia drove away.

26

Jane met Eric and Suzanne at the front door of the theater and walked them up to her office on the second floor. Cordelia and Nolan were already there, Nolan behind his desk, Cordelia standing with her back to the windows. Jane made introductions as she pulled up a few more chairs, and then she offered to get everyone coffee. Nobody wanted any.

Setting a small tape recorder on the desk before he sat down, Eric said, "When the family talked to Jack last night, I taped the conversation. I keep a small tape recorder in the kitchen that I use to leave myself messages. I grabbed it and hid it in my jeans. Maybe I should have said something to Jack, but I didn't. I thought what he said, and maybe even the way he said it, would be important."

Nolan nodded for him to turn it on.

Jane took out a pen and a notepad and scratched a few thoughts as the tape played.

After the second time through, Suzanne said, "What do you think? I feel like he's holding something back. Is it just me?" She looked worn out, her eyes red from lack of sleep.

Nolan tapped his fingers on the desk. "Describe his demeanor?"

"Subdued," said Eric. "He was tired—and hungry. Nothing unusual in any of that." He explained how he'd found Jack hiding next to the front porch, crouched down away from the worst of the wind and the rain. "He was soaking wet. Relieved to be back home. After he talked to Bill Jennings, the new officer assigned to the case, he went upstairs, crawled into bed, and fell asleep. I didn't hear a peep out of him until this morning."

"Andrew took him to see a doctor right after breakfast," said Suzanne. "He didn't have any scrapes or bruises, didn't seem hurt. The doctor concurred."

"At least nothing anyone could see," added Eric. "But he was scared. That was more than apparent."

"I agree with Suzanne," said Cordelia, folding her arms over her chest. "I feel like he's only giving us part of the story."

"Can we keep the tape?" asked Jane. "I'd like to listen to it again."

"You did the right thing to tape him," said Nolan. "Don't worry for a second about that."

"If he knows something about Gabriel, I don't understand why he won't tell us," said Suzanne. She was close to tears.

"Let's back up a minute," said Jane, folding up the notebook and returning it to her pocket. "Whoever took the boys demanded a ransom, which we paid. That suggests that the reason for the abduction was money."

Everyone nodded.

"I've been thinking about that," she continued. "I've got a few questions I need to find answers to, mainly about three people."

"Name them," said Suzanne.

"Aaron Eld, for one."

"Eld? You think he had something to do with the boys' abduction?"

He'd been the one to find Gabriel's cell phone, which might have been pure serendipity, though it was always possible that it pointed to something more sinister. "I talked to his wife yesterday," said Jane. "Seems he may have had some problems at the middle school this past year."

"You mean that creationism flap?" asked Suzanne.

Eric groaned. "I'd forgotten about that. If I recall correctly, Eld didn't want to teach a unit on young earth creationism. He felt it was completely unscientific, simply a way for those with a fundamentalist bent to get their religious ideas taught as science. I don't know all the details."

"The principal of the middle school, Craig Gilkey, is part of my congregation," said Suzanne. "He was getting a lot of pressure from a group of parents who were trying to force the science department to include the subject. He eventually caved in, ordered Eld to cover it."

"Did he do it?" asked Cordelia.

"I'm not sure," said Suzanne. "I was so involved with church business at the time that I never asked. Winfield is fairly conservative. Eld made a big mistake when he did an interview for the local paper. He talked about the problem of getting all the various dinosaurs onto Noah's Ark. Even if they were babies, as the creationists suggest, it boggles the mind. He made a joke out of it, which it is in the opinion of the larger scientific community, but it made the local supporters of the theory furious."

"He still have his job?" asked Cordelia.

"Far as I know."

The idea of a teacher abducting two children, even if he planned to let them go, was a stretch in Jane's opinion. Still, because of his late-night excursions, she wanted to follow up on it. "I'm also curious about Matt Steinhauser. I know you asked to have him removed from the investigation. I think that was a good call. I can't help but wonder why he did such a poor job on the case. I mean, he covered a few of the important bases, but left some of the most obvious opportunities to discover information completely untouched." Jane could have added, but didn't, that she wondered if his relationship with Gabriel went beyond him being his baseball coach—an ominous thought. If he was behind the boys' abduction, for whatever reason, as a police officer he'd be in a perfect position to know how to go about it—and how to cover his tracks.

Suzanne shuddered. "He has a great deal of anger in him. The odd thing is, he never used to be that way."

"You said three people," said Eric. "Who's the third?"

"Your uncle."

"Yeah, figured as much."

"Where does he go when he leaves on his motorcycle?"

"No idea. Sometimes he doesn't come back for days."

"How does he make a living?"

"He's never said a word about that. He doesn't talk about himself, always deflects direct questions. He was our dad's brother. Suzanne and I rarely saw him when we were kids."

"He was in the navy for a while," added Suzanne. "Never married, at least as far as anyone knew. He was like a ghost. He'd appear out of the blue, and then leave without telling anyone."

"I realize he's a strange man," continued Eric, "but that doesn't make him bad."

The meeting broke up a few minutes after noon. Jane promised that she'd drive down later in the afternoon. She wanted to talk to Jack, though she had to figure out a way to do it without making it seem like an interrogation.

Cordelia said she planned to come along. "I'll make us reservations at that five-star motel again," she said with a resigned sigh. "I think that hazmat suit is really going to come in handy when I travel."

27

On her way to the sanctuary that afternoon, so drained and weary that she felt as if she'd downed lithium with her morning coffee, Suzanne ran into Vivian Brassart, who was steaming toward the church office, her dyspeptic eagle presence ready to shred anything in its path.

"Oh, Suzanne," she said, the sharp features softening. "I just heard the good news. The boys are back."

"I'm afraid you've got only part of that right. Jack's home. Gabriel's still missing."

Her frown deepened the lines around her mouth. "But I was told—"

Suzanne had no desire to explain, but took a moment to do so anyway, thinking that it was best to keep their relationship, such as it was, civil.

"I've been praying for both of them," said Vivian. "I wish I could do more."

Nobody was all bad, thought Suzanne—even the woman who had made the last six months of her life a misery.

"This probably isn't the time to bring it up," said Vivian, crossing her arms over her ample stomach. "The fact that I know why you're behind on your work here doesn't really mitigate the problem. I'm not sure what we should do. You understand my position."

"Of course."

"Perhaps you should take an official leave of absence. I'm sure I could get Haden Daltry to step in for you."

Daltry was a Vivian clone. He was also one of the nicest—and funniest—men Suzanne had ever met. Vivian had hired him as a part-time adjunct pastor in March and had been waiting for just such an opportunity to install him in a full-time position. Once he was so ensconced, even though it was temporary, Suzanne felt sure the board would keep him on. Vivian was lining up soldiers behind her. One day the ultimatum would come down from on high: Suzanne could either join the good fight, as Vivian saw it, or move on to another pastorate.

Fingering a couple of the papers in the folder she was carrying, Vivian said, "I'm starting something new. If you'd been at the board meeting on Friday, you would have heard all about it. We're moving our Sunday service to eleven. The ten o'clock hour will be reserved for our new Sunday Morning Forum. As I envision it, it will be an opportunity to bring in experts to talk about values issues. I've got a list of people I'd like to extend an invitation to, and also a list of topics for which we need to find an expert. I'm really excited about this. Perhaps . . . if you have the time . . . you could look the list over and give me your thoughts. I was going to put you in charge of it, but since you'll be taking a leave, I'll give the job to Haden."

As Suzanne opened the folder and began to read through the

list, Craig Gilkey, the principal at the middle school, shambled to a stop a few yards away to answer his cell phone. When he was done, he smiled at Vivian and nodded to Suzanne. "Ladies."

Suzanne hadn't talked to him since the school year had ended.

"How's your brother doing?" asked Vivian.

Craig's older brother had broken his leg in a skiing accident in March. He was one of the best tenors in the church choir and his strong voice had been sorely missed.

"He's doing much better," said Craig, wiping sweat off his forehead. "But then we got nailed by that storm last night. Had a tree fall right on top of our garage. Thankfully, Suzanne's husband came by with that friend of his, Andrew Waltz. They've got most of the tree cleared away. Can't thank them enough. They're sure a couple of great guys."

"I agree," said Suzanne.

"Yeah. My insurance man will be out in the next couple of days. It's always something, isn't it?"

"I was just talking about you this morning," said Suzanne.

"And up I jump," he said, grinning.

"I'm curious what happened with that unit on creationism you wanted Aaron Eld to teach."

"Intelligent design. We don't use the word 'creationism' anymore. And don't get me started on that."

"Eld flat-out refused," said Vivian. "I believe the school board is planning to let him go. Isn't that right, Mr. Gilkey?"

"You're firing him?" said Suzanne, unable to hide her astonishment.

"Well, not for that. It was poor job performance all around."

"But I'd heard the kids loved him."

"I shouldn't be talking about this, but since I know it will go no further—" He glanced around before continuing. "See, the thing is, I'd smelled alcohol on his breath. That means he was drinking during school hours. We can't have that."

"No," said Vivian firmly. "We're well rid of him."

"It wasn't just the alcohol," added Gilkey, flipping open his cell phone to check the screen. "He'd been late for class a few times. Missed several important teachers meetings. And then there was the parents' petition."

"Right, the petition," said Suzanne.

"I wasn't the one who issued the final verdict about firing him. The school board did that. In fact, the letter went out on Friday. He should have it today."

Suzanne harbored no doubts about the primary cause of Eld's dismissal. She excused herself, said she needed to get back to her office. Vivian and Gilkey could continue to applaud the school board without her.

Four pictures adorned Suzanne's desk—one of her first husband, Sam, a shot of Branch piloting his pontoon, a picture of Eric and Andrew, their arms around each other's shoulders, and Gabriel's sixth-grade school photo. She gazed at the picture of Gabriel for a long time, her hand rising trancelike, wanting desperately to touch his soft, sandy blond hair. Nobody who hadn't lost a child could even begin to know what this was like. It was against nature. Purely atavistic. Wrong clear to the bone.

Suzanne called her neighbor Sandy Anderson, who had offered to stay at the house while she and Branch were away. Someone had to be there at all times. After learning that everything was quiet, Suzanne rose and went down the hall to get herself a cup of coffee. The normality of the activity helped to focus her mind. Even so, her hand shook when she picked up the pot, though nobody was in the break room to notice.

Returning to her office, she placed a call to Burton. After their conversation on Saturday, she felt the need to talk to him again. His phone rang five times before his voice mail picked up. She didn't leave a message. As she carefully brought the paper cup to her lips, her attention fell to the folder Vivian had given her. Opening it, she ran her finger down the lists. She should have expected it. It was standard fare for someone with deeply conservative values.

An invitation was to be offered to a man from Sanctity of Life Minnesota, a pro-life group, and to another from something called the Death Penalty Advocacy Group. Apparently, Vivian saw no irony in this particular philosophical juxtaposition. A woman from the Project for a New American Century had already been contacted. She'd suggested a topic: The need for American "full-spectrum dominance" in the world, including land, sea, air, space, industry, and agriculture. Vivian wanted experts found to discuss such issues as immigration and the pros and cons of the Dream Act; opposition to same-sex marriage; gun control; home-schooling and vouchers for charter and private schools; and finally, the scientific evidence against global warming. Vivian had written a note at the bottom of the sheet: "Feel free to suggest other topics."

Right, thought Suzanne. How about: "The Fires of Hell—How God Keeps Them Stoked"? What kind of sick mind would come up with the idea of eternal torturing fire?

Turning to her computer, she brought up Google and typed in her question. Up popped an article written by an ex-Presbyterian minister, a man who'd left his church because of a similar issue.

Suzanne scrolled down the page, learning about the path his ideas had taken over the years. She was struck by how much they paralleled her own. He'd called his leaving the church a "coming out" process. For years, he'd keep his thoughts to himself, even kept his family in the dark—for multiple reasons, not the least of which had to do with his need for employment.

At the end of the article, Suzanne came across the name of something called the Clergy Project. She quickly returned to Google and typed it in. Up came a Web site that offered her the chance to join a confidential online community for active and former clergy who had lost their belief in God. She was staggered. She had no idea something organized existed for people like her—or even that there *were* others like her. Of course, when she thought about it, it made sense. She couldn't be the only one this loss of faith had ever happened to.

For the next hour, Suzanne devoured the testimonials, the news stories about nonbelieving clergy who had left churches behind. Some identified as atheists, some as agnostics, some as nothing at all. She ran through dozens of links for books, podcasts, and other resources for those who were dealing with "this most fundamental question of human existence." In the midst of a darkness that truly did seem impenetrable, she'd found a tiny ray of light—not a light others would understand, but one that held out hope that she wouldn't have to walk this difficult path alone.

28

After the meeting with Suzanne and Eric, Jane had driven back to her house to talk to Avi, but found, much to her disappointment, that she'd already left. After phoning and reaching her voice mail, Jane left her a quick message, asking her to call when she got a minute. She wanted to talk to her about the potential deal with Ducasse & Ducasse. She had no intention to rain on Avi's parade, and yet she had to warn her about potential problems if she entered into a business relationship with someone like Julia.

Not wanting to stick around her house, with Hattie, Bolger, and Octavia filling up every inch of psychic space, Jane tossed some clothes into an overnight bag and headed over to her restaurant. She worked in her office for the next couple of hours, completing her notes for the late summer menu, and was standing on the deck overlooking Lake Harriet when Cordelia finally arrived.

"Let's hit the bricks," said Cordelia. "No time to waste."

Turning to see what her friend was wearing, Jane was pleasantly surprised to find that she'd removed the hazmat suit and replaced it with jeans and a red T-shirt emblazoned with the name of her new theater across the front and back. "Nice threads," she said.

"Oh, this old thing?" Cordelia grinned.

They settled on taking the CR-V, mainly because Cordelia didn't feel like driving. As they flew down Highway 52, Jane put her friend to work doing what she would have done if her house hadn't been invaded. "Use Pro Search," said Jane. "Do the full background check for Steinhauser. I'll give you the password so you can log in."

Cordelia fiddled with her cell phone. "It's terrible how much you can learn about someone this way."

"For a price."

"Even without paying. I looked myself up the other night." She made a strangling sound, clutching her throat. "Several girl-friends have actually written blogs about me."

"All good, no doubt."

"Oh, sure. Stellar reviews all around."

"You mean to say you've made enemies?"

"I seem to be at the top of several hit lists. And get this. There's even a chat room devoted to moi."

"Your ex-girlfriends set that up?"

"It isn't for romantic payback. It's about my work in the theater, my charitable efforts. My genius as a creative director."

"And your possible sainthood?"

"Mock me at your peril, dearheart." She pressed a couple more buttons and said, "Password?"

Jane gave her the number.

"Score," she said a few moments later. "Steinhauser lives at Ninety-two Olsen Road in Winfield. Wait just a second and I'll bring up a map." Scrutinizing the screen, she said, "I have committed the location to memory."

"What else?"

"He's married to Sherry Steinhauser. No other marriages listed. Son's name is Corey. Age twenty-nine. Daughter-in-law, Madison. Grandchildren, Krista, six, and Noah, eight."

"Arrests?"

"Nope. He's an army vet. Served in the Gulf War. Decorated with the Southwest Asia Service Medal. He's lived at this particular address for the last thirteen years. Still owes money on it. Before he moved to Winfield, he lived in an apartment in Minneapolis—for two years—and before that he had a house in Spring Lake Falls, Minnesota, where he was born and graduated from Cornell High School. That's where he started in law enforcement. Worked for the county sheriff there. He's been at the Winfield Police Department since 2002. No lawsuits, judgements, liens, or bankruptcies. From all this, I'd say he sounds like a pillar of the community."

"The question is," said Jane, adjusting the air-conditioning on the dash, "does he need money? I agree, he's no Hannibal Lecter, but people who are pushed to the wall, who see no other way out but to do something against their values and principles—"

"Well said."

"See what you can find on Truman Lindstrom."

Cordelia tapped in the new name. "No Truman Lindstrom in Minnesota. You know where he was born?"

"There can't be that many Truman Lindstroms in the U.S."

"Sixteen, to be exact."

"He was in the navy."

She did some more tapping. "Ah, here we go. Truman E. Lindstrom. Born in Temple, Wisconsin, in 1954. Graduated from Greenbrier High School. We have three addresses after that, one in Colorado, one in California, and one in Montana. Joined the navy in 1978, and left in 1989. No marriages listed, no current address or phone number."

"Arrests?"

"Three. Two misdemeanors. One, an assault charge in 'ninety-one in Alabama, the other for harassment in 'ninety-two in Arizona. He paid a fine for the first one. For the second he served five months. The final arrest was for simple possession. Marijuana. He was supposed to attend a treatment program after he was let out of jail, but never went. After that, it looks like he dropped off the planet."

It was about what Jane had expected.

"And, before you ask, here's the info on Aaron Eld." She tapped in a few keys, then waited. "Born in Minneapolis. Graduated from Washburn High School. BS in biology from the U of M. Teaching certificate from the U. Taught at Richfield Middle School. Married Holly Berg in 2006. Moved to Winfield, where he currently teaches biology and science. Owns a house at Six thirty-one Tyler. Phone number listed. Has a brother, Thomas, and a sister, Sarah. No children. A DUI in 1995, which I assume was while he was in college. None since. Another reasonably good citizen, at least on paper."

Jane's working theory was that someone who needed money had taken the boys and then demanded a ransom, thinking that the family was financially well off. If that was true, why had this individual— or, perhaps, individuals—let Jack go and not Gabriel?

What was she missing? Was the theory totally off the mark? "Why don't you listen to music or something," said Jane. "I need to process."

"Process away," said Cordelia, continuing to concentrate on her phone. "Since I have your password to this handy-dandy little background service, there are a few people I'd like to check out."

"Such as?"

"For starters, the two ex-girlfriends who wrote blogs about me."

"Nasty."

"Ain't it just."

Aaron Eld pulled his car into the parking lot of Thompson's Gun Shop and Shooting Range outside of Short Creek late Monday afternoon. He'd driven past the place many times, though he'd never had any reason to stop in. Now he did.

The sign above the front door said the business stocked over one thousand new and used guns. Trade-ins were welcome. Moving resolutely inside, Aaron found an older man standing behind a glass counter. Rifles were hanging on the walls, along with rifle cases and cleaning supplies.

"Help you?" asked the man.

"I want to buy a gun."

"Do you know what kind of gun?"

"One that shoots bullets." He'd had a couple of shots of bourbon, a little cheap courage. It wasn't every day that he went looking for firepower.

"That's funny, sir. Shotgun? Rifle? Pistol?"

Aaron ran a finger along the class counter top. "A revolver."

"Why a revolver, if you don't mind my asking?"

"Because I shot a semiautomatic once and the thing kept jamming on me."

"There could be a lot of reasons for that. First off—"

"Yeah, yeah, I know."

The guy shifted his position. "A revolver can jam, too, just FYI."

"Then I guess it's up to you to sell me one that won't."

"Okay. Next question: You got a permit to purchase?"

Aaron had gone down to the police station and filled out the form weeks ago. He'd never thought he would actually use it. He'd apparently passed the background check because, seven days later, he had the permit in his hand. Pushing it across the counter, he said, "What about that one?" He pointed through the glass.

The man removed the revolver and set it on the countertop.

Aaron picked it up. "It's heavy."

"Hey, man, don't point that at anything you don't want to annihilate." He pushed the barrel away. "And never put your finger on the trigger pull unless you plan to fire it. You ever had any gun training?"

"What kind of gun is it?"

"It's an EAA Windicator, three fifty-seven Magnum."

"Is that good?"

"It's a little heavier than some. But virtually no recoil. You sure you're not looking for something more along the lines of a twenty-two?"

"How much?" When Aaron heard the price, he winced. "Look, I've got four hundred bucks. What can I get for that?"

The man moved to the other end of the counter. "Just so happens I've got the same gun used." He checked the price tag. "Three hundred and fifty dollars. A real steal."

"What about the condition?"

"It's in perfect shape. I happen to know the previous owner. He always took great care of his guns. It's cleaned, oiled, and ready to go. Do you need ammunition?"

"Unless I'm going to shoot peas."

The man raised a skeptical eyebrow. "You'll also want a cleaning kit."

"Just pick something within my price range." He wiped a hand across his mouth, rocked back and forth on the balls of his feet. "I'm in kind of a hurry."

"What are you planning to use the gun for?"

He gave a casual shrug. "Rabbits."

"I see. Here's the thing. We offer you a fifty-dollar discount on our firearm safety course when you buy a gun from us. You might want to take something like that before you start—"

"Thanks, but not right now." He pulled four hundred-dollar bills from his pocket and slapped them down on the counter. "Could you put everything in a bag, please?"

29

Jane and Cordelia found Steinhauser's house on a winding county road half a mile from town. The white stucco two-story, complete with a slab of concrete attached to the front that served as a porch, and a backyard that looked as if it hadn't been mowed more than once, appeared distinctly unloved. A dilapidated wicker couch and two matching chairs sat on one end of the slab, an empty can of tuna serving as an ashtray on a low wicker table. The lot was sizable, the setting remote, with a weeping willow close to the back door and a speedboat and a canoe parked in the dying grass next to the garage. Steinhauser's squad car was in the drive. The only part of the property that seemed well tended was a garden, suggesting that someone in the family had a green thumb. Surprisingly, the yard was filled with toys.

"Not exactly my dream mansion," said Cordelia, climbing out of the front seat.

Jane would have liked to walk around the property to take a closer look, but figured, with Steinhauser inside, it wasn't smart.

The only thing that looked new in the yard and thus seemed entirely out of place was a Weber gas grill sitting by a side door. It was a six-burner stainless-steel propane unit that easily cost two thousand dollars or more. She knew the cost because the Lyme House had several just like it that were used by her catering crew.

"I'm not sure what you expect to learn," said Cordelia, following Jane up to the front door.

"Likely nothing," said Jane, ringing the bell. The scent of garlic and frying meat wafted through the screen. Steinhauser appeared a moment later, dressed in a blue polo shirt and jeans, a kitchen towel tossed over his shoulder. "Yeah?" he said. Then, recognizing Jane, he added, "I know you. You're Andrew and Eric's friend."

"Jane Lawless." She handed him her card. "And this is my friend Cordelia Thorn."

"You're a PI?"

"Could we talk?"

"What about?"

"Gabriel Born."

His bushy eyebrows dipped. "Um . . . let's sit on the porch. It's a nice evening."

Clearly, he didn't want them inside.

Turning around, Steinhauser called, "Corey? Could you do me a favor and turn the heat off under the spaghetti sauce?" He paused, listening to a muffled response. "Yes, in the kitchen. The knob on the front of the stove. The one way to the right." He paused again. "Yeah, right now."

Cordelia commandeered the couch as Jane and Steinhauser sat down on the chairs.

"Make this quick," he said curtly. "I'm making dinner."

Before Jane could get started, two kids burst out of the front door, one a girl with curly dark hair, and the other a boy with a *Star Wars* light saber strapped to his waist. They raced down the steps out into the grass, where they jumped on bikes and took off across the yard.

"My grandchildren," said Steinhauser, his scowl lifting. "Hey, you two. We're eating dinner soon. Don't go far."

The boy waved.

"You've got your hands full," said Jane.

"Tell me about it."

"Do they live with you?" asked Cordelia.

"Yeah, for the last year and a half. My son was serving in Afghanistan up until a few months ago. He's home now. His wife . . . well, let's not get into that. She's not part of their lives anymore." Removing the towel from his shoulder, he continued, "So what do you want?"

Jane leaned forward in her chair. "I know this may be a sensitive subject, but I was told you coach a Little League baseball team that Gabriel is on."

"Yeah? Nothing sensitive about that. I love coaching."

"I'd heard that you and Gabriel got into it a week or so ago."

"Who told you that?"

"Is it important?"

"It was Branch Born, right? That guy is a total shit. Okay, I admit it. I lost it with Gabriel. It happens. He wasn't paying attention. He never used to be like that. Never. I coached him last year, you know. Even spent some time one-on-one with him after school. He's a hard worker. It's like . . . I don't know. Like sometimes he just loses focus. He's not being fair to his teammates when he plays like that, or to himself. So, okay, I gave him a serious talking-to. I got a little hot. But I talked to him the next day. Apologized. I was out of line. Branch, on the other hand. That guy really yanks my chain. Always so silent, so above the fray, so full of himself. He had no right to come at me like that. I should have arrested him for assault."

Jane was about to ask another question when a tall, muscular young man in cutoffs and an army-green T-shirt limped out onto the front porch. The left side of his face was badly scarred, as was his left arm. "Where's Mom?" He glanced at Jane and Cordelia with little interest.

"She's working, son."

"When will she be back?"

"Not until late. You need something?"

"My meds."

"They're on the tray table right next to your chair."

"I can't find the . . . the—"

"Xanax?"

"Yeah."

"It's there. Look a little harder. We're having dinner in a few minutes. I hope you're hungry."

"I thought we were having rib eyes."

"We had rib eyes last night."

"We did? Oh, yeah. Right." He turned and limped back into the house.

His eyes on the screen door, Steinhauser waited a few seconds and then, lowering his voice, said, "My son. For the last two years he's served in Afghanistan. He was in a Humvee in the Sangin district of the Helmand Province when it hit a roadside bomb. I saw a picture of the truck. Can't believe anyone came out of it alive. His best friend died. Another friend lost both his legs."

"I'm so sorry," said Jane. "How's he doing?"

"He's got some physical damage, but mostly it's his spirit, his mind that's messed up. He's depressed, can't remember things, has terrible headaches. Nightmares. He jumps at the slightest noise. Sometimes he gets upset, doesn't know where he is. That scares his mom because he's so strong, and his anger can flare so quickly. He doesn't scare me. I can handle him, but—I get lots calls from my wife to come home and help talk him down. Kind of plays havoc with my work. I've driven him up to the VA hospital in Minneapolis a bunch of times. They keep promising stuff, but mostly all they do is give him drugs. He needs more than that—and he needs it now. Before—" He cleared his throat. "Kids, you know? It's like having your heart walking around outside your body. We finally found him a therapist. It's costing an arm and a leg, but I think it's helping. It's been a rough time for all of us."

"Is your wife the gardener?" asked Jane.

"Yeah, she loves it. Saves us a little money, too. She retired a few years back, but with all the added expenses, she had to find another job. She's home in the day with Corey and the kids, and when I get off work, she leaves for hers. We hardly ever see each other anymore. I'm not complaining," he added quickly. "I'm damn proud of my son. He served his country, just like his old man. It's just—" His voice grew husky. "Don't mind me. We'll make it through. I'll make sure of that."

Using the kitchen towel to wipe the sweat off his forehead, Steinhauser continued, "Now, to get back to the subject at hand. You're here because of Jack and Gabriel, right? You think I did a lousy job, that I should have found them, that the chief had every right to take me off the case. Pardon me if I disagree. There's been something hinky about those kids' disappearance from the very first."

Steinhauser didn't know anything about the ransom and Jane wasn't about to tell him. "In what way?"

"Think about it. Jack came back. Gabriel didn't. Why? Makes no sense. Unless."

"Someone stopped him from coming back," said Jane. "You think it was Jack."

He lifted his eyebrows. "Exactly right. You're not as dumb as you look. Hey, I didn't mean that. You're very attractive. I just meant—"

"I understand," said Jane.

"Jack and Gabriel were abducted," said Cordelia firmly.

"Were they? Sounds like a load of BS to me. Those kids left of their own free will. I got a right to my theory of the case and that's it. You wanna know what happened to Gabriel? Why he hasn't come home? You talk to Jack. He knows. Now get out of here. I've got a family to feed."

Shortly before five, Jane pulled her SUV into the farmhouse driveway next to Branch's pickup.

Cordelia had been unusually quiet on the ride over. As they walked toward the house, she said, "Are you actually entertaining the idea that Jack prevented Gabriel from coming home? That he, like, has Gabriel locked up somewhere?" She seemed indignant. "Isn't that blaming the victim?"

"Steinhauser and I agree on one thing," said Jane. "Jack's the key."

A motorcycle cruised into the yard and stopped a few feet away. "Afternoon, Jane," Truman said pleasantly. "Cornelia."

"Cor*delia*."

He smiled, then squinted. "You theater directors sure have a lot of free time on your hands."

She cocked her head. "How did you know I was a director?"

"Is it a secret?"

"Well, no, but—"

"What's the latest on the boys?"

"We're here to celebrate Jack's homecoming," said Jane.

Nodding to the half a dozen cardboard cylinders strapped tightly to the back of his bike, Cordelia said, "More cylinders."

"Yup."

"And you're not going to tell us what's in them."

"Treasure," he said, smirking. Over the sound of the motor, he called, "Diamonds. Rubies. Gold doubloons."

"Right," said Cordelia.

Branch emerged from the front door looking red faced and sweaty.

"Jesus, take a shower, man," said Truman, waving the air away from his face as Branch approached.

"I been cutting down trees all day, helping people clean up after last night's storm. You might want to pitch in, Truman. Give the good people of this town a little of your sweat."

Truman offered nothing but a pained look.

"We're having a family dinner for Jack tonight," said Jane. "You're invited."

"You're celebrating? Isn't Gabriel still missing?" Truman flexed his legs. "Kind of cold, if you ask me. 'Course, nobody around here ever does. I don't know what those kids have been up to, but it isn't good."

" 'Up to'?" said Jane. "You said that once before. I'm not sure what that's supposed to mean."

He flattened his hands against his thighs. Turning off the motor he said, "I was in town last week and I saw them walking down Main. Man, let me tell you. I may be wrong, but they sure as hell looked like they were up to something, so, being the curious sort, I stopped and asked them if they were on a shopping spree." He laughed. "They were each carrying a paper bag. And boy, they didn't want to show me what was in them either. So, me being me, I grabbed them."

Branch pulled up his T-shirt and wiped his face. "And?"

"Fritos," said Truman. "Four big sacks. What the hell does a kid need with four big sacks of Fritos?"

"Anything else?" asked Cordelia, clearly out of patience with his snarkiness.

"Yeah, as a matter of fact, there was. Jack had a five-pack of this funky multicolored electrical tape. And a couple of scissors. Think they were working on a science project?"

"Did you ask them about the tape?" asked Jane.

"They gave me some lame answer about helping a friend put posters up in his bedroom. I know bullshit when I hear it. When I gave them the sacks back, they took off running. Bats outta hell, that's what I thought. Up to *no* good."

Branch studied Truman for a few seconds. Shaking his head, he walked back to his pickup. "Jack's inside. There isn't much food in the house. If you're going to make dinner, Jane, you may need to hit the grocery store in town. I'm planning to pick up Suzanne when I'm done. Andrew and Eric will be back around seven."

He was either disgusted by Truman or angry at his attitude about the boys. Climbing into his truck, he backed up and drove away.

"Friendly guy," said Truman, watching the dust kicked up by the oversized tires.

"You should talk," said Cordelia.

He smiled. "Later, m'ladies. By the way, don't expect me for dinner. I got other plans." He started the motor, gunned it a couple of times, and then shot back across the yard to his RV.

"Absolutely charming man," said Cordelia, shuddering. "It's a shame he's living down here. If he were up in the Cities, I'm sure my sister would have married him by now. That would make him what? Husband number eleven? I've lost count."

30

Aaron cracked the front door of his house and stuck his head inside. "Holly? You around?" When she didn't answer, he came in and shut the door behind him. He called again. "Holly, honey. I'm home."

Still nothing. His luck was holding.

Walking into the kitchen, he found a note in Holly's neat handwriting propped against a bottle of dishwashing liquid next to the sink.

> Aaron—I went over to Peg's house for
> coffee. I should be home by six. I made
> egg salad for dinner. Thought we'd have
> sandwiches and some of that leftover coleslaw.
> And the rest of the Jell-O mold I made
> on Saturday. Hope that's okay. Love you. H.

After removing the paper bag from under his shirt, he placed it on the kitchen table, pulled out a chair and sat down. Firing up a cigarette, he took a long inhale and then blew smoke over his shoulder. He'd actually done it. Bought himself a handgun. He'd lied to the man at the shop. He'd never fired a revolver—or any sort of gun—before. He'd heard someone at a party once talk about the problem he was having with the new 9mm he'd just bought. The jamming problem. As if Aaron had ever had a problem like that.

Opening the sack, he tilted his head and peeked inside. Yup, still there. With the cigarette dangling from his lips, he slipped the gun out and placed it carefully so that the barrel was pointed away from him.

And then he watched it. Several minutes went by. He tapped ash into an empty juice glass and thought about what it would be like to pull the trigger. For just an instant, it felt as if he was watching a wild animal curled there in front of him, seemingly quiet, though capable of striking in an instant, making anyone near it a victim. Then again, no. It wasn't going down that way.

He'd take the revolver out into the woods and fire off a few rounds. Get used to the way it felt in his hand. It was possible that he might even like the way it felt. If that turned out not to be the case, it wouldn't matter. He'd bought the gun for a reason. His letter-writing campaign was finished. So were the blogs. He suspected it was all downhill from here. People would probably call him crazy when it was over. Maybe he was. This turn of events had surprised him as much as it would others. Little doubt remained that he'd go to prison. "Better be worth it," he whispered, not at all certain it would be.

Jane sat on the back steps waiting for Jack to bring out the grocery sack filled with fresh corn on the cob. He'd agreed, reluctantly, to help her do the shucking. Cordelia had spent the last hour watching *Simpsons* reruns with him, all the while attempting to engage him in a conversation. He claimed he was bushed after a day of helping his father and Branch clean away trees and brush. He had the beginnings of a sunburn on his face and arms, which he kept scratching until Cordelia ordered him upstairs to take a shower and apply some aloe vera gel. When he came back down, Jane was in the kitchen, trying to figure out what to make for dinner. Branch had been right about needing to hit the grocery store in town. But first, Jane wanted her chance with Jack. The noninterrogation interrogation.

After hefting the corn sack out onto the steps, Jack set a large plastic bowl between them and sat down.

"Appreciate the help," said Jane. "So how are you doing?"

"Okay," he said with a diffident shrug.

"You've been through a lot."

He nodded.

"Can I ask you a question about Gabriel?"

"I suppose. I'm kind of sick of questions."

She smiled. "I know. But this is important. Did Gabriel like guns?"

Another shrug. "Sure."

"Do you?"

"Well, I mean . . . they're useful."

"For . . ."

"Hunting. Stuff like that."

"Does Gabriel like to hunt?"

"Uh-huh."

"Do you?"

"Papa says I'm too young."

"But Branch has brought Gabriel up to his hunting cabin."

"I know. I told Papa it wasn't fair. I mean, Branch even took Gabriel to a gun store to show him the rifle he planned to buy him when he turns fourteen. There's nothing like that in *my* future."

This was news to Jane. She assumed it would be news to Suzanne, too. "Do you think that's cool—that Branch has promised to buy Gabriel a rifle?"

"Well . . . yeah. I guess. Dad—that's Eric—doesn't like guns. He won't allow one in the house."

"And you think that's wrong?"

"No, I get it. Sort of."

"Did it make Gabriel happy—knowing he was going to have his own gun?"

"Oh, yeah. Super glad. He was trying to talk Branch into buying it for him when he turned thirteen next fall. He didn't want to wait another year."

"Because?"

"You know. It would make him feel safer."

"He doesn't feel safe?"

"No, not like that, as in he thinks someone's out to get him. Just in general. It would be cool to have firepower if somebody tries to hurt him or someone he loves."

"Like his mom."

"Yeah."

"Or Branch."

"Uh-huh."

"I'm curious. Would you say Gabriel was depressed?"

"No."

"Are you depressed?"

239

"No. Sometimes. I don't know. No more than anyone else is."

"You'd be happier if your dads got back together."

"Well, duh."

She looked off toward the woods. "These last few days must have been pretty frightening for you. Eric told me that you were kept in a room with just a mattress and a lamp. No windows. No bathroom either?"

Jack grabbed an ear of corn and began pulling off the outer leaves. "There was a bathroom."

"How did you get food?"

"They guy brought it to me on a tray. Crap. Like soup. Bread without butter. Sandwiches with weird meat."

If he was lying, he was good at it.

"And Gabriel. You never saw him, never heard his voice?"

"Nope."

"The man who kidnapped you . . . he didn't hurt you?"

He shook his head.

"I wonder why he took you?"

"Dad said that he wanted money." One leg began to vibrate as he shifted away from her. "I didn't know anything about that. Honest."

"Hey, do you know what time it is?"

"Huh?"

"The time," she said, pointing at her wrist. "I forgot to put my watch on this morning."

"Nah. No idea."

"You don't wear a watch?"

"I don't like the way they feel."

"Then, I guess there's something I don't understand."

"Like?"

"Well, you don't wear a watch. The room you were dumped in didn't have a window. But you told your dad that when it got light the kidnapper came back with some food."

"Yeah."

"How did you know it was light?" She turned to look at him. It didn't matter what he said next. They both knew she'd caught him in a lie.

"I . . . I guess I just assumed it was light. Time passed. You know?"

"How much time?"

"I'm not sure. I fell asleep."

"So it could have been minutes or hours."

He clearly didn't know what to say. "I'm not lying, if that's what you think. I just assumed it was light out. Why are you making such a big deal out of it?"

"I'm only trying to understand."

Gazing down at the ear of corn in his hand, he said, "I've already said what happened. There's nothing more. I wish I could help find Gabriel, but I don't know where he is. That's the truth." His eyes swelled and he looked like he was about to cry.

Jane put her hand on his back.

"He's my best friend," said Jack. "If I could help I would."

"I believe you," she said. She didn't believe everything he'd said, but his concern for Gabriel seemed genuine. Just then, her cell phone rang. Checking the caller ID, she saw that it was Avi. Maybe this was a good time for a break.

"Give me a sec," she said, getting up and walking out into the yard. "Hey."

"Hey yourself," said Avi. "Where are you?"

"At Andrew and Eric's farmhouse."

"How's everything going? Did you get a chance to talk to Jack?"

"A little."

"Are you getting anywhere?"

"Not sure."

"I assume you called to talk to me about the deal Dr. Martinsen put on the table this morning."

"You still considering it?"

"More than considering."

"Did you talk to your agent yet?"

"She wants to have a powwow with Elaine Ducasse to nail down all the details, but she agreed it sounded promising."

Not what Jane wanted to hear. "Does that mean she won't even try to take the book to any of the major publishers in New York?"

Avi laughed. "Boy, you really don't like Dr. Martinsen. Tell me again how you know her?"

Jane didn't want to discuss this over the phone, and yet she had to say something. She should have told Avi about Julia. The thing was, she didn't want Julia to exist in any way between them. "Julia and I were together for a couple years."

"She was your girlfriend?"

"I ended it and she's never been able to accept it."

"Lord, I had no idea."

"That's why I think you could be stepping into a hornet's nest if you do business with her." When Jane received nothing but silence in reply, she said, "Are you there?"

"Yeah."

"I'm not trying to rain on your parade."

"Right. You know, Jane, you have to consider that this may not be about you. It could be that she believes in my book. Her interest could be perfectly legitimate."

"She's not a healthy woman," said Jane.

"How could someone that successful—"

"There's a big difference between doing well in business and being a decent human being—trustworthy, honest, ethical."

"I don't know," said Avi, clearly resisting Jane's analysis. "Your romantic experience with her could have biased your judgment."

Julia had been right. If Jane pushed too hard, sounded too negative, Avi would begin to see *her* as the problem. Once again, Julia had played her hand perfectly. "Maybe we can talk a little more when I get home."

"Okay. But you should know that I'm going to rely on the advice of my agent. She's the professional."

Meaning that Jane, if she knew what was good for her, should butt out. "I really want to see you get that book published—and published well."

"I realize that."

"Don't be angry with me."

"I'm not. Except, you have to understand that this is *my* life. I make the decisions. We clear on that?"

"Absolutely."

"Good. Now. Any idea when you'll be back?"

"A day or two."

"I'm staying clear of your house. Cordelia's sister is a real pain in the ass. I like Bolger and Hattie, but—"

"I hear you. And I love you. You be safe."

After Jane clicked off, she stood quietly for a few moments, her gaze drifting off toward the meadow. When she finally sat back down, Jack said, "Everything okay?"

243

"Not sure." She noticed that he'd shucked half a dozen cobs of corn while she'd been talking. "Have you ever had a friend who you knew was about to make a bad decision? Something that might end up hurting them? But when you tried to talk them out of it, they wouldn't listen. All of a sudden, *you're* the bad guy."

It was Jack's turn to gaze silently at the distant grass.

"It's not easy to know what to do. Makes you feel helpless."

He picked up another ear of corn and began ripping off the leaves with a startling ferocity.

She wondered if she'd hit a nerve. "But still, you have to try. Right? You can't just let the person you love make a terrible decision without doing what you can to stop it. I mean, you have to do *something*."

"You do," said Jack. "Absolutely."

Cordelia pushed open the back screen door. "If we're going to get a meal on the table any time soon, I think we better head into town."

"Can we have sloppy joes?" asked Jack. "And baked beans?"

"Sure we can," said Cordelia. "Anything you want."

"And rocky road ice cream?"

Jane's chance with him, at least for now, was over. Perhaps, later tonight, they could resume their conversation.

31

Jack directed them to a small grocery store on the south end of Winfield. Jane remembered seeing a bigger store in the center of town, perhaps one that would have more choices. Then again, if she followed Jack's menu, she didn't need much.

"I'll get the ice cream," said Jack, racing off as soon as they entered the store.

"You learn anything new?" asked Cordelia, pushing a shopping cart toward the meat department.

Jane had mainly learned that Andrew had been right—Jack was unusually stubborn. Most people, when caught in a lie, admitted it. "Not much," said Jane. She wondered which aisle held the Manwich, Jack's favorite. "Get at least four pounds of ground beef," she called.

"Will do. Meet you at the front, okay?"

Jane was about to head into the bowels of the store when she caught sight of Jack rushing toward the entrance. Skirting several shopping carts, she raced after him, all the while wondering where the hell he was headed.

Once outside, she saw him running toward an alley. He was young and quick, though her strides were longer. She trailed him at a distance, ducking behind a garage when he looked around to see if he was being followed. She silently counted to five, then moved into the open again and saw him turn into a backyard. She quickened her step, continuing to follow him through two more yards until he approached a run-down house with a red-and-white FORECLOSURE sign prominently displayed in the front yard. The storm winds had come through this block with a vengeance. Jane counted four downed trees and one house where a large section of shingles had blown off. Some of the debris had been cleaned away, but not all. She stood behind a lilac bush and watched Jack open a window on the first floor and hoist himself through.

Sprinting across the street, she noted the name and the number of the house. All the windows had been covered with newspaper. Standing under the open window, she noticed now that the newspaper had been taped to the glass with colored tape. Red. Green. Blue. Yellow. Was this the tape Truman had seen in the bag Gabriel was carrying in town last week? As far as Jane was concerned, this was the smoking gun. The abduction story was a lie. It had all been all a lie. As she crawled in through the open window, questions swept over her. Did *the boys* send the ransom note?

As she dropped down into the room, her eyes lingered on the scraps of newspaper and tape scattered on a threadbare rug. She paused under the living room arch, listening to the sound of footsteps, the creek of a door opening, then more footsteps. She followed the sounds until she came to a stairway that led to the basement. Behind her, it looked as if someone had kicked in the back door. It stood open, allowing her a clear view of the garage.

She listened a moment more before starting down. When she reached the bottom, she found Jack sitting cross-legged on a blanket spread over a deeply pockmarked concrete floor. Next to him was an empty fifth of Popov vodka.

Moving closer, she glimpsed something terrible in the dead stillness of his eyes. "Jack?" Though she'd said his name softly, her voice was like a roar inside her head.

He didn't move.

"Where's Gabriel?"

No response.

"Jack? Answer me."

"Gone."

"Gone where?"

He shook his head, staring at a spot on the floor a few feet to the right of where he was sitting. "I don't know."

"You expected him to be here?"

He nodded.

She stood over him. "It's time to stop this. There was no abduction. You and Gabriel came here on your own. Tell me the truth," she all but shouted. "Tell me!"

"I can't!" he shouted back, breaking into sobs, rocking back and forth.

Her immediate instinct was to crouch down and put her arms around him, try to comfort him, and yet she couldn't. "Where would he go?" she demanded.

He shook his head, raked a hand through his hair.

"You must have some idea."

"Maybe he hitchhiked."

"Where?"

"Away from Winfield. Anywhere but here."

"Or maybe he went home," she said.

"No. He wouldn't do that. Ever."

Jane made a quick call to Cordelia, explaining what had happened and giving her the address. "Call the family," she said. "I'll stay here with Jack until you get here."

Still holding the cell phone in her hand, she crouched down. No matter what he'd done, seeing him there, so upset, so vulnerable, her heart nearly broke. "It's going to be okay."

"No. It's not," he said, wiping a hand over his eyes.

"Did you and Gabriel drink that vodka?"

"Yeah. It was awful."

"You got sick?"

"What do you think?"

Empty bags of Fritos and smashed cans of Mountain Dew and root beer littered the floor. "Was that your only food?"

"The people who used to live here left some stuff. Soup. Canned fruit and vegetables. We thought we could live here for weeks. Maybe months. I guess we didn't realize how much we eat."

"And the vodka?"

"Gabriel found it in back of the furnace. We thought we'd hit the jackpot. That we'd have a great time."

"Why did you leave?" asked Jane. Since the shock of finding Gabriel gone had opened him up, now was the time to strike. She needed the truth.

"Because."

"That's not an answer."

"I had to. I couldn't stay here any longer."

"Why?"

He looked down. Shook his head. And then he stopped talking.

Suzanne and Branch were the first to arrive. Jack was still refusing to talk. Suzanne cradled him in her arms while Jane filled them in what she'd learned, and Branch looked around the basement.

"What's this?" asked Branch, bending down, touching the floor by the stairs.

Jane stepped over. "Looks like blood."

"Blood?" repeated Suzanne, her head snapping up.

"Feel it," said Branch. "It's sticky."

Suzanne scrambled to her feet. She bent over to look, then nailed Jack with her eyes. "Talk to me," she all but screamed. "Why is there blood on the floor?"

"I . . . I don't know," he said, his eyes growing big and desperate. "If I knew, I'd tell you."

"We need to call the police," said Jane.

Branch took out his cell phone and made the call.

Continuing to scan the room, Jane found a pocketknife with more blood on it. Holding it in front of Jack's face, she asked, "Who does this belong to?"

"Gabriel."

"Why would there be blood on it?"

"How should I know?"

"They'll be here soon," said Branch, returning his cell to his pocket.

Jack crawled over to a dark corner of the room, covered his face with his hands.

A few minutes later, Andrew flew down the stairs, followed by Eric.

In the distance, the wail of a siren drew everyone's attention. It didn't take long for it to reach the house. Boots hit the stairs as two men shuffled down.

With his fathers on either side of him, Jack stood, wetting his lips, a kid preparing himself for the gallows.

Cordelia, out of breath and panting, appeared at the top of the steps and trotted halfway down before stopping. "What did I miss?" she asked conversationally. Searching the faces of those standing around the basement, she squeezed out a guilty smile and said, "Oh. Sorry. My bad." She gave a little wave. "Don't mind me. Just continue on as if I weren't here."

Lucas Xavier, the narrow-faced chief of police, led Andrew and Eric into a conference room at the rear of the police station. Suzanne and Branch asked to be allowed in, but the chief said no. At the last minute, Andrew said he wanted Jane with them. If the chief didn't allow it, they could all wait until a lawyer was located.

Looking disgruntled, Xavier nodded his assent. He took the chair at the head of the table. Andrew and Eric sat on either side of Jack, with Jane across from them.

"Just tell the truth, Jack," said Eric, giving his son's shoulder a reassuring squeeze. "Everything's going to be okay."

As Xavier fiddled with a voice recorder, Andrew asked if the basement of the foreclosed house was considered a crime scene.

"Yes, sir, it is," said Xavier.

"I didn't hurt Gabriel," Jack began even before a question was asked. "I never would. He's my best friend."

Xavier pushed a button on the recorder, then opened his notebook, stated the date, the time, and who was in the room. "No one said you did, son." Adopting a fatherly tone, he said, "I just need you to answer a few questions. I think the best place to start is the beginning. Tell me why you and your cousin ran away."

Jack shifted in his chair. "We . . . were pissed at our parents."

"Because?"

"My dads have been fighting a lot. Makes me feel crazy when they do that. And then Papa left a few weeks ago. It's like they don't care what I think."

"That's not true," said Andrew.

"So you were mad at your dads and you wanted to hurt them," interjected Xavier before Jack could respond to his father's denial. "You wanted them to worry about you, where you'd gone."

"I guess."

"How long were you planning to be gone?"

"We didn't talk about that."

"Okay," said Xavier. "What about Gabriel? Why did he want to run away?"

"He . . . wasn't happy."

"About what?"

Jack shrugged. "His mom was gone all the time. He really hated that. When we found the house, we both had the same idea. We could live there. Nobody would know. We'd put newspaper on the windows so people couldn't see in. There was this closet under the basement stairs. It locked from the inside. If

251

anyone came, we figured we'd go in there and hide. But we never needed to."

"Why did you leave and Gabriel stayed?" asked Eric.

"Please, Mr. Lindstrom," said Xavier firmly. "Let me ask the questions. Go ahead and answer that." He motioned for Jack to continue.

Making direct eye contact for the first time, Jack said, "I don't know about Gabriel, but I got sick of hiding. The basement smelled bad. We didn't have enough to eat. We found a bottle of vodka and drank it. We both threw up in one of the upstairs bathrooms. That stunk even worse. We were always afraid someone would come in the house and find us. I missed being home. I kinda thought that Gabriel might go home after I left, but when he didn't, I figured I should check up on him, which is why I left the grocery store. I didn't know she was following me." He eyed Jane sullenly.

"I'm glad she did," said Andrew.

"So you have no idea when Gabriel left that house or why," said Xavier.

"No. And I don't know anything about the blood. It wasn't there before. I swear."

Reading through the notes he'd taken while talking to the family outside the foreclosed home, Xavier asked, "Why did you lie and tell everyone you'd been abducted?"

"I—" Jack crossed his arms over his chest. "See . . . when Dad found me under the front porch—after the storm—the first thing he asked me was how I got home. If *they'd* let me go. I didn't know what he was talking about. I was scared to death that he and Papa were going to be furious at me for taking off again after promising I wouldn't. Then he started asking me all these

252

questions, like if I'd seen the kidnapper's face. Did I know him? Would I recognize him if I saw him again? He wanted to know if they'd let Gabriel go, too. I mean, I couldn't tell him the truth. I didn't want to rat out Gabriel, especially if he was planning to stay there a while longer. That's when he said that the family had paid a ransom to get us back." Jack's eyes grew large and round. "I didn't know anything about a ransom. There *was* no kidnapper, so who would have asked for the money? I still don't get that. All I know is, Gabriel and me left the tent about three in the morning. We walked into town. We climbed through an unlocked window and we stayed there. That's it. So help me God. That's all I know."

The room was silent as everyone digested his words.

"Can I ask something?" said Andrew.

Xavier gave a grudging nod.

"Gabriel never said *anything* to you about where he might go if he didn't come back?"

"Nothing," said Jack, picking at a scratch in the table. "I guess I just assumed we'd both go home. Eventually. And live with the consequences."

Jane found his manner troubling, and at the same time, telling. When he'd been answering Xavier's last questions, he'd looked everyone in the eye. Now, answering Andrew's, he was back to staring at the table. He'd been telling the truth, then stopped. Why?

"Okay," said Xavier, tossing down his pen. "That's all for now. Thank you, Jack, for being so forthcoming."

"What about Gabriel?" asked Eric.

"You have my promise. I'll put every person I have on it. We'll do our damnedest to find him."

Without Jack's help, Jane wasn't sure their efforts would be enough. Gabriel had to be found, and fast. As hard as Jack had insisted he'd given up everything he knew, the fact was, he hadn't. He remained the only key that would unlock the door.

And he wasn't talking.

32

Wearing a white terry-cloth robe, Cordelia sauntered out of the motel bathroom, a towel wrapped around her head. "I feel human again," she said, easing down on the bed next to a stack of scripts.

Jane was sitting in an uncomfortable comfy chair by the window, sipping from a can of Sprite, making a mental list of questions.

Grabbing a package of red licorice twists, Cordelia stretched out and put on her reading glasses.

"Is that what you plan to do for the rest of the evening?" asked Jane.

"I need to make this decision, like, *yesterday*. I'm meeting with Octavia on Wednesday. She'll have her selection, I'll have mine. And then, just an FYI, expect all-out thermonuclear war to ensue." She gazed at Jane smugly over the rim of her glasses. "Good thing I have my BFF in my corner. I don't even know why Octavia bothers. No matter what Octavia wants, you'll vote with me."

Jane attempted a smile. "Unless you pick the wrong play."

"Hilarious. Always the comedian."

"Before you start work, talk to me a minute about what just happened tonight," said Jane.

"Specifically?"

"The ransom note. If the boys weren't kidnapped, who sent it?"

"Ay, there's the rub."

"I mean, the motive—money—sill seems plausible."

"Except that motive, such as it is, doesn't exactly cull many from the herd." Cordelia ripped open the licorice package. "The problem, as I see it, is that everyone in town who can read or who hasn't been locked in a closet for the last week would have known about the boys' disappearance."

"A crime of opportunity. I still think we're looking at three primary suspects. Truman, Steinhauser, and Eld."

"Or," said Cordelia, whipping off her glasses as if an idea had just occurred to her. "It could have been a member of the family."

Jane sat up straight. "You mean—"

"Any one of them. They all need money. Well, except for Suzanne. She's got a job that seems solid."

"And who would be better positioned to know what was going on?"

"Maybe it was all of them," said Cordelia. "Sort of like a modern *Murder on the Orient Express*. Except without the murder."

It was an intriguing solution.

"I know," said Cordelia. "Too out there."

"Afraid so. What about the blood on the floor and the stairs at the foreclosed house?"

"I guess you better do more digging, Janey. While you're unearthing, will you pick me up a burger?" She adjusted her reading glasses, picked up a script, stuffed the end of a strip of licorice into her mouth, and began reading.

Jane assumed she'd been dismissed.

Winfield was a town that turned in early. As twilight descended, fingers of scarlet stretched across the western sky, promising another beautiful summer day tomorrow. Jane lowered the window of her CR-V and, resting her elbow on the door, cruised slowly through the neighborhoods. She would occasionally come across a white vehicle parked in a drive, but never a Chevy Avalanche.

Just before ten, she stopped at a hamburger stand and ordered a couple of cheeseburgers. They were in the process of closing, but the young man behind the counter said it wasn't a problem. She sat down on a chair by the window to wait. When he returned with a white sack, she paid him. "I don't suppose you know anybody who drives a white Chevy Avalanche." She was sick of asking the question.

"Nope," he said, pressing his hands on the counter. "Sorry. They're kind of pricey. You looking to buy one?"

"Yeah."

"I know where they got one for sale. My dad's been shopping around for a new truck. I went with him the other day. He tried out an Avalanche. I'm pretty sure it was white. You know where Magic Motors is? They sell used cars and trucks?"

"Sorry, I don't."

"You know where Bay Point Park is, right? Follow the street—Kenyon—that runs next to the bandstand and it will take you out to County Road Fifteen. Turn right, or north, and go about two miles. It's on your left. They wouldn't be open at this time of night, but you could try them tomorrow."

A used truck, thought Jane. Sitting on a used car lot. Could it be that simple? She thanked the guy and left.

By ten, after parking a few doors down from the Tudor revival home Eld had entered two nights ago, she sat and ate her burger. She might be wasting her time, and yet she continued to be curious about his "runner" subterfuge—what he was really doing in that house.

Halfway through the burger, he appeared. He stood on the corner and looked around, then flicked a lit cigarette into the street and trotted across the front yards and up the steps. He rang the doorbell, and the woman appeared and let him in.

This time, Jane was prepared. She'd added a monocular to the gym bag she kept in the backseat, one that was filled with equipment she might need on the job.

Feeling for a mini-flashlight and the monocular in her pocket, she dashed across the street. Viewing the basement room through the monocular, she was hoping she'd be able to read what Eld was looking at on the computer. She hid behind a hedge in the next yard and watched for a few seconds. When a light came on in the basement, she crept up to the window. As expected, Eld had found his way to the desktop computer. This time, however, instead of staying there, he shot out of the chair and began punching the air, shouting at the woman, who had seated herself on the couch.

Bending closer, Jane struggled to hear what he was saying. Though muffled, she thought she heard the words, "could kill him." The woman spoke softly, so Jane had no idea what she was saying. Her body language suggested that she was trying to calm him down. At one point in his rant, the woman grabbed his arm and pulled him down on the couch next to her. Holding his hands, she looked him squarely in the eyes and spoke, once again, softly.

Eld listened without speaking, eventually pulling away, his face tight with anger, though his general agitation seemed to have lessened. He sat with his forearms resting on his knees, running his hands through his hair. When he lifted a pack of cigarettes from his running shorts, the woman shook her head.

"I am so screwed," he all but screamed. Looking defeated, his shoulders drooping, he got up and left the room.

The woman sat for a few moments, her eyes fixed on the computer, then rose and followed him.

Jane stayed by the basement window and waited for Eld to leave. After he'd run off down the street, she pulled a business card out of her pocket and approached the front door. She assumed the woman would answer, even though it was late, thinking that Eld had come back. When she appeared, Jane was surprised to find a much older woman than she'd expected.

"I'm sorry to bother you," said Jane. "I know it's late. I saw someone just leave, so I knew you were up." She handed over the card.

Slipping on the reading glasses hanging around her neck, the woman looked at it. "You're a private investigator?"

"That's right."

"Lawless? Any relation to Raymond Lawless, the St. Paul defense attorney who ran for governor a few years back?"

"He's my father."

"What a small world," she said, standing back and beckoning

Jane to enter. "He came to Winfield, you know." She led Jane into the living room, where she sat down on a green brocade wingback chair by the cold fireplace and nodded for Jane to sit opposite her. "I worked for his campaign in the county. I'm Myra Taft."

"Nice to meet you," said Jane.

"I'm sorry your father lost. I thought he would have made a great governor."

"He would appreciate that."

"He seemed like such a decent man."

"He is." When Jane's father's political aspirations helped break the ice in a conversation, Jane usually ran with it.

"Is he still working as a lawyer?"

"He is," said Jane, surveying the room, taking in the antiques, the Impressionist reproductions on the walls. It was an elegant home, as was the woman who owned it. "He sits on a number of boards. And he has several projects that claim a lot of his time, some charitable, some law related. He stays busy."

"There was a young man with him when he spoke at the high school gym," said Myra. "He was filming the talk."

"That's my brother, Peter. He shot a documentary of my dad's run for office."

"Handsome fellow."

Jane smiled. "He's continued to work as a documentary artist."

"You have a fascinating family. And you're a PI."

"I came because I'm hoping you could answer a couple of questions."

"About?"

"Well, first, I should tell you that I'm in town because of the disappearance of two boys."

260

"Oh, of course. Jack and Gabriel. I know them well. I'd heard that Jack had returned home."

"He has. But Gabriel's still missing."

"I'm sorry."

Jane glanced over at the front door. "I saw Aaron Eld leave your house a few minutes ago."

"You know Aaron?"

"We've met. What I'm curious about is his nightly running regimen."

She lifted her chin, gave Jane an evaluating look. "I'm not sure why that should interest you."

"The thing is, he was the one who found Gabriel's cell phone the day after his parents discovered the boy was missing."

"So?"

"My concern is that he may know something about Gabriel's disappearance that he hasn't told anyone. Or, perhaps, that he had something to do with a ransom note that was sent to the family."

"Ransom? Aaron? I can't imagine it."

"Does Aaron have any special need for money right now? Anything that would cause him to act rashly? He seemed upset when he left here a few minutes ago. I know my questions seem intrusive, Myra, but Gabriel is still missing. The family is crazy with worry. I'm trying to understand what's going on so I can help bring the boy home."

"Aaron would never hurt a child. Never."

"I've heard that he had some trouble at school this past spring. The principal wanted him to include creationism in his curriculum and Aaron refused."

She adjusted the hem of her skirt over her knees. "That's all true."

"Were there any repercussions?"

Myra looked into the fireplace. "Oh, I suppose I can tell you. It's not a secret, or at least it won't be by tomorrow morning. Aaron received a letter this morning telling him that his contract won't be picked up for next year."

"He was fired?"

"I'm afraid so. The principal had already taken summer school away from him. That was a big financial hit. It's terrible timing, too, because Holly, his wife, was diagnosed with lupus last year. She hasn't been able to work. If they lose their health care through the school, her disease could easily bankrupt them. Add to that the problems with a ballooning mortgage payment on a house that's completely under water, and you have yourself one very upset young man."

"The house is under water?"

"There were some local shenanigans. All part of that subprime mortgage disaster. Aaron and Holly bought one of the homes that Andrew Waltz rehabbed and Branch Born landscaped. They always did such beautiful work. What I've heard was that the appraiser that worked for the bank inflated the worth of those homes. Aaron and Holly had no way to know about it. Because of the price, and their credit history, they were given one of those low-quality loans that the bank turned around and sold to someone else at a profit. They didn't understand that the monthly payment they started with wouldn't last. A very bad business all around."

"Did they think Andrew and Branch were in on it?"

"Yes, I think so, though Aaron has no proof."

"What do people in town say?"

"Nobody really knows what went on. I think some people do

blame Andrew and Branch, and the appraiser and the bank, of course. The problem now is, Aaron's been keeping all these financial problems from his wife because stress can cause her symptoms to worsen. He was worried when he left tonight because he had to go home and tell her he's been fired. He's been coming here almost every night since school ended looking for another teaching job."

"In this area?"

"They'd probably have to move."

And sell a house that was already under water? Aaron was the poster child for financial desperation. "Has he found another teaching position?" asked Jane.

"He's applied for several, but so far, he hasn't heard anything back."

"Why does he come here to use your computer? Doesn't he have one of his own?"

"Yes, but he and his wife both use it. He didn't want her to know about his applications."

"So he came here." It was all beginning to make sense.

"Aaron blames the principal, Craig Gilkey, and rightly so, for being let go. I hate to say it, but Gilkey is a people-pleaser. He's not the guy you'd want to send into a meeting hoping he'd fight for your side. I feel so badly for Aaron. My husband died two years ago. Aaron and Holly were incredibly kind to me during that time. That's when we first became friends. Aaron would come by when the grass was long in the summer and offer to cut it. He'd be out there in the winter, first thing in the morning after a snow, shoveling the walk. Holly would come by with a hot dish and a comforting word. They had me over to dinner at least once a week for the first few months. They're good people. Kind people. I understand that you're trying to figure out what happened to Gabriel. I just don't believe Aaron had anything to do with it."

Jane moved to the edge of the chair. "I'd pick you to be the person to go into a meeting and fight for my side."

Myra smiled. "If there's any other way I can help—"

Jane stood and held out her hand. "Thanks for your candor."

33

"So, what do we do?" asked Eric. He and Andrew had come out-side to get away from the house, not wanting their conversation to be overheard. Andrew sat cross-legged in the grass, looking up at the stars. Eric, his shirt off, sat next to him, staring up at Jack's bedroom window. Jack had turned the light off a few min-utes ago. "Do you think he's telling the truth?"

Andrew didn't answer right away. After sticking a blade of grass between his lips, he said, "I think much of it was the truth, as far as it went."

"I'm worried about what might have happened between him and Gabriel."

"Like what? They got into a fight?"

"Maybe," said Eric.

"We can't force him to talk."

"Yeah. Thumbscrews are out." Sighing, Eric stretched out on the grass.

"Hey, look," said Andrew, lowering his voice and pointing to-ward the house.

They watched in silence as Jack opened his bedroom window and crawled out onto a narrow section of roof.

"What's he doing?" whispered Eric.

Jack inched his way toward the porch, where the roof flattened and widened. Drawing his feet up to his chest, he sat there, unmoving, his head tilted up.

"I'll bet he does that all the time," whispered Andrew. "It's a nice night. He's just getting some fresh air. Probably helps him think."

"What's he thinking *about*?" asked Eric. "That's what I want to know."

Andrew stretched out next to him. "Suppose he can see us?"

"Too dark."

Rolling over onto his side, Andrew said, "We need help."

"I know."

"No, I don't just mean with Jack, but for us. The two of us."

"Like a therapist?"

"Yeah."

"You'd do that?" asked Eric.

"I don't want to split up. Not if there's a chance we can make it work."

"Sometimes I think if we'd just stop and actually listen to each other, stop the knee-jerk reactions and just be open to the other's thoughts and feelings—"

"Neither one of us is very good at that," said Andrew.

"We used to be."

"How did we become so . . . distant?"

"Just happens. It's life." Eric turned toward him. "I've been thinking. We should move."

"We should? Seriously?"

"Back to the Cities. It would be better for us, better for Jack. A new start."

"What about the café?" asked Andrew.

"It's dying. I've known that for a while, I simply wouldn't admit it to myself. I can't keep the thing open just because it's a piece of my family history. If we moved back, you could come home every night. I'd get a better paying job—maybe work full-time as a speechwriter again. We could tighten our belts and pay off our debts."

"You really think we could make that work? You'd leave your sister? Especially if . . . I mean, if the outcome with Gabriel isn't a good one."

Eric rolled away onto his back. "Why is nothing ever simple?" Reaching for Andrew's hand, he said, "All I know is, I love you. I never stopped. I may not be able to see what our lives will look like moving forward, but I do know, without a doubt, that I want to move forward together. As a family. You and me and Jack."

"Contra mundum?"

Eric closed his eyes and smiled. They'd first heard the Latin words in a TV adaptation of *Brideshead Revisited*. They used to say it to each other in bed at night, after they'd made love. "Yes," said Eric, pulling Andrew down next to him. "The three of us. *Contra mundum.*"

Against the world.

Suzanne was in the kitchen pouring herself a glass of iced tea when Branch came in the back door carrying a six-pack of beer, which he set on the round oak table.

"Where were you?" she asked.

"Driving around. I had to get my head straight after what we discovered in that basement."

"I see you found a destination." She nodded to the six-pack.

"Want one?"

"I'll stick with tea." She had the letter in her pocket, the one from the genetic studies institute. It was in the mailbox when she got home.

He screwed off the cap on one of the bottles and then drifted out into the living room.

"Honey?" she said tentatively.

"What?" He took several long pulls on the bottle.

"I have to tell you something. It's good news. Gabriel has no genetic link that would predispose him to ALS. We got the letter today."

"Oh, wow, that's wonderful," he said. He looked so preoccupied that she wasn't sure her words had even penetrated.

Things couldn't get any more chaotic, thought Suzanne. There was no perfect time to tell him about leaving the church. She didn't really think he'd care all that much. He could still attend services—go to any church he wanted. She stood in the doorway and watched him walk over to the window and adjust the shades so that he could look out. "There's something else."

"Crap, Suzanne. Can't we have five minutes of peace?"

"Nothing about Gabriel. This is about me."

He eyed her warily.

"I'm leaving the church."

"Vivian fired you?"

"No. I guess the simplest way to say it is: I've lost my faith in Christianity."

"Is this a joke?"

"It's something I've been thinking about for a long time. I know I haven't said anything. To you, or to Vivian. I didn't feel I had a choice because we needed my paycheck and the health care. You know I haven't been happy since Vivian took over the senior pastorship. But now that you're about to get that job in Prior Lake, I can come clean—to you, and to the church, to the congregation. To Vivian. I don't have to be in the closet anymore."

"I . . . you're not making any sense."

"I don't believe, Branch. I'm not an atheist. That position seems as ridiculous to me as absolute belief in a deity. I mean, maybe there is a God. The only thing I'm sure of is that, if there is, Christianity's version is much too small. I can't use the idea of a God anymore to give weight to my own opinions. I think it's insane for humans to think they know the mind of God. It would be like an ant trying to know mine."

"But . . . but—" He circled around the room, struggling to express himself.

"You must have guessed that something was different."

"No," he said. "Not at all. How can you not believe in Jesus? He died for us. Without him, without His sacrifice, there wouldn't be any forgiveness. Don't you get it? It's *all* about forgiveness."

She was stunned by his reaction.

"It's everything, Suzanne. I've made mistakes. I'm not always a good man. If God can't forgive me—if you can't—what's the point?" He got down on his knees, as he often did at times of stress. "Pray with me. You start. I'm not good with words."

"Branch, no. I can't do that anymore."

He grabbed her hand and jerked her down next to him.

"You're hurting me."

"If we can't pray, how do we ever get God to listen to us?"

"Honey, you can pray. You can believe in God, go to church, read the Bible. I'm not taking any of that away from you. I'm just telling you how I feel, what I believe."

"I married a *minister,* Suzanne. You think that has no significance to me? That it's some inconsequential part of why I love you?"

"I never really thought about it."

"You can't change. You have to be the same. You're godly. You understand things other people don't. Things *I* don't."

She shouldn't have brought it up. It was the wrong time. She'd been so excited to tell him about the organization she'd found on the Internet, too headstrong to realize how vulnerable he was right now.

He dropped her hand as if it were a hot coal. Standing up, he snatched the beer bottle off the floor and hurled it at the wall.

Suzanne ducked as shattered glass flew at her.

"My whole world . . . it's all gone. What am I supposed to do?"

"Branch—"

"I can't be here right now," he said, bolting for the front door.

34

Tuesday

While Cordelia slept the early morning away at the motel, Jane walked into town find herself some breakfast. Before she reached Main Street, her cell phone vibrated in her back pocket. Checking the caller ID, she saw that it was Nolan.

"Anything new on your case?" he asked. He rarely exchanged pleasantries before getting to the point.

Jane filled him in.

"Are you in Winfield?" he asked.

"For the next few days."

"Makes sense. You got any leads?"

"A few. How are you doing?"

"Oh, okay."

He sounded down. "Just okay?"

"Well, you know. Pain. Limited mobility. It takes some of the joy out of life."

"Have you been over to the new office?"

271

"Not since I saw you there with Suzanne and Eric."

She wanted to ask if he'd taken on a new case himself, but didn't want to push.

"I spent part of the afternoon yesterday watering the plants in the backyard," he said. "Big deal, right?"

It was a big deal. It was the first time he'd tried it. "How did it feel?"

"It was kinda nice being outside. But this neighbor woman— she moved in last fall—stood behind her fence and scolded me for watering plants in the sunlight. She's a retired librarian. Ruby Johnson. A real know-it-all type. We got to talking. She'd been baking pies all morning—mostly strawberry rhubarb."

"Yum."

"She brought one over later in the day. Surprised me. Since it was close to dinnertime, I invited her to stay. I ordered a pizza. We ended up playing cribbage."

Jane smiled. This was the best news she'd heard in ages. "Nice to have a new friend in the neighborhood."

"She could drive a normal person batty. Never stops talking."

"Was the pie good?"

"Not bad. Would have been better with ice cream. When do you think you'll be back?"

"Hard to say. A day or two." This was the first investigation Jane had taken on since Nolan had left the hospital. She'd been spending so much time at his house that she couldn't add anything more to her plate. When Andrew had called, coinciding with the completion of their new office at the theater, it seemed like the perfect opportunity to start moving them both back toward a more business-as-usual footing. Nolan was physically able to handle it. The emotional side of his recovery was another matter.

"It would be nice to see you—when you're back and have the time," said Nolan.

She saw the comment for what it was—his way of feeling out her intentions without asking a direct question. He wanted to know if she would continue to come by, get his groceries, bring him meals from the restaurant, help him around the house, watch movies with him in the evening. The answer was a qualified yes. She would never leave him in the lurch if he truly needed her help. Of course they'd get together for dinner, movies, et cetera. The full answer, however, was more nuanced. If Jane kept doing things for him that he should be doing for himself, he was never going to get back on his feet—figuratively, if not literally. She understood that this would present difficulties for him, but none that he couldn't solve.

"I'll call you when I get back," she said. "We'll figure something out."

"Ruby was telling me about this grocery store. All I have to do is call and place an order and they deliver."

"Sounds perfect." One hurdle down, thought Jane.

"Well, I won't keep you. I'm planning to head over to the office this morning. Do a little work."

"Great. You hang in there, *Pops*." It always tickled him when she called him that. They both understood that their relationship had progressed far beyond business partners, or even friends. They were family, the only word that really covered it.

After saying good-bye and cutting the line, Jane continued on into town, coming upon an outside stand with a sign that asked, GOT FRY BREAD? She ordered herself a large topped with powdered sugar and cinnamon. As she ate, leaning against a lamppost, surveying the businesses along Main, a police cruiser pulled up next to her.

The window rolled down. "I just heard about Gabriel," said Steinhauser. "Thought I'd say I'm sorry."

"Thanks."

"Also wanted to say I told you so. I knew we weren't dealing with an abduction. I also wanted to clarify something I said yesterday—about Branch Born. Maybe I was a little too hard on him. I'm sure he loves Gabriel. It's that whole NFL thing that bugs me."

Jane had no idea what he was talking about and asked him to explain.

"Everybody knows he spent a year playing for the Indianapolis Colts. If you don't know, he tells you."

"He never said a word about it."

"That surprises me. It's all part of his big-man persona. I've been around guys like him before. Winning is everything. They beat on their kids to be disciplined. Well, not actually *beat,* but you know what I mean. Branch started coming to the games two or three weeks ago. Before that, I guess he was working some part-time job. When he was there, Gabriel's skills would turn to shit. He'd drop balls. Fail to make throws. He couldn't live up to Branch's unrealistic expectations. It was those expectations that got in the way of his playing, not Gabriel's lack of ability. Not me getting hot under the collar at him every now and then. You ask me, Branch might be one reason he ran away."

Jane took a last bite of her fry bread, chewing while she considered his comments.

"Oh, crap," said Steinhauser, putting his car in gear. Up the street, two men had begun a shoving match. Abruptly excusing himself, he swung his cruiser away from the curb and took off.

Back at the motel a while later, Jane stood next to Cordelia's bed, listening to her snore. She felt a twinge of guilt for waking her. She'd been up reading scripts deep into the wee hours of the morning.

Waving food under her friend's nose, Jane waited for the inevitable.

Without opening her eyes, Cordelia mumbled, "Smells greasy. Grease is one of five essential food groups."

"Five?"

"A taco?" she said, sitting up in bed. "You must think I'm a cheap date."

"A fry bread taco."

"I need caffeine to go with it."

Jane pulled a can of Pepsi from behind her back. "It's cold." She set it all on the nightstand and then sat down on her bed. "We need to leave."

"Not before I eat."

"After you eat."

"Where to this morning, Sherlock?"

"A used car lot."

Lowering her eyes and raising her eyebrows, she said. "A taco and a used car lot? When I'm with you, Janey, the fun just never stops."

While Andrew and Jack made breakfast, Eric went outside to water the daylilies on the west side of the house. Waking up with Andrew in his bed, making love, then coming downstairs to find Jack watching TV in the living room—it all seemed so right. As they puttered in the kitchen, Andrew suggested that he and Jack

275

make waffles. Eric set the table. Andrew turned on the radio. Eric was certain that each of them felt guilty for feeling even a crumb of happiness when Gabriel still missing.

Hearing a metal door scrape open and then shut, Eric turned to see Truman leave his RV and head into the woods. Instantly angry that his uncle was so damned closemouthed about everything in his life, he stomped across the yard. "Screw you," he said, opening the RV's door and climbing inside. "Oh . . . my . . . God," he said, his jaw nearly hitting the floor.

No wonder Truman kept the blinds drawn on all the windows. It appeared that he and Truman were living in parallel—though opposite—universes. While the outside of Eric and Andrew's house looked well tended, the yard manicured, the interior was anything but. In Truman's case, the exterior of his RV was badly rusted and run-down. The interior, however, was expensively appointed, with a long leather couch and matching chairs, an entertainment center complete with a Bang & Olufsen components and a huge flat-screen TV, several pieces of bold artwork on the custom cherry woodwork walls, an open bedroom at the back with designer bed linens, and a galley kitchen with high-end appliances. At the front, just to the right of the door, was an extra-large drafting table. Two swing-arm lamps were attached at each side, with a flat file cabinet behind the table, and a narrow console table along the opposite wall.

It was the contents of the console table that compelled Eric's attention. Stepping closer, he picked up one of the hundreds of bones Truman had assembled. They'd all been meticulously cleaned. Several were mounted on pieces of rough-sawn cedar, as if they were works of art.

"What the fuck?" came a gruff voice. "Get the hell out of my place."

Eric was startled, but stood his ground. Coming eye to eye with Truman, he said, "Not until you answer my questions."

"I don't need to answer shit."

"Who *are* you?"

"You know who I am."

"Do I? What do you do with those animal bones?"

"That's a 'need to know' kind of thing, and you *don't*."

"All those weird dead animal displays in the woods. What's that about? It's ghoulish. It's not normal."

"And you're the poster boy for normality? Give me a break."

"I've tried to be tolerant, to be patient—"

"Get out."

Eric sat down defiantly on the stool in front of the drafting table. "How do you make money?"

"None of your goddamn business."

"You go around extorting cash from unsuspecting relatives? Say, sending ransom notes when the opportunity arises?"

A muscle twitched in his face. "I don't know jack shit about that ransom note."

"Then tell me how you can afford all this." His eyes swept the room.

"Okay, yeah. It is extortion. But my kind. Doesn't hurt anyone. It's even legal."

"You're clever, I'll give you that. Deflecting every question about who you are, what you do. You create this aura of mystery around you because you like to play with people's heads."

"It's nice to know I'm so transparent."

"You live like a king, but you hide it. You've obviously got bucks, but you scrounge food in our pantry because you're too cheap to spend a dime."

"That's not why."

"Why, then? Why come over to our place all the time to scrounge for something to eat?"

"That's my business."

"Why?" Eric demanded, almost shouting the word.

"Because I'm lonely," said Truman. He ran a hand over his face. "There. Are you satisfied now?"

Eric was momentarily thrown. "I don't believe you."

"Fine. Don't."

"You know something about Gabriel. Where is he?"

"Don't pin that on me."

"Tell me!"

"Prove it!" Truman yelled back. "You think I had something to do with that ransom note, with Gabriel's disappearance, all I got to say is fucking prove it." He stared down at Eric. "You can't, can you."

Eric didn't answer.

"Get out. I've got some business up in the Twin Cities. When I'm done with that, I'll be moving on. You won't have Truman to kick around anymore." His scowl turned to a smirk.

"You're a sad little man," said Eric.

"Out," said Truman, clearly done talking. "Out of my RV and out of my life." He moved aside so that Eric could step around him. "I should never have come."

"No," said Eric, brushing past him. "We agree on that much."

35

Aaron crept into the kitchen though the back door, being careful not to make any noise. Standing in the doorway that faced the living room, he found Holly on the couch, knitting in front of the TV, watching a cooking show. Feeling a sense of relief that she was happily occupied, he made his way down the hallway to his study. Once the door was closed—and just to be on the safe side, locked—he sat down behind his desk and opened the top drawer. From a locked metal box, he removed the revolver and set it in front of him. The box of bullets was hidden behind his two staple guns. He pulled it out and set it next to the gun.

Even now, with everything set and ready to go, he still wondered what he was doing. Had it come down to this? A gun? Really? Who the hell was he? He didn't have to go through with it. Even the sight of the revolver made his heart pound. Nothing, he supposed, was written in stone.

"There it is," said Jane, pointing at a tall sign along the county road that read, MAGIC MOTORS USED CARS & TRUCKS.

"I wonder what it would be like to own a truck." Cordelia unwrapped a lump of bubble gum and tossed it into her mouth.

"You had one. That Hummer."

"That wasn't a truck. It was an armored command vehicle."

"Every theater director needs one of those."

"Damn straight."

Jane made a left into the parking lot and rolled up next to a low, glassed-in building. "Do you see it? The Avalanche?"

Cordelia swiveled around. "Nope."

Once inside the showroom, they were virtually tackled by an eager salesman in tan khakis, a white shirt, and a striped tie, his hand outstretched. "Morning. Morning. You two looking for a used car? Truck? I'm sure I've got the perfect vehicle for you."

"Do you have any Chevy Avalanches?" asked Jane.

"Ah, let me think." He snapped his fingers. "I do. I believe it's on the back lot."

"What year?" asked Cordelia.

"Newer model. Maybe oh eight or oh nine. Any specific reason you're interested in an Avalanche?"

"What color is it?" asked Jane.

"Of course. Of course. I know color is important to the fairer sex."

Jane and Cordelia exchanged glances.

"It's white. Tan interior. I'm sure we can agree on a price that would fit your budget. Which one of you is shopping today?"

"Do you ever let people do a test drive?" asked Jane.

"Definitely. I don't want to sell you something you're not happy with."

"Have other people been in looking at it?" asked Cordelia, snapping her gum as she sidled up to a Ford Mustang GT.

"Oh, yes," said the man. "By the way, my name's Arnie." Again he stuck out his hand.

"Jane," said Jane, giving it another shake.

"I feel like being Veronica today," said Cordelia.

Arnie gave her a quizzical look. "Veronica?"

"Yes, Arnie?"

"I mean, that's your name?"

"Do you doubt me, Arnie?"

He blinked a couple of times, then turned back to Jane. "Would you like to take a test drive?"

"Could we take the truck out ourselves? Would you need to come along?"

"No, no. That's fine. Except, management says I have to hold your driver's license, keep it here while you're gone. It's not that we don't trust you—"

"Do you keep track of who drives what?" asked Jane. "And when?"

"Well, of course. It's always possible that we may not be able to agree on a price today, but I do work closely with my manager. I need to know who to call if I can offer you a better deal."

"Did anyone drive that truck last Saturday?"

"Well, now, I have no idea."

"But you could find out for me?"

"Why would I do that?"

Jane pulled a fifty dollar bill out of her pocket, held it out to him. "Would this be a good enough reason?"

He glanced over his shoulder.

Jane continued to hold on to the bill.

"So, let's clarify: You're not really interested in the Avalanche?"

"We're interested in information, Arnie." Cordelia plucked the fifty out of Jane's hand and waved it under his nose. "Easy money is hard to come by."

"That's true," he said.

"Veronica."

"Veronica." Grabbing the bill and stuffing it in his shirt pocket, he added, "My manager drove into town to have breakfast."

"I highly recommend the fry bread tacos," said Cordelia, stifling a burp.

"What I mean is . . . yes, I could find that information for you. Just stay here. I'll be right back."

"This could be it," whispered Jane after he'd gone. "This may tell us who was behind the ransom note."

Cordelia blew a bubble as she slipped into the front seat of the Mustang.

It took Arnie a few minutes, but he finally returned to the show floor, a piece of paper in his hand. "Here you go," he said.

Jane unfolded it and read the name.

"I was off that day, but I remember Tim—he's my manager—saying that the truck was gone for several hours. He almost called the police."

"You've been a big help," said Jane.

"You little ladies stop in again any time," said Arnie. "Bye now." He walked away quickly.

"Did he just call us 'little ladies'?" asked Cordelia as they headed back outside. "I think we've entered a time warp."

Jane wasn't listening. All she could focus was the name she'd read on that piece of paper.

"So, who drove the truck?" asked Cordelia as she hooked up her seat belt. "Come on, give."

Before Jane started the engine, she sat back in her seat and took a deep breath. "Someone I never suspected."

36

Holly came to the front door, the look on her face friendly, though apprehensive. "Hi," she said, fingering the top button on her blouse. "Aaron isn't home."

"We were hoping to talk to you for a few minutes," said Jane. Again, she took out one of her cards, pressed it to the screen.

Holly didn't immediately unlock the door. "What about?"

"You know Gabriel Born is still missing."

"Neither of us know anything about that."

"I'm not suggesting you do. But you might be able to help."

"Who are *you*?" she asked, directing the question to Cordelia.

"Thorn, Cordelia M. Civilian backup. Jane's BFF."

"If we could just come in for a few minutes," said Jane.

Reluctantly, Holly allowed them into the kitchen. "I just made fresh coffee. If you'd like—"

"Coffee would absolutely save my life," said Cordelia, sitting down at a round kitchen table covered with a red-and-white checked tablecloth.

"If it's not too much trouble," said Jane. The rash on Holly's face seemed less pronounced today. She moved slowly, as if her body hurt. Jane was used to seeing this in older people, but never in someone so young.

"Cream? Sugar?"

"All of the above," said Cordelia.

"Black for me," said Jane.

Once they were all settled at the table, Jane began with a straightforward question. "Could you tell me about the test drive you took at Magic Motors last Wednesday?"

Holly looked stricken. "Test drive?" she answered weakly.

"The white Avalanche. You drove it for several hours. Where did you go?"

She twisted the coffee mug in her hands. "Well, I mean—"

"You and Aaron were the ones who sent the ransom note."

"Excuse me? What did you say?"

"You might as well admit it," said Cordelia, stirring a third teaspoon of sugar into her mug.

"I saw the Avalanche drive past us when we were waiting at that mailbox," said Jane. "And I saw it again behind the trees at the housing development."

"You did?"

"Why did you do it?"

"You're wrong. You've got no proof for any of this."

"I have enough to persuade the police to get a warrant to search your house." Jane wasn't sure that was true, though it didn't matter as long as Holly believed it. "What would they find?"

With trembling hands, the young woman set the mug down. "Nothing."

"I think you know that's not true."

"I want you to leave," said Holly, pushing away from the table and standing.

"If I do, I'll be back with the police," said Jane.

"And I'll stay outside while Jane drives to the station to make sure you don't leave with the money," said Cordelia.

Holly covered her face with her hands.

"You might as well tell us the truth," said Jane, feeling more sorry for her than she'd anticipated.

"Tell us why you and Aaron did it," said Cordelia.

Holly shook her head. "It wasn't Aaron. It was just me."

"Where's the briefcase?" asked Jane. Once she had that, all questions of proof would be moot.

"In the basement."

"How much money have you spent?"

Dropping back down on the chair, Holly said, "About eight thousand."

"On what?" asked Cordelia. "That's a lot of cash to spend in a couple of days."

"I paid our overdue mortgage payments. Made next month's payment. Paid all the overdue bills. And then I bought some food. I filled up the freezer with meat and fish and chicken. Filled the pantry with canned food." She began to cry. "I bought some underwear. How pathetic is that? I've been mending ours, but it's all so threadbare." Looking up defiantly, wiping tears from her eyes, she said, "I didn't head to the nearest department store to buy diamonds and furs. Aaron and I are drowning in debt. I'm ill. The way we're going, it won't be long before the bank starts foreclosure proceedings. I saw that those boys were missing and I thought it was my chance. I didn't figure asking for money would really

286

hurt anyone. I mean, Eric Lindstrom and Andrew Waltz have that beautiful house, two expensive cars. Gabriel's mother is a minister. She's had a steady job for years." Turning her head away, she said, "I know it was wrong. I *know* that. But I was desperate." Weakly, she added, "I'm sorry. I'll go to jail now, won't I." It wasn't a question.

"Holly," said Jane softly. "Listen to me for a minute. Go get the briefcase, okay? Can you do that?"

She nodded.

As she descended the basement steps, Cordelia said, "We've got her now. At least you'll be able to pay your dad back most of the money."

Holly wasn't the only one with secrets. "I didn't borrow the money from my father."

"No? Where'd you get it?"

Before Jane could figure out how to answer, Holly was back. She placed the briefcase in the center of the kitchen table.

Jane opened it. She did a quick count and found that Holly had told her the truth. "What you did was wrong," she said.

"I already told you I know that," said Holly, her face red with shame. "Just call the police and get it over with."

Jane picked up one of the bundles. One hundred hundred-dollar bills. Ten thousand dollars in each bundle. After closing up the briefcase, she handed the bundle to Holly. "This won't help you for long, but it's something."

Holly's eyes widened. "I don't understand."

"I'm not going to call the police."

"But . . . why?"

"I don't know. Just leave it at that."

"But the money."

"Take it," said Jane. "In exchange, you have to promise me that this stays between us. You don't tell Aaron, you don't tell anyone. This ransom business remains forever a mystery."

"I don't know what to say."

"Say thank you," said Cordelia, raising her eyebrows.

"Thank you," said Holly.

On their way out to the Honda, Cordelia said, "Boy you're an easy mark."

"Shove a sock in it," said Jane, unable to explain why she'd given Holly the money and unwilling to give it another moment's thought.

Easing his hand into the pocket of his jeans, touching the gun, checking his courage, Aaron knocked on Craig Gilkey's back door.

The principal's wife, Monica, appeared a few moments later. "Aaron, hi." She didn't look happy to see him.

"Is Craig around?"

"He's out in the garage working on the car."

"Great," he said quickly, before Monica could engage him in a conversation. She was one of those nonstop talkers who never seemed to take a breath. Nodding his thanks, he trotted around the back of the house. Sure enough, Craig's PT Cruiser was parked in the driveway. Stepping up to the side of the car, Aaron said, "Problems with the motor?"

Craig was inside the garage, digging through a tool chest. Seeing Aaron, he grabbed a rag and wiped off his hands. "Yeah. Always something wrong with the thing. What can I do for you, Aaron?"

"Thought I'd come by. Had a couple of things I wanted to say to you."

"That right?"

With his right hand sunk casually in his pocket, Aaron moved into the garage. "I'd like you to talk to the school board. I want them to reconsider my termination."

"Not going to happen," said Gilkey. "You know that, Aaron."

"If this were, say, 1498 instead of 2013, and you were, oh, I don't know . . . Torquemada——"

"Who's that?"

"The Spanish Grand Inquisitor. You remember the Inquisition?"

"I'm not going to stand here and listen to this."

Aaron moved on without missing a beat. "Then I could understand why I might be fired for refusing to teach creationism as science. The church used to believe that the sun revolved around the earth. The earth was the center of the universe. It was considered a settled fact because it fit with the going theological assumptions."

"This conversation is over. It was over a long time ago." Gilkey bent back over his tool chest, pulling out a different drawer. "Just accept the inevitable and move on."

"Is that what I should do?" asked Aaron.

Gilkey jumped.

"Don't turn around," said Aaron.

"What's that? What are you doing?"

"What do you think?"

"Is that a gun in my back? Are you out of your mind?"

"Highly possible." Aaron shoved harder. "Now that I've got your attention, I want you to shut up and listen."

Gilkey raised his hands.

"Don't do that." He glanced back to the drive. Thankfully, nobody was around. It was a quiet summer afternoon. This was the best chance he was going to get. "It's like this. Say you believe the earth is flat. Just to clarify, do you believe the earth is flat, Craig?"

"Of course not."

"Okay. But let's say you do. And I think it's round. CNN decides to cover the issue. They bring me on to point out all the proof we have that the earth is round. Then they bring you on with your proof that the world is flat. They give us equal time, treat us like our ideas are of equal weight and probability. Is that fair?"

"Well, I mean . . . maybe. There are some people who think that. Can you lower that gun? I promise, we can still talk about it."

"If the earth *is* flat, then how can satellites orbit the earth? If scientists are wrong about something so fundamental, how have they been able to make precise calculations that allow us to send men and machines to distant planets?"

"I told you I didn't believe it."

"But if we present one view as having equal weight with the other—don't you get it? People who don't study the issue, those who are scientifically ignorant may be swayed into thinking that the flat-earth theory has merit."

"I hear what you're saying. Take that gun out of my back and we can have a real conversation."

"We're having a real conversation, Craig. Here's the deal. In six months, if I don't find another job, our health care goes away. My wife is sick. She'll have the illness for the rest of her life. If we don't have health care, the disease will sink us."

"I'm sorry, Aaron. But the school board made the decision. Not me."

Aaron shoved Gilkey forward, bent him over his toolbox.

"Look, you weren't fired because of that creationism business. It was the drinking issue."

"I had a beer, Craig. One stinkin' beer. I'd taken my wife to the doctor that morning. She was diagnosed with lupus. Do you know what that is?"

"Sure, but—"

"We went out to lunch. I was upset. I took her home and then I came back to work."

"I didn't know that—about your wife."

"Even if I came to school out of my mind drunk, one incident isn't enough to cause the board to terminate my contract."

"I'm afraid you'd need to consult a lawyer about that. You have that right. You can certainly sue the school board to reinstate you."

"And who would pay for a lawyer, Craig?"

"Well, I . . . I don't know. Come on, put the gun down. *Please.* There's nothing I can do. I would if I could."

"No, you wouldn't. At least tell the truth about that."

"I don't know what to say. This is just plain crazy."

" 'I'm sorry' would be a good place to start. But you're not, are you."

"Aaron, please. You're not in your right mind. We can get help for you. The board would pay for it. I believe I can promise you that."

"I need a *job.*"

"I understand. But . . . hurting me isn't going to get you one. Think about your wife. Your future." He was panicking. Sweat

291

bled through his shirt, with big, sour-smelling drops dripping off his chin. "I won't press charges. Swear to God."

"Press charges for what?" asked Aaron.

"For . . . for threatening me with a gun."

"What gun?" Aaron pulled his index finger out of Gilkey's back.

Gilkey turned around. When he saw that Aaron didn't have a weapon, he reached for the biggest wrench in his toolbox.

"Let's frame it this way," said Aaron. His hand slipping back into his pocket, he continued, "You had a theory. Aaron Eld is holding a gun on me. You felt you had good reason—proof—for your theory. But turns out, it was just my finger. Sometimes what looks like proof really isn't."

"You're insane," said Gilkey, raising the wrench.

"No. Just making a point. You gonna hit me with that?"

"I should. I have every right to."

Inside his jeans, Aaron pulled back the hammer on the revolver. It was a loud click.

Gilkey heard it. "What was that?"

"What was what?"

"That click?"

"Maybe I have a gun in my pocket."

"Get the hell out of here."

"I guess that means you're not going to help me get my job back."

"Get out!"

Aaron drove his rusted Ford around for a while, finally stopping at Hammermill lake. He stood on the sandy, deserted shoreline and spent a few minutes thinking about Holly and how much he loved her, about how much he loathed guns, and about trust. "You're a fool, Eld," he whispered, removing the revolver from his pocket and heaving it as far out into the water as the strength in his arm would allow.

And then he got back into his car and drove home.

37

Eric carried a basket of clean laundry up from the basement, thinking that the house seemed unusually silent. The TV blared as usual, with Jack on the couch watching, but for some reason, it accentuated the quiet, almost made it unbearable.

Passing through the living room, Eric looked over at his son. "You doing okay?" It was a warm afternoon, which was why the blanket Jack held up under his eyes made no sense. Unless he was crying.

He blinked, nodded.

"Why don't you come upstairs? Papa and I are sorting laundry. You could help."

"Sounds like a laugh riot," mumbled Jack.

"Suit yourself." Eric wasn't sure how to handle his son, who had been emotionally up and down all day. He and Andrew had tried talking, tried not talking, tried playing cards. Nothing seemed to penetrate.

Heading up the stairs, Eric's felt a sudden urge to order Jack not to leave the house. Jack already knew he wasn't supposed to.

Saying it again would only irritate him, and yet Eric had to force himself to remain silent when his every instinct shrieked at him that if he came back downstairs again in five minutes, Jack could be gone. Again. He had to trust his son, which was nearly impossible because Jack had done nothing recently to earn that trust.

Returning to the bedroom, Eric found Andrew making the bed. He set the laundry basket down, then walked around the side of the bed and kissed him. "I'm so grateful your work gave you some time off."

"Me, too," said Andrew, drawing Eric down on the bed.

"Jack hasn't moved in the last two hours."

"This is so hard. All of it."

Hearing the landline ring, Eric reached over to pick it up off the nightstand. He said hello.

"Eric? It's Jane."

At Andrew's questioning look, Eric mouthed her name. "What's up? You sound out of breath."

"I figured it out. I know who took Gabriel."

"You do?"

"Remember the door that was kicked in at the house, where Gabriel and Jack were hiding?"

"Yeah?"

"Here's my thought process. Cordelia and I had just arrived at your house last night when Truman roared up on his motorcycle. While we were talking, Branch came out of the house. He'd brought Jack home because Jack said he was tired, didn't want to work on the storm cleanup anymore. We all stood around for a couple of minutes. Truman let it slip that he'd seen the boys in town last week, before they took off, and that they were both carrying brown paper bags. Truman grabbed them so he could look inside. Mostly it was food, but in Gabriel's bag, he found a scissors and some multicolored electrical tape, the kind that was used to tape the newspaper to the windows of that old house. Are you with me so far?"

"Yes," said Eric. "Go on."

"That electrical tape was a dead giveaway to anybody who knew about it and had seen that house. I think Branch must have noticed it when he was out cleaning away storm debris. It probably registered, but he didn't think anything of it until he heard what Truman had to say. That's when he put it together. I think he drove straight to that house to check out his theory. He kicked the door in and found Gabriel."

"If that's true, why wouldn't he tell us he'd found him?"

"Did Branch ever come back after he returned Jack to the farmhouse?"

"He said he was going to, but he never showed up."

"It fits. Branch has Gabriel, but we don't know why and we don't know where he's taken him. I still think Jack's the key. You've got to get him to talk."

"How? We've tried everything we can think of."

"Cordelia and I are heading over to your place right now. Let's put our heads together when we get there."

"Branch would never hurt Gabriel." Eric resisted the idea with all his might.

"I hope you're right. The thing is, if you are, then why didn't he bring Gabriel home?"

Eric's gaze collided with Andrew's.

"What, *what*?" demanded Andrew, his eyes pleading. "What's she telling you?"

"Can you call Suzanne?" asked Eric. "Tell her what you just told me?"

"That was my plan. We'll be there in a few minutes."

Eric said good-bye and cut the line.

Hearing Jack's footsteps on the stairs, both men stood.

"Hey," said Andrew, seeing Jack in the doorway. He smiled.

"Come in," said Eric.

"Do I have to fold clothes?" grumped Jack.

"No, but there's something I'd like to ask you," said Eric, sitting down on the foot of the bed.

"Now what?" said Jack, his mouth pulled together into a pout. "I've already told you everything."

"Just humor me."

He dragged himself over to a chair by the window. "What," he said morosely.

Eric knew it was now or never. He had to get it right. Thinking there was one question he'd never asked his son, he said, "The night you slept in the backyard—the night you and Gabriel took off—we found a bunch of cigarette butts and the tip of a marijuana cigarette in the grass about ten yards from the tent."

"They're called roaches, Dad. I'm not four years old."

"Fine. A roach then. Do you know who might have been standing there smoking them?"

Jack's expression grew wary.

"Did you see someone?" asked Andrew, sitting down next to Eric.

"Maybe."

"Who?"

"Uncle Branch."

Eric felt his pulse speed up.

"Branch?" repeated Andrew. "It was the middle of the night. What was he doing out there?"

And why had he never mentioned anything about it, thought Eric.

Again, Jack shrugged. "Watching the tent, I guess. We didn't know he was there until he climbed inside. I think he was pretty stoned. He laid down between us, started talking about when he was a kid. Boring stuff. We'd both been asleep. I was pissed."

"How long did he stay?"

"I don't know. Maybe half an hour. After he left, Gabriel said that we shouldn't wait. That we should head into town right then. I didn't think we'd stockpiled enough food, but Gabriel figured we'd be fine. I kept dragging my feet until he said that he was going with or without me. Hell, I couldn't let him do that. We were in it together. Friends forever."

"Your friendship with him means a lot to you," said Andrew.

Jack scratched his face to hide the fact that he was rubbing a tear away.

Instead of trying to comfort him, Eric let him sit there with his feelings, raw and exposed. "If that's true, then why did you leave that house without him?"

"I didn't want to. I never would have."

"But you did."

"Yeah," he said, his shoulders beginning to shake.

"Why? There must have been a reason."

Wiping a hand across his mouth, Jack said, "It was that bottle of vodka. Gabriel got real drunk. I mean really *really* drunk. He started telling me stuff I didn't want to hear. Awful stuff."

"About what?"

"About—" He couldn't bring himself to say it.

"About Branch," said Eric.

"Yeah. How did you know?"

Eric felt a shiver. "What about him?"

Squeezing his eyes shut, Jack said, "I'm so sick of keeping secrets."

"We know," said Eric. "Now's the time to tell it all."

Jack covered his mouth with his hand. Removing it after several long moments, although only partially, he said, "For the last couple of years, Branch has been taking Gabriel out with him on his pontoon. Fishing trips. Gabriel loved it. Last fall, when they got out into the center of Arbor Lake, Branch started messing with him. He insisted it was completely normal. That his father had shown him love the exact same way. He told Gabriel that he was proud of him. That he loved him more than anything in the world. He made sure Gabriel understood that he wasn't gay. He wasn't like you two. At first, I think Gabriel was too ashamed to admit what was happening. But he hated Branch. He told me he wanted to kill him. Branch had promised to buy him a rifle when he turned fourteen, but Gabriel didn't want to wait. As soon as he got it, he was going to use it on Branch. A few days before we took off, Gabriel found a pocketknife. He said that if his stepdad ever tried to touch him again, he'd use that."

Andrew looked stunned. "We had no idea."

"Nobody did," said Jack.

"But why did you run away from that house?" asked Eric. "Was it because Gabriel started telling you about Branch? Because he was drunk?"

"No way."

"Then why?" asked Andrew.

"Because——" He drew his legs up to his body, turned sideways in the chair and covered his head with his arms. In a barely audible voice, he said, "Because he tried to freakin' kiss me."

"Oh, Jacko," said Andrew.

Both men kneeled down next to Jack's chair. Eric squeezed his son's arm. Andrew held back. "Jack, you have to listen to what we're going to tell you," said Andrew. "Are you listening?"

With his arms still covering his face, Jack nodded.

"Gabriel had no right to do that. He forced himself on you. Nobody has a right to touch you unless it's something you want. Do you understand what I'm saying?"

"I know," Jack mumbled.

"What Branch did was even more wrong," said Eric. "He's an adult. What he did to Gabriel was a crime. It has nothing to do with being gay or not being gay. And absolutely nothing to do with love. You may not want to hear this, but you and Gabriel are both still children. Adults have no business initiating sex with a child. Ever. Period."

Hearing more footsteps on the stairs, Eric turned to find his sister rushing into the room.

Suzanne stopped in the doorway. By the look on her face, Eric could tell that she'd talked to Jane.

"Oh God," groaned Jack, seeing his aunt. He started crying again.

"You stay with him," said Eric, touching Andrew's back.

Once out in the hallway, Eric led Suzanne into Jack's bedroom. "Are you okay?"

"What do you think? Did Jack confirm that it was Branch?"

"Yes."

Suzanne seemed dazed by the news.

Andrew came into the room. "I'm sorry, Suzanne. So very sorry."

"I know where he'd take him," she said, a fierceness blooming in her eyes.

"Where?" asked Andrew.

"The hunting cabin."

"I've never been there," said Eric.

"I have," said Suzanne and Andrew, almost in unison.

With renewed energy, and for the first time in days, some real hope, Eric charged down the stairs. He was about to grab his cell off the coffee table when he saw Jane's SUV pull into the driveway.

"Call the police," said Suzanne, racing past him. "Have Andrew show them how to get there. I'll go with Jane. Someone needs to leave right away."

"I love you, sis," called Eric. It was all he could think of to say, and yet at a time like this, it hardly seemed enough.

38

"Why didn't I see it?" demanded Suzanne, sitting in the front seat so that she could give Jane directions. She yanked on the neck of her thin cotton sweater, shifted in her seat, tapped on the armrest, unable to quiet her nervous energy.

"It's not your fault," said Cordelia from the backseat.

"Of course it is. Don't you get it? If I'd been there, if I'd spent more time with Gabriel—"

"Let the responsibility rest where it belongs," said Jane.

"I'm sure Branch would be happy to let you take the blame," offered Cordelia.

"All those new books up in his room. The athletic gear. We didn't have the money for that stuff, but Branch kept on buying him things. Promising more. I assumed it was because he loved him, wanted the best for him."

Jane thought back to the conversation she'd had with Steinhauser this morning, how he'd said that Gabriel had turned into an athletic klutz every time Branch showed up at one of his games. Steinhauser had put it down to the pressure Branch was putting on Gabriel to be a star athlete. He'd diagnosed part of it correctly, just not all of it.

They drove in silence until the road veered off to the north and headed into a thickly wooded area.

"Up there," said Suzanne. "It's not a road we're looking for, just a dirt path. But it's wide enough for a car."

Jane slowed and then turned. She slowed even more when the tires hit a series of deep ruts.

"Kind of like being a pioneer in a covered wagon," said Cordelia, gripping the back of Jane's seat. Under her breath, she added, "Never wanted to be a pioneer."

Jane drove on, branches scratching at the sides of her car. While still hidden in the trees, she said, "We should probably stop here."

Up ahead, she could see the cabin. She guessed that it was maybe twenty feet long by twelve feet wide, with two small windows on either side of the front door. It looked ancient, covered in cracked cement siding painted a dull grayish green. There were no electrical lines, no propane or oil tank sitting in the yard. Without heat or electricity, and probably without plumbing, this was more of a shack than a cabin. Branch's truck was parked in the grass next to it.

Suzanne had already taken off her seat belt. She was out of the SUV before Jane could stop her. "Branch," she called, rushing up to the door and banging on it. "It's me. Let me in."

Jane jumped out and ran after her. They should have discussed their options before she took off.

"Branch," Suzanne called again, banging even more loudly. "I know you have Gabriel. We have to talk."

Moving up behind her, Jane whispered, "Take it slow."

"Unlock the door," demanded Suzanne. "Now!"

"Get away from there," came Branch's voice.

Jane stood on her tiptoes, trying to see in through one of the windows.

"I need to see my son," called Suzanne.

"He's fine." His voice sounded thick, as if he'd been crying—or drinking.

"He's *not* fine," called Suzanne. "If you won't let me in, then send him out."

"Or what?" came Branch's petulant reply.

Jane wondered if she could circle around and come at him from the rear.

"And tell Jane to get back in her car and go home. You wanna talk? That's the deal. This is between you and me."

"I'm not leaving her here alone," called Jane.

One of the windows shattered as the barrel of a shotgun was forced through it. "I'll use this if I have to. On both of you."

Backing up, Jane held up her hands. She didn't see that she had much of a choice. "Okay. I'll go. Just . . . take it easy with that thing." Returning to the Honda, she backed it up, but stopped before she reached the main road. She had no intention of leaving Suzanne alone.

"What do we do now?" asked Cordelia, sitting hunched in the backseat, her shirt pulled up over the lower part of her face. "I think this one's above my pay grade, Janey."

"Stay put," said Jane. She ran back toward the cabin, ducking down, then crawling the last few feet before finally hiding behind the trunk of a pine tree. Up ahead, Suzanne and Branch were still talking.

"Gabriel told Jack what you did," called Suzanne. She'd backed away from the door. The woman had guts, thought Jane, standing there with a shotgun pointed at her, speaking the truth to a man with his hand on the trigger—a man with very little left to lose.

"So it's Jack's word against mine," called Branch. "What if he's lying?"

"Why would he lie?"

"Because he's a little shit. Because he hates me."

"It's not just your word against Jack's. You're forgetting about Gabriel." She looked back over her shoulder, appeared to spot Jane, but gave no visible sign that she had. "Just let him talk to me. To know that he's okay."

"What about me?" yelled Branch. "Don't you care how I am?"

"Sure. Yes. Of course I do."

"This . . . mess," called Branch. "It's not all my fault, you know."

Keep him talking, thought Jane.

"Why did you bring Gabriel here?" asked Suzanne.

"Why do you think? Where else could I go?"

"If you ever loved him—"

"Of course I love him."

"Why don't we all go home? I'll make us dinner. There's cold beer in the fridge. Let's rewind the clock."

"How I wish," he called.

In the distance, Jane heard a siren. With each passing second, it grew louder.

"Oh, Jesus," called Branch. "You called the police on me?"

"Honey, please. Be reasonable. If you'll just let Gabriel come out—"

"Shut up!" he screamed. The barrel of the shotgun disappeared, replaced by a thinner barrel.

"What's that?" asked Suzanne.

"A hunting rifle. With a scope. In case you're interested, I'm a great shot."

"Did you bring an arsenal with you?"

"What if I did? What are you going to do about it?"

Two police cruisers roared to a stop just before the clearing. Andrew was in the second car. Jane was glad to see that Steinhauser was driving the first. Crawling back toward them, she waited for the men to get out, then crouched down next to Steinhauser and said, "He's got a shotgun. Looked like a twelve-gauge. And a hunting rifle."

"Is Gabriel with him?"

"Yes."

"You tell those cops to get out of here," yelled Branch, firing off a shot to punctuate his demand.

Steinhauser pulled a megaphone out of the front seat of his cruiser. "Branch, this is Matt Steinhauser. Looks like we've got ourselves a situation here. I think we'd all like to keep this from getting out of hand. I understand you've got Gabriel in there with you."

"Leave," screamed Branch. "I'm done talking."

"Branch, please," called Suzanne. "You don't want to hurt Gabriel."

"I'll go to prison," he cried. "I'll rot there for the rest of my life." The rifle barrel disappeared.

"What are you doing?" asked Suzanne.

"Branch," came Steinhauser's voice again. "Would you let me come in? We may have had our differences, but you know I'll give you a fair shake."

"Branch?" called Suzanne. "What's going on? Where did you go?" She charged up to the door and began banging on it again. "Branch, please. Let me in. I know we can work this out."

"Something's happening," said Jane. She didn't like the fact that he'd disappeared.

"We need to get in there," said Steinhauser. He was conferring with the other two officers when the rifle barrel reappeared.

"So, let's talk about forgiveness," said Branch. His tone was more conversational now.

Suzanne backed up. "Are you going to use that thing on me?"

"Eric and Andrew," he continued, ignoring her question. "They're never going to forgive me. Neither will a judge or a jury. What about God? Will He forgive me?"

"Yes," said Suzanne without hesitation. "If you're sorry for what you've done."

"Do you know that for a fact? You're the one who doesn't even believe in God anymore." He waited. When she didn't respond, he said. "What if I'm not sorry? What if I believe I didn't do anything wrong?"

"Branch, listen to me. I don't know what God thinks or what He'll do."

"You are a freakin' minister. You *should* know."

"I'm sorry I'm such a disappointment to you."

"You are. You're not the woman I thought I married."

"Honey?" she said, more softly this time. "Please. Don't do this."

He withdrew the gun.

"Let Gabriel come out to me. Please," she begged.

"So that leaves us with one last question," he called.

Jane didn't like the finality of the comment. She crawled toward the edge of the clearing. Suzanne wasn't more than fifteen yards away. She stood in the grass, looking so small, so thin, so desperate.

"Do *you* forgive me?" asked Branch.

Say yes, thought Jane. Just say it. It doesn't matter if it's true or not.

"Suzanne? Can you at least give me that much. Just say you forgive me."

"I forgive you."

"No you don't. You never loved me."

"That's not true," she cried. "I loved you with all my heart."

Jane waited for the rifle to reappear.

"What's he doing?" whispered Steinhauser.

A gunshot split the silence.

In an instant, the officers were up and rushing the cabin. Suzanne reached the door first, beating her arms against it, calling Gabriel's name, crying for him to come to her. Jane got to her just as Steinhauser pulled her away. He held her back as the other two cops kicked the door in.

"I have to go in there," she screamed, trying to buck and squirm out of Steinhauser's arms.

In an instant, Andrew was by her side. "Let the cops make sure it's safe."

Since nobody was holding her back, Jane bolted inside. Branch was lying on his back on the bare wood floor. The wall behind him was covered with blood and what was left of the top of his head.

"Must have put that nine mil in his mouth," said one of the officers, nodding to the gun a few feet from the body.

As Jane took in the scene, she felt an overwhelming sense of emptiness. It took a few more seconds for the truth of the situation to sink in. Gabriel was nowhere in sight.

"Gabriel?" she called. With no furniture in the cabin, there was nowhere for him to hide.

"Where is he?" screamed Suzanne from outside, her voice hoarse. "Honey, come here. Gabriel, please. Come to me."

Stepping back into the doorway, she saw that Suzanne was still struggling to get away from Steinhauser.

"Where is he?" she screamed. Seeing the look on Jane's face, she stopped fighting.

"He's not here."

"He has to be," said Suzanne. "Do you hear me? He *has* to be."

Jane shook her head.

"No," she cried, breaking away finally. She ran for the door, lunged through it. "Oh God," she said, wincing at the sight, sinking to the floor. Covering her mouth with her hand, she said, "Oh, God, oh God, oh God."

Andrew kneeled down next to her. He put his arms around her, held on as she wailed her son's name.

Jane walked back to the edge of the woods, where Cordelia was standing next to one of the squad cars. "Gabriel's not there."

"Lord."

"I know."

"Now what?"

"This is a crime scene," called Steinhauser, coming out of the cabin door. "I want everyone except the officers to clear the area. Immediately."

The light was starting to fade as Steinhauser and his crew finally drove away. One of the officers had driven Andrew and Suzanne back to the farmhouse, while Jane and Cordelia—after much heated negotiations—were allowed to stay. It took the local coroner a good hour before he arrived and officially pronounced Branch dead. After that, the body was removed to a waiting van.

Cordelia had been chewing bubble gum madly for the last hour. She removed the last two lumps from her pocket and offered one to Jane.

"No thanks."

"I guess we better go."

"I guess."

Cordelia's cell phone rang. "Can you believe there's cell phone service out here?" She glanced at the caller ID. "I need to take this. It's Hattie."

"I'm going to walk around. Let me know when you're done. We should probably go find ourselves some dinner."

She drifted toward the cabin. Following a dirt path that ran around the side of the property, she saw that there was a small deck jutting off the back. She walked up the rickety steps and stood for a few minutes looking up at the trees. It was a beautiful spot. Quiet. Hearing the sound of geese, she searched the sky until she located them.

Sometimes, she thought, no matter how hard you tried, it wasn't enough. It was easier being a restaurateur. At least, unless you poisoned someone, you weren't dealing with life and death.

A rustling in the woods caught her attention. There, about ten yards away, was a deer moving slowly through the underbrush. She watched it until it disappeared. Lovely, she thought. So lovely.

That's when she heard it. The muffled sound of crying. Hurrying down the steps, she crossed through a grassy patch, then stood for another moment, listening, trying to determine where the sound was coming from.

She plunged deeper into the brush, jumping over a downed tree, pushing branches out of her way.

And then she saw him. "Gabriel?" she called, a shiver rumbling through her.

He was huddled next to a rock.

She didn't want to spook him. Moving tentatively forward, she said, "Gabriel? Do you remember me? My name is Jane. Are you okay?"

His eyes were hooded and dark as they gazed up at her.

"What are you doing out here?" She crouched down.

"Branch. He told me to run."

" 'To run,' " she repeated. "When did he do that?"

"Few hours ago. He said not to come back. To run straight and I'd get to a highway. But I got lost. And then I saw the cabin. I didn't mean to come back. Honest."

"It's okay," said Jane. He reminded her of a wounded animal. Skittish. Frightened. "It's fine," she said gently. "I'm glad you came back."

"You are?"

"Absolutely."

He touched a cut on his arm.

"How'd you get that?"

Looking scared, he said, "A knife. It was an accident. Could you . . . I mean, I need to get home."

She held out her hand. "I can take you. I know where you live. I even know your mother, Suzanne."

"What about . . . Branch?"

"He won't be there."

"You're sure?"

"Positive. He won't be coming back."

"Ever?"

"Ever."

"You know my mom?"

"She'll be so happy to see you."

"I don't know."

"I do," said Jane, feeling an overwhelming rush of tenderness when she smiled at him. "Seeing you is going to make her the happiest woman in the world."

39

One week, thought Jane. It had been one week since Andrew had first called her. Both boys were home now, where they belonged, and Jane and Cordelia were on their way back to Minneapolis.

Sitting in the passenger's seat, a stack of scripts next to her on the floor, Cordelia threw her head back and hooted. "This new PI occupation of yours," she said. "You're going to go broke if you don't change your business model. I don't know how much you charged Eric and Andrew. Whatever it was, it's hardly going to cover the eighteen thousand dollars you gave Holly Eld."

"Shut up."

"Just saying."

They talked about Gabriel for most of the way home. About Suzanne. Before they'd left Winfield, she'd confided to them that she was leaving her position as a pastor at Grace Fellowship— leaving town for good. Gabriel needed to see a counselor to help him deal with what had happened to him. She needed a good counselor, too. As it happened, she had a friend in Minneapolis, an ex–probation officer turned therapist who could make recommendations.

"A sad business," said Cordelia as they pulled onto Jane's street.

Seeing Octavia's limo parked outside her house, Jane realized she'd put her own house's "infestation" out of her mind while she'd been gone. Oh joy, she thought acidly.

As they carried their overnight bags into the front foyer, Jane noticed a suitcase next to the door. "I wonder if your sister is leaving?" she asked. She hoped.

"Octavia would never buy a cheap suitcase like that—unless it's a theater prop."

Hearing laughter coming from the living room, Jane and Cordelia walked in to find Octavia entertaining a guest. Bolger was filling up champagne glasses as Octavia stood by the fireplace, holding court.

Noticing what she thought looked like a familiar head of hair, Jane said, "Truman?"

"Huh?" sputtered Cordelia.

"Why Cor*nelia*," said Truman rising from the couch and grinning. "And Jane."

"What are you doing in my house?" asked Jane.

No doubt sensing a confrontation, Bolger made a hasty exit. "I have to go pick up Hattie from camp."

"I invited him," said Octavia, clearly annoyed by the need to state the obvious. "And why are you calling him Truman?"

"That's his name," said Cordelia. "It's axiomatic that if it's his name, that's what we call him."

"It's all right," said Truman, planting a delicate kiss on Octavia's cheek.

Cordelia's mouth dropped open.

"Your sister knows me by my more well-known name, T. Everett Lind."

"T. Everett Lind," mumbled Cordelia. "T. Everett Lind. T. Everett Lind." Then, eyes narrowing, she said, "The artist T. Everett Lind? That's you?"

"Guilty."

Jane had never heard of him.

"He's in Minnesota because the Wolker is doing a show of his newest work," said Octavia.

"Let me guess," said Jane. "Bones."

"Pencil drawings of nonhuman bones, to be exact," said Truman.

"They're utterly amazing," oozed Octavia, clearly enchanted by everything about him.

He did clean up well, thought Jane, eyeing his gray linen suit, immaculate white shirt, and pink tie.

"Where did you two meet?" asked Cordelia.

"Was it Rio?" asked Octavia.

"Madrid," Truman responded.

"Just to clarify," said Cordelia, her eyes fastened on her sister. "You're not marrying him, right?"

Octavia tittered.

"Oh, Lord," said Cordelia.

"I'm not the marrying kind," said Truman.

"Don't bet on it," muttered Cordelia.

"Since you two are finally home," said Octavia, "why don't we move briefly to my study and discuss some business."

"*My* study?" said Jane.

"Well, your study, I suppose. But share and share alike, right? Truman," she said, drawing her hand seductively across his chest, "I shall be right back."

Octavia led the way down the hall, sitting behind Jane's desk as Jane and Cordelia stood in front of her like naughty children.

"I'm tired," said Cordelia. "Whatever it is you want to say to us, make it fast."

"All right," she said, casually crossing her legs. "I've made my decision. Selected our first play."

"As it happens," said Cordelia, hands rising to her hips, "so have I."

It occurred to Jane that she should run.

"State the name," said Cordelia.

"*The Zebra Hunt,*" said Octavia. "By Erin——"

"O'Brian," said Cordelia, finishing the sentence for her. "I can't believe it."

"Believe what, dear?"

"After a long and difficult deliberation, it just so happens I picked the same play."

The sisters cocked their heads at each other like little animals in a Disney cartoon.

Jane felt a wave of relief so strong that it almost knocked her over.

"How is it possible that we agree on something?" asked Octavia. "That's not right. Not right at all."

"Just enjoy the wholesome camaraderie," said Jane, inching her way toward the door.

"Wait," cried Octavia, holding up her arm. "One more thing.

You should stay and hear this, Jane, since it affects you." She picked up Jane's letter opener and tapped it against the pencil holder. "You know I've been looking for a permanent residence. A place I can lay my weary head at night and call home when I'm in town."

"Just spit it out," said Cordelia.

"I've found a place. In Kenwood."

"A mansion," sniffed Cordelia. "So what else is new?"

"It's utterly gorgeous. Think Sunset Boulevard."

That analogy seemed to catch Cordelia's interest.

"Eight bedrooms. Four bathrooms. The kitchen has all been redone. The rest of the house is period elegance. My real estate agent negotiated the deal last night. I move in next week."

Jane sent up a silent thank-you to the universe.

"Here's the bottom line," continued Octavia. "You, my dear sister, should move in with me. You and Hattie and dear, dear Bolger. The place is so large we'd never need to see each other if we didn't want to. And when I'm gone, to Europe or wherever, you can look after the place for me."

"You're suggesting I become your servant?"

"No, no. I'll *hire*. Think about it. Your loft will be out of commission for a long time. Perhaps months. I know Jane is unusually generous. She'd let you stay here forever if you wanted."

Jane cleared her throat.

"But if you move in with me, you'll never need to worry about bedbugs again. Think about *that*."

Cordelia jumped.

Octavia rose from her chair. "Now, I must get back to my guest."

"Quick question," said Jane, raising a finger. "There's a suitcase in the front foyer."

"Oh, that." Octavia made a sour face. "It belongs to that woman. Avi Greenberg."

"She's here?" said Jane. "I didn't see her car."

"A friend dropped her off. Last I saw, she'd run upstairs to that room she's using as an office."

"Later," said Jane, dashing out. She rushed back down the hall to the kitchen, saw that the dogs were out in the backyard, and then headed through the dining room back into the foyer and up the stairs.

Out of breath, she came to a stop in the bedroom doorway.

Avi was stuffing file folders into a briefcase. "Jane," she said, looking up and smiling. "Hey. I sent you a text."

"You did?" She slid her phone out of her jeans pocket. There it was. "I must not have felt the vibration. Are you going somewhere?"

Outside, a horn honked.

"New York," said Avi, stepping to the window and pulling back the curtain.

"By yourself?"

"With Julia."

So now it was Julia, not Dr. Martinsen.

"Don't get that look."

"What look?"

"Listen for a second." She slid her arms around Jane's waist. "I know you don't like her, but this is my life. We're flying to New York to meet with my agent. We'll be there for two, maybe three days. Then, if all goes well, we'll stop in Chicago on the way back to talk to Elaine Ducasse."

"You're going with that press? For sure?"

"No, not for sure. I'll talk my agent. My agent can ask Julia all the necessary questions. If the answers are the right ones, I'll sign. But only if my agent says I should."

Jane could hardly argue with that. All she could do was search her soul for the courage necessary to achieve resignation. Such as it was. "I only want what's best for you."

"I know. And I love you for it."

"You . . . love me . . . for it?"

Avi's fingers played with Jane's hair. And then she gave her a long, slow, greedy kiss. "It's been good to have this time away. I've done a lot of thinking. I'm more and more certain that you're the one."

"But not completely."

Once again, the horn honked.

"I'll call you when I get to the hotel," said Avi.

"Where are you staying?"

"No idea. Julia made the reservations." She picked up her briefcase and headed downstairs.

By the time they reached the foyer, the doorbell was ringing.

Jane opened it, finding Julia outside.

"Jane," said Julia. "You're . . . home."

Avi kissed Jane and then picked up her bag. "I'm all ready."

"Go on. I'll be there in a second."

Once she was on her way, Julia turned to Jane. "Amazing how these things work out."

"You do anything to harm her career—"

"You need to get off that dime. I'm going to take very good care of our Avi."

"*Our?*"

"She's part of my life now, too. She's quite something, isn't she? Believe me when I tell you that I'm planning to take very good care of her. Very good care indeed." She flashed her eyes at Jane, then turned and walked back to the waiting cab.